Praise for Like Water for Weary Souls

Liisa Kovala writes with wisdom, heart, and intuition. She knows instinctively what drives justice-seekers, especially when they're women—what they carry in their bones, what they'll risk to unearth secrets and bring truths to light. And why, sometimes, hearts must break before they can be healed.

— Susan Scott, ed., *Body & Soul: Stories by Skeptics and Seekers*

The resiliency of the characters is embodied in the Finnish word sisu, an idea that conjures the tenacity and strength of not just existing—but thriving—in a new world. Beautifully written and aptly evocative of a specific time and place in Northern Ontario history, *Like Water for Weary Souls* is a story that will stay with the reader long after the last page is turned.

—Kim Fahner, author of *The Donoghue Girl*

This wonderful elixir of story is steeped in the bitter herbs of reality and the sweetness of possibility.

—Eleanor Albanese, award-winning author of *If Tenderness Be Gold*

A touching story of family secrets and dreams, *Like Water for Weary Souls* beautifully delineates the opportunities and dangers of life in a Northern Ontario mining community in the grinding poverty of the 1930s.

—Marion Agnew, author of *Making Up the Gods*

As young Essi Kivi searches for answers about Hanna's tragic death, the novel explores themes of love, loss, and quiet determination. Kovala offers a vivid and honest look at a difficult time, crafting a story that stays with you, showing how powerful the human spirit can be even in the face of great sorrow.

—Caroline Topperman, author of *Your Roots Cast a Shadow*

Like Water for Weary Souls will make you holler at injustice, cry at betrayal, and cheer at triumph. It embodies the tenacity and hopefulness of the human spirit.

—Emily De Angelis, award-winning author of *The Stones of Burren Bay*

Like Water for Weary Souls

Also by Liisa Kovala

Sisu's Winter War
Surviving Stutthof

Like Water for Weary Souls

A Novel

LIISA KOVALA

Copyright © 2025 by Liisa Kovala

All rights reserved.

No portion of this book may be reproduced, distributed, or transmitted in any form or by any means, including photocopying, recording, or other electronic or mechanical methods without the prior written permission from the publisher or author, except as permitted by copyright law. No part of this book may be used for or reproduced in any manner for the purpose of training artificial intelligence technologies or systems. For permission requests, please contact House of Karhu Publishing at houseofkarhu.com.

Publisher's note: This book is a work of fiction. Names, characters, places, and incidents are products of the author's imagination or are used fictitiously. Any resemblance to actual persons, events, or locales is coincidental.

ISBN: 978-0-9950834-3-1 (softcover)

ISBN: 978-0-9950834-4-8 (EPUB)

Book Cover: Mark Karis

Author Photo: Westmount Photography

Published by: House of Karhu

First Edition 2025

We acknowledge the generous support of the Ontario Arts Council.

For John

> As cold water for a weary soul,
> So is good news from a far country.
> —Proverbs 25:25

> For this I weep all my days
> and throughout my lifetime grieve
> That I swam from my own lands
> towards these strange doors
> to these foreign gates.
> —Elias Lönnrot, *The Kalevala*

Prologue

My dreams of Karelia are buried with me, beneath a thin sheet of ice in a shallow creek. From where my body lies, frost paints the steel girders of the bridge above me, blending its footings with the snow-covered embankment. Dark clouds will soon obscure the slate sky, dotted with stars, and the snow will fall.

It is the kind of Northern Ontario night that envelops one in its complete stillness. The kind of air that transforms one's breath as it balloons and stretches, spirals, and dissipates. No one will see my body, nearly covered in water so cold I would be numb if I could feel it. My exposed face reveals eyes wide open, and so blue they are almost translucent. They see nothing, yet I see all.

With little will, I rise from the creek that has released my weary soul, from my heavy body, from the water tugging at my clothes. No signs of life within my empty shell, and yet everything is awake to me now. A cacophony surrounds me: creeping growth of frost, cracking of snow, colliding of water and ice, sighing of cold air, shifting of stars, scraping of snowflakes against sky. I am apart from it and yet a part of it all.

A low rumble, a tremor in the air—the night train approaches. The light, a pinprick in the distance, expands toward me until it illuminates the scene below in blinding clarity. The clack and whine of wheels against steel tracks are enough to wake the dead, or so I've heard.

A gust awakens the trees, their branches cracking along the shore, and passes through me, threatening to drag me in every direction. I will myself to stay. For how long, I cannot tell. I only know I am tethered to this place, to this one lifeless body, to this one space in time, despite the powerful pull from some force wishing me away. Not yet. Not until.

PART 1: ESSI

Chapter One

April 1933

I set aside my fountain pen and journal and pull open the thin lace curtains to the early morning sun. A fresh layer of snow blankets the rows upon rows of two-storey brick houses with their sashed windows and snow-covered verandahs. If I crane my head just so, I can follow Kathleen Street to the railroad tracks, and further down across the blackened rock, toward Nolin Creek. I open the window a crack and take a deep breath, thankful there is no sulphur in the air, and absently touch the smooth button sewn into my bracelet.

A fresh layer of snow hangs over the pines and drapes across the small front yard and into the distance. No vehicles, no people, nothing to suggest our Donovan neighbourhood is awake or has any cares in the world. On a Saturday morning like this, people sleep off the night before, still in a stupor or varying states of regret. I glance at my sister's bed, nestled in the corner across from mine. It, too, is untouched. It's not the first time she hasn't made it home before morning, but it still makes me uneasy, like a worried parent wondering where her child is.

A black Ford Model A rumbles to a stop outside the boarding house. I pull back from the window and catch my breath. The police. If they are at Rouva Ruusa's door, it means trouble. My mother, a strict Finnish Lutheran woman from the old country, would be horrified.

I rush down the staircase, past the parlour, and burst into the kitchen at the back of the house. Rouva Ruusa—Madame

Rose as her girls call her—is sipping coffee and reading a newspaper at the kitchen table.

"Essi? What's wrong, girl?" Rouva Ruusa stubs a cigarette into a saucer with one hand, then swigs the last bit of coffee from her cup with the other.

I grip the back of a chair. "There's a police car outside."

Rouva Ruusa's eyes widen ever so slightly. She sighs and pushes herself up from her wooden chair, tucks her blouse into her skirt, and sweeps a hand over her slightly dishevelled hair, pinning a stray grey section in place. "It's becoming routine with these goons. They want either a piece of my girls or a piece of my profits. You should make yourself scarce."

I follow her into the parlour at the front of the house. She glances around, the evidence of last night's party still on display. Cigarette butts crushed into ashtrays and empty bottles of whisky litter the tables. A gramophone seems poised to play a polka or waltz, maybe some jazz. On the floor under the table, a pile of discarded records. The miners get paid on Friday and release the stress of days underground with a night of carousing.

"Is it about the girls? Or the bootlegging?" Yvonne has told me Rouva Ruusa sometimes has to pay them off. "Aren't they supposed to uphold the law and not break it by taking bribes?"

Rouva Ruusa laughs. "You're a sweet girl, but you have a lot to learn." She parts the curtain just enough to see the police car outside. "I hope you never change."

A year and a half of living in Sudbury has already changed me and the people I trust. It took me months to reconcile myself to the fact that my landlady runs a brothel and sells bootlegged liquor, and yet now I trust her more than most people I know.

I tug at the button on my bracelet, wondering why the police haven't approached the house yet.

Rouva Ruusa turns her back to the window and casually looks me up and down, as if she has all the time in the world to chitchat. "You could be quite a looker. Not a stunner like your sister, but there's something pleasant and downright homey about you that would appeal to some of my clients. You could make a good living working for me."

Heat rises into my cheeks at the idea of working here. "No, thank you. Hanna has a steady paycheque that can keep us going until I find a new job." If I can find another situation. I avoid telling potential employers where I live in case they don't understand I'm just a boarder, not an employee. "Aren't you concerned about the police?"

Rouva Ruusa shrugs. "This life is tough. Get it where you can, just like men. Do you think they care a whit about honesty? Why should we women take any less?"

From behind the chesterfield, a leg sprawls out with a boot attached. Rouva Ruusa gives it a kick. "Time to get up," she says. He groans, brushing greasy hair from his forehead. It's Billy, one of Rouva Ruusa's strays. Yvonne says he's slow, but sweet, and Rouva Ruusa finds him odd jobs to do around the place and makes sure he's fed.

"Nyt!" Now! Even I jump at Rouva Ruusa's commanding voice. There's no denying who is in charge here. She's a large woman, big-boned some might say, and the equal of any man entering her establishment. Her clients know not to mess with her or her girls. Anyone who makes trouble is thrown to the street, often by her hands.

"Menen, menen." I'm going. Billy staggers to his feet.

I peek through the curtains. The two officers navigate the snowbank and move toward the porch. "Hurry, Billy. The police are coming up the stairs." Billy will be of no help if the police ask questions. He can't tell anything but the truth.

My heart is pounding now. Although I have nothing to do with Rouva Ruusa's business, I don't want to see anyone in trouble. "Your hat!" Billy turns to catch it.

"Näkemiin." Goodbye, he says, waving behind him. From the side door, he'll enter the back alley and disappear into the neighbourhood.

"Go to your room. I'll handle them." Her thick Finnish accent reminds me of my mother's, but otherwise they have nothing in common. Rouva Ruusa nods towards the stairs across from the parlour in her calm manner. Nothing suggests she is worried, except the slight twitch at the corner of her eye revealing her irritation. Rouva Ruusa's movement to the door is unhurried.

I climb the narrow stairs to the landing where the staircase turns so I can observe the foyer without being seen, avoiding the steps with the creaky boards. Rouva Ruusa lets in the cold air and the stiff-looking officers.

"Officer O'Rourke. What do you want?"

O'Rourke is known throughout the Donovan neighbourhood. Some residents refer to him as Tiny Tim. His portly belly enters a room before he does, and his face is permanently flushed. Apparently, he likes his drink.

"Ma'am." O'Rourke nods and removes his hat while Rouva Ruusa checks her wristwatch as if she has somewhere else to be. "This is Officer Robert Cane. We're looking for a girl."

I peer down at the younger man's striking features, firm jaw, and dark hair. If Hanna were here, she'd call him a looker.

"You've come to the right place," Rouva Ruusa says. She turns to Officer Cane. "You're new. Haven't been here before, have you?" Rouva Ruusa's reminding them who is in charge. I smile from my perch on the stairs.

Cane's cheeks redden, and he stares at the floor. "No, ma'am. We're here because—"

O'Rourke interjects. "We're looking for Esteri Kivi. Hanna Kivi's sister."

What do they want with me? The stair squeaks under my feet, and I freeze.

Rouva Ruusa's gaze never leaves the officer's face. "And what would you want with Essi Kivi? She's probably at work right now."

O'Rourke takes out a small notebook and pencil. "And where does Miss Kivi work?"

"Mrs. Johnson's a few streets over on Antwerp. About halfway up the hill on the left. Essi cares for the children and does housework," Rouva Ruusa lies. "What has Essi done?"

"And Hanna Kivi, her sister. One of your tenants? An employee?" O'Rourke asks.

"Essi and Hanna are my tenants. I'm not at liberty to discuss my boarders' personal lives. Do you mind telling me what's going on?"

"It's not about your business, if that's what you're concerned about. Not this time." O'Rourke stares at Rouva Ruusa. "We need to question Esteri Kivi about her sister."

I can't suppress my gasp. All three look my way before I pull back into the shadows.

"Essi?" Rouva Ruusa leans against the bannister and peers up at me. "I think you should come down here," she says in Finnish.

The worn bannister feels cold under my fingertips. The stairs groan under my weight as my legs threaten to give out from under me.

O'Rourke straightens his stance and clears his throat; squishing his hat between his thick fingers. "Miss Kivi?"

I stare at them, unable to form any words. Visions of my parents in Wanup flood my mind. I've seen this expression before.

O'Rourke turns toward Rouva Ruusa, his eyebrows knitted together. "Does she speak English?"

Rouva Ruusa nods. "Fluently. She immigrated as a child with her family, who live in Wanup. She speaks perfect English and Finnish, I assure you. A little Swedish, too, I believe."

O'Rourke clears his throat a second time and turns his attention to me. "Will you sit down, please? I'm afraid we need to give you difficult news." He looks around the trashed parlour and gestures toward the bench in the hall.

I shake my head, eager to hear what they have to say. The knot in my stomach grows, and my hands shake. I clutch them in front of me.

"Unfortunately, it is my duty to inform you that your sister, Hanna Kivi, is deceased. Our sincerest condolences, Miss Kivi."

"She's ...? That's impossible. Hanna went to work yesterday. She could just be late getting home. Not ..."

"I'm so sorry," Officer O'Rourke says, sounding fatherly.

"What happened?" The words barely escape my constricted throat. I look from O'Rourke to Cane.

"A local man found her this morning in Nolin Creek. I know this is very difficult for you, but ... we would like you to make an identification," Officer Cane says.

I stare at him but can't form any words, can't breathe. Rouva Ruusa wraps an arm around me, holds me up. My face and hands are cold, and my body shivers uncontrollably.

"I'm sorry for your loss." Cane's kind voice delivers the words no one wants to hear.

Rouva Ruusa and O'Rourke's lips are moving, but I cannot discern their words. It's as though they are talking under water while my ears fill with liquid and my body drags down.

"Essi? Essi?" Rouva Ruusa squeezes my shoulders and leans her face closer to mine. "Do you understand what Officer O'Rourke is saying?"

I draw my eyes towards hers and nod my head, but I don't hear him. What is he telling me? I am treading water against a current, incapable of moving forward or back. The force threatens to pull me under.

"You'll need to come with us, Miss Kivi," Officer O'Rourke repeats.

"Go on, girl. Do what needs to be done." Rouva Ruusa nudges me forward. "I can go with you if you like." Her offer is kind, but I say no. I need to see my sister alone.

I reach for my winter boots and pull them on, unable to register what I'm doing. Rouva Ruusa helps me with my wool coat and cloche hat from the stand. I stop at the door, taking a long look at Rouva Ruusa's face. She is paler than usual, and her kohl-lined blue eyes are wide with concern, but her dark red lips give me a reassuring smile.

"It'll be all right," she says. I've never seen grief on Rouva Ruusa's face before, but now it creeps to the edges of her eyes.

I nod and pull the door closed behind me, allowing Officer Cane to take my arm as we navigate the snowdrifts, and willing myself to breathe deeply, despite the cold sending spikes through my lungs.

Chapter Two

April 1933

We pause just outside the doorway of the coroner's room, and I realize I've been holding my breath. My lungs hurt as though filled with liquid.

Officer O'Rourke is on my right, and Officer Cane is still holding my elbow on my left, supporting my weight as I stumble. He releases my arm, and I clutch my hands together, trying to keep them still. Is it the cool of the early spring day, the starkness of the corridor, or my fear? The cold has seeped inside me and will not give way.

"Are you ready, lass?" O'Rourke speaks in a gentle tone.

Absentmindedly, I reach for my bracelet with Martta's button until I feel its smoothness under my fingertip, inhale deeply, and try to release the tension in my body. I nod. O'Rourke opens the heavy door to the well-lit space.

A clean white sheet drapes a still figure. I can't look away, but I can't move toward it either. During our short ride from Kathleen Street to the coroner's office, I could not help but think it was a mistake. It is some other girl. Someone else's sister. Hanna is still at Dr. Wright's house. Hanna is in the kitchen sipping coffee, chatting with Yvonne or Rouva Ruusa. Making her bed with the quilt she sewed with her own hands when we lived on the farm. Daydreaming by our window. Humming the latest Irving Berlin tune.

O'Rourke gives a discreet nod to the coroner, a tall, balding fellow with kind eyes. He doesn't speak a word and barely looks my way. The coroner lifts the sheet and folds it down, taking great care not to disturb the body, as if she is in a deep sleep from which she might awake.

Below the sheet is a bloated body, pale and waxy. I'm drawn to the hand, with its swollen fingers and bleached skin. The face is distorted. Unrecognizable from where I'm standing.

"Is this Hanna Kivi?" O'Rourke asks. His words hang in the air like mist rising from a river.

I move closer, both repelled and drawn to the figure. Not Hanna, not Hanna, not Hanna.

I creep toward her.

And then I see. My sister. My beautiful sister. Skin waxen under my fingertips. I stroke her matted hair. Hanna's soft features and smooth skin, and the beautiful blond hair I envied, distorted on this grotesque figure. But I know it's her. Only her eyes, still open wide, are familiar.

I grip my handbag until my fingernails burrow into the flesh of my palms, my breath shallow. I want to scream. To cry. But I am frozen, staring at my sister's lifeless body, willing her to return to me.

Something is missing. I look for her *Hannunvaakuna* pendant, the St. John's Arms charm she wore on a gold necklace, but it's gone. It was meant to protect her.

I look at the coroner. "She wore a … a necklace … every day since she turned thirteen."

The coroner shakes his head. "I'm sorry, miss. I didn't find any jewellery." His voice is surprisingly deep, and he speaks slowly, as if not to disturb her. "She may have lost it in the creek when she passed."

How is it possible? Hanna is gone. Martta, our younger sister, is gone. Our mother Ida's unborn child is gone. I am the last of the Kivi girls. "My parents?" I ask. "Have they been told?"

Officer O'Rourke shakes his head. "Not yet. We wanted to identify her first. It's best they are told in person, and we can certainly send somebody to inform them today. It might make the news ... a little easier."

"It should be me. I'll tell them myself." I picture my mother and wonder if she can survive another devastating loss. If I can survive the telling.

Officer Cane steps forward. "I'll take you to your parents. If you don't object."

I shake my head. "I have a friend from Wanup, a neighbour. Fredi Virtanen. He does a lot of deliveries between Sudbury and Wanup. He'll take me." The last time Hanna and I visited was for our father Edvard's birthday. My mother, Ida, was out-of-sorts, as she often is, and she didn't get out of bed the whole time.

"That's just fine." Officer O'Rourke has his hands folded in front, feet slightly apart, but his voice contrasts with his formality, much like the way adults spoke to Hanna and me after we lost Martta, as though their voices alone were enough to crack us in two and expose our grief to the world. Nothing about having grieved for Martta makes this fresh loss any easier. No amount of time heals, although it is the line everyone gives to those left behind. It isn't true. I know. I've lived it.

"What happened?" I lean in toward her, my gaze on her unwavering stare. My question remains unanswered. We always told each other everything, but now she will not reveal her secrets to me. I'll never hear her voice again. I weep.

Officer Cane offers me his handkerchief, and I wipe my tears, repeating my question. "What happened to her?"

O'Rourke nods at Officer Cane. "We believe she was trying to cross Nolin Creek to get to Frood Road, but the ice was too unstable. The recent warm spell, followed by last night's storm, would have made it difficult to judge the safety of the ice. She must have lost her footing, fallen through. There's some bruising and a contusion on the left side of her head. Probably hit a rock when she fell. If she were unconscious, drowning was inevitable. Last night's snowfall covered any trace of footsteps, but there is no sign she was with someone."

"Who found her?" I ask, trying to absorb every word.

"Someone from the neighbourhood," Officer O'Rourke says, "out walking his dog this morning. The dog pulled toward the creek, and the man noticed a red scarf under the snow. He recognized your sister and even knew her name. That's how we located you. By then, her body was submerged in the water, a layer of snow covering her." Officer O'Rourke recites the facts with detached professionalism, as though he were informing a reporter instead of a grieving sister.

"No." My voice is a whisper. They have it all wrong.

Officer O'Rourke furrows his brow. "Pardon?"

"That's not what happened." I try to control my tone. They can't just assume it was an accident.

"Do you know something about this, Miss Kivi?" O'Rourke's tone is serious, but the look in his eyes reveals his surprise. He readies his pencil over his notepad. Cane crosses his arms, but he leans in with a puzzled look on his face. Do they think I'm going to confess?

"Hanna always walked the same way from Dr. Wright's house. I've gone with her hundreds of times. We never considered crossing the creek beneath the railroad tracks, even though it might save a few minutes. It wasn't worth it. She understood water. And ice. Hanna would never risk it." I look O'Rourke squarely in the eyes. "Hanna has seen what water can do."

Officer Cane raises his eyebrows and seems about to speak, but he remains silent.

O'Rourke rubs his chin. "There's one other possibility. I'm sorry, but it is not very pleasant to discuss. Lots of young people, especially immigrants, struggle in the city. Times have been difficult for everyone ever since the stock market crashed. At least for ordinary folk. No offense, but we don't know what your sister was experiencing. If she were having difficulties, she might have wanted a way out. It happens more than you think. Was your sister in trouble?"

Sadly, there was truth in his words. "No, that wasn't Hanna," I reply. Men and women from our community were struggling; there just wasn't enough work. Some people migrated to bush camps up north. Some left Canada altogether, returning to Finland, moving to America, or venturing to Soviet Karelia. Others found a permanent way out, taking a last walk on the railroad tracks.

But not Hanna. Hanna was always optimistic about life and full of dreams for a grand future. A handsome husband, preferably wealthy, and her own house—at least two storeys. Children some day. Nice clothes, jewellery, money in her purse. She envisioned a bigger life for herself.

"If Hanna had problems, I would have known. It's been difficult, but we'd been doing fine since moving into the city. And she was excited about the future. She had plans." I want to sound confident, but I worry doubt has entered my voice. Was it possible Hanna was in trouble and hid it from me? Impossible. "When you investigate, you'll see. She wouldn't take such a risk."

Officer O'Rourke sighs. "Listen, Miss Kivi. We're scouring the area for clues, but they're under a foot of snow. Your sister fell, hit her head, drowned, and subsequently froze in the creek. There's no evidence of foul play. Let me reassure you, if any new leads appear, we'll do what we can to find out what happened to your sister, but the current evidence points to accidental drowning. Our department is understaffed and underfunded. There is simply nothing to suggest a crime. It's best for your family if you let this go. Tell your parents. Bury your sister. Grieve and move on."

I glance at Cane. He looks regretful, embarrassed even, but he says nothing.

O'Rourke's words anger me. He clearly has no intention of investigating Hanna's death. Robert Cane might be of more help, but I doubt he'll work behind his superior's back to help a girl like me, just another nobody in their books.

It's because we're immigrants and Finns. We're troublemakers, rabble-rousers, union activists. I've heard it all before. But we're also hard-working human beings wanting to build a better life than the ones we have, just like everyone else in this mining town. What's wrong with that? I purse my lips to keep my anger from spewing across the room on these police officers who have sworn to protect everyone, even me, but have no interest in justice. I take one last long look at Hanna, kiss her forehead and touch her hair.

"I'll find out what happened. I promise." My voice is a whisper. Then I brush past the officers and stride out of the building.

Before I can do anything else, I need to go home and tell my parents. A single black crow swoops down and lands on the path in front of me, tilts its head, squawks once, and eyes me as if he dares me to act. Father told us that in Finnish mythology the crow carries messages between the living and the underworld and guards the threshold between the worlds. What message is this crow carrying to me now? After a few moments, he squawks again and takes flight. I watch his dark figure until it disappears into the distance.

Chapter Three

April 1933

Fredi turns on the ignition of his beat-up old Ford delivery truck. It sputters and fails, then sputters again before coming to life. We sit in silence as he navigates through the Donovan and the downtown, past Borgia Street where he lives, over the iron bridge, and past the Bedrock gates towards Paris. Another twenty kilometres and I'll be home. I dread the moment I see my parents' faces.

Fredi grips the steering wheel as the truck lumbers down the pitted road. There is very little traffic; only a dairy truck and a horse and buggy pass by on their way to Sudbury or farther north. Watching the landscape through the passenger side window, I wipe away my gathering tears with my sleeve. I rest my forehead on the cold glass, closing my eyes and reminding myself to breathe. My focus on doing something about Hanna's death has left me little time to feel anything. Maybe that's the point. But now, as we get closer to home, I feel Hanna's absence so acutely my body feels weighted down. I fear I will dissolve into tears here, in Fredi's truck, but I don't want to see my parents in that state. I need to keep myself together, if only for them.

Fredi reaches into his pocket and passes me a handkerchief. We drive in silence for several minutes before he wipes his own eyes. More emotion than I had expected to see from him. He's a man of few words. We've known each other since childhood, long enough not to have to fill the silence with idle chatter, especially on a day like today.

Fredi pulls off the dirt road and onto the long gravel driveway leading to my family's farmhouse, slowing to a crawl to navigate the potholes.

"Do you want me to come in with you?" He parks the truck beside the barn with its chipped paint, the greying wood. A crow caws from the rooftop, as if reminding me of my task.

I shake my head. "No, I have to do this alone. I owe it to Hanna."

Fredi looks straight ahead. "Got a few deliveries to make and then I'll go home and see the old folks. Pick you up in a few hours?"

I agree and move to open the passenger door, but it sticks. I glance at Fredi, and he shrugs before reaching over to whack it open.

"Thanks for doing this. It means a lot to me." Driving here with a police officer, even Officer Cane, would have been awkward. I prefer comfortable silence with an old friend.

Before backing down the drive, he raises a few fingers from the steering wheel in a brief wave.

Slushy snow covers the wooden steps to the old house. I glance around the property from the familiar porch where I played with my sisters, trying to steady myself for what is coming. The latest snowfall has crushed the fields with its weight, but already bare patches are visible. Distinctive odours from the barn waft toward me, reminding me of the hours we spent jumping into the hay bales, milking the cows, and mucking out the horses' stables. Freya and Inkeri are outside grazing on some hay, swishing their tails, and shaking their heads as if they are gossiping with one another. I let out a low whistle, and Freya's ears prick. She stares at me. I'm tempted to visit my old friends, stroke their manes, and share my grief, just as I'd told them all my secrets as a girl, but I'm not here to be comforted.

I hesitate to walk in. Hanna and I scarcely visited over the time we've been gone—there was never enough time—so they might think someone is intruding. Instead, I knock. The storm door, almost off its hinges, creaks as I turn the handle.

I hear my father's booming voice call out in Finnish. "Ida, someone's at the door."

A gust of wind carries flakes of snow from the roof, and sending strands of hair across my face. My mother opens the door. "It's you," she says in Finnish. "Why are you here?" Her voice is quiet, and her tone is cold. She looks behind me and scans the yard. "Where's your sister?"

I don't know what to say, although I rehearsed it in my mind so many times. Mother's expression shifts as she studies my face.

"Something has happened to Hanna?" My mother's already aged face drops, and the creases from the corners of her lips to her jowls seem to deepen before my eyes.

My tongue feels thick. The words are stuck, but I force them out. "I'm sorry, Äiti."

My mother's eyes are wide with shock. "No! Not Hanna." She grabs the doorframe with her strong, knotted fingers to steady herself. Before I know what is happening, she stands tall and slaps me across the cheek. My skin burns from the pain and the unexpectedness of it.

She turns into the house, and I follow her, holding my hand against my hot cheek, eyes stinging.

My father's sitting at the pine table, a cup of steaming coffee between his calloused hands, too large for the dainty cup. He could crush it with ease and not feel the sting of the jagged pieces in his hands. His eyes widen as I approach, and his lips form a smile, but when he sees my expression, his face transforms. He knows something is wrong.

I pull out a spindle chair and sit across from him, holding my mittens in my lap. My winter coat feels stifling now in this small space. Then, I tell them. Hanna is dead. Here, at this same table where we ate meals, where we did homework by candlelight, where I wrote countless stories, where we baked with our mother as children. The same table where we sat silently after Martta's funeral, unable to eat our neighbours' offerings or speak to one another as the sun gradually set across the fields and the room darkened around us.

Now, the afternoon sun streams in from the windows, and light dances across the pine table, at odds with the heaviness within.

Father clutches my mother's hand. "What happened?"

I lower my eyes. Anything is better than looking at them directly. "Someone found Hanna's body in Nolin Creek. The police call it an accidental drowning." I force myself to look up at my parents.

My mother's body shrinks, her dull grey eyes become lifeless, and she squeezes and twists her gnarled fingers. Father retrieves his tobacco from his breast pocket, but his hands are shaking so much he can't roll it. I take his pouch and paper and roll a cigarette for him. He accepts it with trembling fingers. I strike a match, and he inhales deeply.

The room is silent save for my mother's uneven breathing and the relentless ticking of the wooden clock on the buffet table.

"I'm sorry," I say. "I didn't want you to hear it from a stranger." Would it have been better for them to learn of their daughter's death from someone else, like unshakeable O'Rourke or sympathetic Cane?

He shakes his head. "You did the right thing. What did the police say?"

"That she shouldn't have tried to cross Nolin Creek while the ice was unstable. The snowfall covered everything, so it's impossible to see if she was alone."

"It was no accident," my father says, looking directly at me. Ash gathers at the end of his cigarette.

"No, Isä. It wasn't." What can I say to comfort my parents? What words would make it better?

We sit in silence for a few minutes. It's always been this way in our house. Good news or bad, we internalize our reactions. I know their suffering is overwhelming, as is mine, but we gather our strength to show a brave face to one another and to outsiders. Is it Finnish stoicism, as I've heard it called, or is it an inability to face the tragic truth?

"Something must be done," my father says. He takes a drag from his cigarette, his gaze on the rolling fields. Clouds obscure the sun, darkening the afternoon. A sudden chill strikes me, although the stove is throwing a fiery heat.

"I'll take care of it. I promise you." As soon as the words escape my lips, I know I cannot take them back. My father nods his approval.

His face relaxes slightly. "Good," he adds in English, sounding satisfied. Someone has a plan. A plan is always good. But I have no plan. My heart sinks.

Mother stares at me, her eyes narrow and her features pointed. "This is your fault," she says in Finnish. "You left home, where we protected you. Where God could keep you safe. You moved to the city, and I warned you something bad would happen." No tears well in my mother's eyes. Her rage is palpable. "You're the oldest. You should have protected them. Saved them."

Them. My mother is blaming me not only for Hanna's death but also for Martta's. I avert my eyes and stare out at the empty fields. I am fourteen again. The weight of Martta's death is drowning me under my mother's anger and sorrow. The guilt of Martta's death is a burden I've carried for nine years, and my mother has never let me forget it. But Hanna's death? Am I to blame? Could I have saved her?

"I'm sorry, Äiti." I don't know what else to say. It is not enough. It will never be enough.

My father butts out his cigarette, helps my mother rise from the table, and guides her to their bedroom. She looks smaller now. Frailer than I've ever seen her. I am motionless, wondering if I should leave them to their grief, an anguish my mother clearly condemns me for.

Father drops himself back into the chair across from me, gripping his coffee cup, but he does not bring it to his lips. His hands still tremble. "She never recovered, Essi. She's never been the same since Martta went to God. And now Hanna. It's too much." Tears form in his eyes, and he stifles a sob.

"She blames me." I say it so softly perhaps he doesn't hear me, but I know it to be true, and so does he.

"Your mother blames everyone. She blames the world. Even God."

"I'll uncover the truth about Hanna. She wouldn't dare cross the creek at this time of year." I don't know how I'll do it, but I vow I will. I have to do something.

My father and I stare out the window as if the answer is written on the fields. "What do you think happened? Did someone want to hurt her?"

"I don't know," I say, holding back my tears. I want to be strong.

He reaches over and touches my hand, squeezing it for a moment before letting it go. His eyes cloud over with new grief, layered on top of the old. He tries to give me a weak smile. It is something. Our desire to know the truth unites us. I won't let him down.

We spend another hour together, my mother cocooned in her darkened bedroom, my father sitting still like a defeated statue in his chair. I brew more coffee, and encourage my father to eat some leftover stew, but he leaves it untouched. I tidy the kitchen and stoke the fire. Anything to be helpful, but the house feels darker and colder than it was when I arrived. It occurs to me I should stay and be with them, and I say so to my father.

For a moment, he is silent, considering my question or not hearing it. "You take care of yourself. Go back to town. I'll take care of your mother. It's for the best."

I understand what he wants. He is strong enough for them both, I hope. For all these decades, he has been at her side through joy and loss. Too often grief. He has been her rock. As I take a last sip of coffee, I search the dark circles under his eyes, the way his shoulders droop. He's aged before my eyes. He'll need every ounce of *sisu* he can summon, but not even his courage, his determination, will bring his daughter back.

The rumble of an old truck and tires crunching on the gravel driveway fills me with relief, for which I feel immediate guilt. I should want to stay with my parents, but the house feels suffocating, the pain seeping from the walls and rising from the floorboards. I need to leave before it envelops me completely.

"Fredi's here. I have to go," I say. I am torn between this place, this old life, and returning to my new life without her.

Father nods and follows me to the front door.

I hesitate at the end of the hall leading to my mother's room but decide to pass it without a sound. The last thing she wants right now is my interference in her sorrow. If I can find her answers, maybe she will forgive me. Knowing how Hanna died may give her some peace.

My father stands at the doorway as he has always done when visitors leave his home. Usually, he has a broad grin on his face, but not today. I embrace him, breathing the scent of tobacco and the fields emanating from his clothes, trying to gather strength. If only a little of his Finnish sisu could rub off on me. It would keep me going.

Chapter Four
May 1924

The chirping of birds outside our farmhouse breaks the early morning silence and I turn over in my bed. The sun, brighter than it has been in months, sneaks into our upstairs bedroom through cracks in the curtains. I squint and close my eyes, not ready yet to face the day. Hanna had kept me up with her tossing and turning.

"Get up, Essi. It's here! It's my birthday!"

I flop on my side and hide my head under a pillow. "Go away, Hanna. It's too early."

Hanna jumps on my bed until I giggle. "Come on, say it!" She swings a pillow at my head.

I sit up, cross my arms, and try to look puzzled, but a look of disappointment crosses her face, and I relent. "Happy Birthday, little sister."

Hanna jumps up and down with joy on her face. "Happy Birthday to me!"

From the kitchen, I hear Martta chattering away to our mother. The aroma of bacon frying and pancakes on the griddle wafts up the stairs.

"Look who's up." Mother wipes her hands on her apron and greets us with a rare smile. "My little girl is becoming a young woman. How time flies!" She adds in English, "Happy Birthday."

A blush rises on Hanna's cheeks. She's been talking about turning thirteen for ages. "Where's Isä?"

"Probably in the barn," I say, swiping a slice of bacon. Hanna takes her place across from Martta, and I place the cups and saucers on the table for Hanna's birthday breakfast.

Our mother glances towards the barn. "Your father said to start without him. He'll be in soon." She serves buttermilk pancakes, blueberries, bacon, and eggs. Martta chomps eagerly on a pancake, maple syrup running down her chin, while Hanna sits like a lady, tall and upright, her pinky raised as she sips her milky coffee.

I pull a small package wrapped in butcher paper and red ribbons from my skirt pocket and pass it to her, hoping she'll like it. "I made it myself."

Hanna unwraps the ribbon and carefully opens the paper to reveal the bracelet I've woven. My mother taught me how to plait the straw in such a pattern it looked delicate but felt strong.

"It's beautiful, Essi." Hanna places it on her wrist and studies it in the light. Last year, for my thirteenth birthday, she embroidered a bookmark with my name surrounded by stars.

Our father arrives at the door, retrieving a small package from its hiding place under the wooden bench near the entrance. My parents have not let me in on their secret gift, so I wait with as much anticipation as Hanna shows on her face. When I turned thirteen, they gave me a brooch that had belonged to my great-grandmother. I keep it safely in a box with my favourite things: my old stories, a few family photographs, some pebbles collected by the river.

"This is a precious gift. It's been in the family for generations," Mother says.

Hanna gingerly opens the packaging to reveal a small carved box.

"Let me see!" Martta teeters on her chair with her hands on the table to peer inside, and I lean over.

"This necklace belonged to your grandmother in Finland. She gave it to me before we boarded our ship to cross the sea. It's called Hannunvaakuna or St. John's Cross. It brings luck and protection," our mother explains. "You're old enough now. Take good care of it. Someday you'll give it to your own daughter."

Hanna traces the engraving of the outward-pointing loops beneath her fingertips.

"The old folks say it will ward off evil," Father says, helping with the clasp.

I laugh. "What evil are you going to find in Wanup?"

Hanna shoots me a look. "That's not the point. It's a family heirloom. I love it," she says, looking from Mother to Father. Hanna reaches her arms around him, and he embraces her warmly. His eyes glisten with pride. She turns to Mother and gives her a more polite embrace and a peck on the cheek.

After clearing the breakfast table and completing our morning chores, Hanna and I, with little Martta trailing behind, make our way to the banks of the Wanapitei to watch the yearly flow of logs floating downriver. A small group of curious children and a few adults have already gathered, but I couldn't care less about the logging. We watch it every year. It's only exciting when the logs get all bunched together, and the logger uses his pole to dislodge them, dancing across the shifting logs. Most of the time, the logs move along with a few men showing off for the onlookers. Big deal.

"Look, Essi." Her eyes are wide. Martta opens her tiny hand to reveal a shiny button, blue like the river, with little stones encircling it. "Can you fix it?"

The button has fallen from her hand-me-down dark blue spring coat. I kneel to see where it came from: the second from the top, closest to her heart. "Give it to me." Martta places it in my open palm. "I'll sew it on when we get home." I put it in my pocket where it will be safe.

Martta's face brightens, and she skips toward the water's edge.

"Don't go far, Martta," I call out to her. "Stay away from the edge." The roar of the spring thaw always makes me nervous: too raucous, too out of control.

Hanna groans and nudges me. "Oh no, there's Fredi. He's getting gawkier the older he gets, don't you think?"

Fredi has grown taller this last year, pants a little too short and his arms a little too long for his sleeves. "He needs friends, Hanna. You know he's having a tough time at home."

"I know, it's just I have nothing in common with him, and he's always staring at me with those puppy-dog eyes."

Fredi waves from a distance. "Don't you think we should say hello to him?"

Hanna shrugs. "You go right ahead. But do not, I repeat, do not invite him over for birthday cake."

Fredi heads to the water where Martta is tossing rocks. Her face lights and she talks animatedly, probably about all the rocks she'd collected.

"At least Martta likes him," I say. Of course, Martta likes everyone. Of the three of us, she is the most outgoing, with Hanna a solid second.

"Äiti said I could ask the girls from school for cake this afternoon. I'm going to find them. You look after Martta."

"Why do I have to watch her?" I can't help complaining, even though it's Hanna's day.

"I played with her all afternoon yesterday while you and Äiti were baking together. It's your turn." Hanna's eyebrows knit together. She knows how to make me feel guilty with just one look.

"I helped Äiti make pulla in a hot kitchen, and we made *your* cake. I would rather have been playing in the barn with you and Martta," I say. But the truth is, I enjoy the time with our mother. Over the years, she's taught me to cook, sew my own clothes, darn socks, and how to make a doll from a corn husk. Hanna took little interest in any of these activities, although we both made our own quilts last summer. "Fine. Go find your friends. I'll watch Martta."

Hanna's forehead relaxes, and she flashes me her best smile, touching my arm in reconciliation. "You're a peach. There's Helen and Miriam. I'm going to invite them to my party," she says, and saunters off toward a group of girls on the ridge.

"It's not a party, Hanna," I call after her. "It's just cake."

"Don't be such a spoilsport. It's my birthday, and I'm calling it a party," Hanna yells over her shoulder as she heads up the hill.

"I'll be there in a few minutes." Martta is going to tire of her game soon enough. Her pigtails bob as she skips along the river's edge.

"Watch your step. Don't get too close to the water!" I shout to make myself heard over the crash of waves and wallop of logs.

Martta reaches down to gather rocks in her small palms. I know she wants to watch them disappear into the waves, a game we often played in the creek in the woods behind our house. Fredi crouches beside her, smiling patiently as Martta puts the rocks in his outstretched hand.

A few shouts signal excitement upriver, and a group of kids runs toward the sounds. From my vantage point, I can see a logger scampering across the logs. There must be a jam.

"Essi!" Miriam yells over the ruckus of the river. "Look!" She points toward the water. Her expression is one I've never seen before. Her mouth gapes, and her eyes are wide with fear.

Fredi is standing motionless, knee-deep in the current, gripping a protruding rock to keep himself from being pulled downstream. Where is Martta?

I scan the river's edge, trying to make sense of the chaotic scene. Logs hurtle down the bulging river. More people are gathering, looking frantic. They run along the bank, shouting at one another. My stomach churns. Where is she? I glanced away for only a second.

I stumble down the embankment, tripping on loose rocks and calling her name over and over again. She'll jump up from behind a boulder or run toward me from the bushes. I'm going to find her lying in the tall grass watching the clouds. *Look, Essi: a fish, a bird, an angel.*

Hanna is beside me now, gripping my hand and shouting, "Where's Martta? Where is she?"

My heart pounds against my chest. I can't breathe. I can't speak. Inside my head, someone is screaming.

"I was holding her rocks in my hands," Fredi is saying. "She was taking them, one at a time, throwing them into the water." Fredi looks at the waves, his face white. "She stepped forward to throw a stone ... too close to the edge. She tumbled in ... I reached for her ... her fingers ... I tried to grab hold ... she ... slipped away."

Hanna throws her arms around my shaking body, tears drenching her face. The logs jostle down the rapids, crashing into each other, relentless in their path of destruction. I'm helpless to stop them. As if waking from a dream, we run downstream, my screams silenced only by the roaring water stealing my sister away.

Chapter Five

April 1933

I shift on the hard pew, trying to concentrate on the sermon. Paster Antero is saying something about death and God and the arms of Jesus. A small, wiry man, he's been our minister at the Evangelical Lutheran Church in Wanup since our confirmation. He speaks as if he knows her.

There are only a few people in the small church, including the pastor and his wife Anna, both from the old country. Fredi is sitting in the aisle across from me with his parents, Hilja and Samuel. I hear my mother's cousin, Aunt Marjatta, sniffle behind me, but her husband, Uncle Timo, sits silently beside her. There are others—Helen, Miriam, a few friends from our school days—but I can't look their way.

The air is stifling. I long to go outside and breathe the cool air, feel the rain on my face, but I know I must sit still and attend to every word. My mother clasps her hands in front of her, and my father holds on to his hymnal as if his life depended on it.

After the pastor concludes his sermon, the congregation sings a hymn, and I feel a sense of relief from all the talking.

Pastor Antero eyes me and nods, gauging my ability to stand before the congregation. He says, "Esteri, Hanna's sister, will now read from Ecclesiastes."

"For everything there is a season, and a time to every purpose under Heaven," I read, choking on the words. It isn't the right time for Hanna to die. She was too young, full of life and dreams of the future. I force myself to finish the passage. In the back pew, a man in uniform listens intently. Robert Cane. Why is he here? I sit down beside my father, holding back tears.

After the service, I stand beside an open grave, the plain wooden coffin my father built in the barn only days before slowly being lowered into the ground as the wind howls and spiky raindrops prick my skin. I sense Fredi's presence near me and feel a little comfort in it. I touch my bracelet with Martta's button while Pastor Antero says a prayer. Someone behind me sobs, but my eyes are dry.

My mother's face is pale against her black dress, and her eyes are red-rimmed and puffy from crying. Now, she stands like a statue, her outward composure masking her intense grief. Father stares at Pastor Antero, watching his every move, as though he might find some answers in the minister's words or actions. Father throws the first handful of earth. As a child, I thought my father was a strong and sturdy man, but now he looks smaller and frailer with every passing day.

Two Wanup men wait at a distance with shovels, a pile of earth ready to be heaped unceremoniously over the coffin when we've turned away. They must see me staring because one turns his back, and the other lowers his hat as if to protect himself from the rain.

When it is done, I slog behind my parents to my father's horse and wagon, pull myself up, and tuck my coat around my legs. There is some comfort in the wagon's jostle on the uneven roads and the soft snorts and whinnies from the horses. The small group of friends and neighbours from the churchyard follows us. A dark vehicle pauses before turning toward the road to Sudbury. I try to glimpse inside, but I can't tell if it is Officer Cane or someone else. Will this day never end?

As we make our way down the driveway, the house looks lonely and neglected. There is no joy in this gathering and little to offer our guests, but I've done my best to supply a spread. Ruby even sent some baking with me. Although our neighbours have so little to spare, everyone brings an offering for our shared meal. I am grateful for this act of kindness, but I can't bear making small talk with them. Instead, I hide in the kitchen, preparing trays with the food the neighbours bring, and serving cup after cup of coffee.

I lean against the kitchen table and feel the aching in my bones, wishing everyone would go away. Is this how my mother feels? I was younger when Martta died and never imagined I'd feel such intense grief again. Makes you want to hide away from all human contact. Makes you feel a hundred years old and ready to fall on the bare earth until it swallows you whole for one last, long sleep.

In the other room, I can hear the guests conversing and offering their condolences to my parents. I'm grateful Fredi is here. He is chatting with Pastor Antero and Anna, even though he's not one for conversation.

Aunt Marjatta brings me a container with her *karjalanpiirakat*. Her delicious Karelian pasties usually make my mouth water, but not today. "Is there anything else I can do to help, Essi?" she asks.

I thank her and say no, placing the pasties on a serving plate.

"She was a beautiful person," Aunt Marjatta says, her eyes welling with tears. She dabs them with her handkerchief. "You'll get through this."

I try to smile and nod, but I can't find the right words. "I just want to know the truth."

Aunt Marjatta takes the coffee I offer her. "The truth isn't always what we need to hear. Sometimes it's better to let things go. Accept what's happened and make peace with it."

She's wrong, but I don't say so. I need the truth about what happened to my sister. So do my parents. I don't want to talk. Not today. Not about Hanna.

After some time, Fredi enters the kitchen with a pile of dishes. "Need any help?"

I pause for a moment, surprised he has offered. "Can you bring me home after this?"

Fredi picks up a tea towel and a plate to dry. "Sure thing, but I thought you wanted to stay for a few days."

I glance at my mother through the kitchen doorway. She is sitting alone, staring out the window, her back to the guests. "I don't think I'm wanted right now." Pastor Antero approaches and places a hand on my mother's shoulder. He says a few words, but she doesn't acknowledge his presence. I don't blame her. Being in the kitchen is just a busier way of avoiding people.

"She'll forgive you in time," Fredi says. "What happened wasn't your fault."

I sigh and return to the soapy water and dirty dishes. "I hope you're right, but until I find out what happened to Hanna, I don't think she'll ever speak to me again."

"You still think someone did this ... intentionally?" Fredi stacks the clean dishes in the cupboard.

"There is no other explanation. You know Hanna would never risk crossing the creek, especially with the spring current and fragile ice. We always crossed at the tracks. You saw what happened to Martta."

A shadow crosses Fredi's face.

"I'm sorry, Fredi. I didn't mean ..." It was careless of me to mention Martta.

"It's okay. I'll never forget that day. She was so little. Only five. And everything happened so fast. If only I had ..." His eyes tell of his deep sadness, and his voice reveals the guilt I know he still has for not saving her. "If there's anything I can do to help, just ask."

"Thanks. I can always rely on you." Hanna may not have appreciated Fredi, but he and I have been friends for a long time, and after Martta's death, we shared a sense of guilt. No one else could understand, not even Hanna.

When the last cup is dry and put away, I glance back at my mother, still alone in her chair. "I suppose I should go over there," I say, drying my hands on my apron. Fredi nods but hangs back.

I pause beside my mother's chair, wondering if I should sit. "Can I get you anything?" She hasn't eaten a morsel all day, and her hands tremble as she clutches her handkerchief. "You should eat something."

Memories of Martta's funeral flash through my mind. My mother was younger then, with less grey in her hair and fewer wrinkles across her face. She had changed in the days after Martta's death. I didn't know how to help her then, and I don't know how to reach her now. What will become of her with both Hanna and Martta gone?

I wait for a response. It feels like an eternity, but it is only minutes of silence, each one seeming to stretch the distance between us. My father observes us from across the room, a frown on his face, but his attention turns back to Uncle Timo. He won't say it, but I know he is fearful about my mother's health. He's watched her slip away for years. We all have, but our father has always been her pillar, and we left him to take on the whole burden when we moved away. The guilt gnaws at me.

My mother grips the arms of the chair and pushes herself up, unsteady on her feet. I reach out to support her, but she swats my hand. "Go away. I don't want to see you." She turns to face the guests, her voice booming. "You can all go away now. Leave me be."

My cheeks flush with heat. "Äiti, our guests just want to offer their condolences," I say, my voice low.

"I don't want their words. They can't give me what I've lost," she says in Finnish.

The guests look surprised and confused, glancing from my mother to my father and to me.

"Get out!" She makes her way down the hallway and slams the bedroom door.

Samuel rises from the couch and shakes my father's hand. "Let's go," he says to Hilja, and she follows without protest, glancing at me with a familiar pity in her eyes.

Fredi trails behind his parents. "I'll be back to pick you up." He lifts his hand in a half-wave, as if in apology.

One by one, the guests disperse, stopping to say a word to me or my father before going into the dreary afternoon. They are thankful to leave us to our grief, I suspect, as much as I am relieved to be left alone.

Pastor Antero and Anna approach me. "If there is anything, please don't hesitate," he says. Anna touches my arm. For the first time today, tears well in my eyes. I bite my lip to stop it from trembling and nod, knowing any words I try to say will catch in my throat. They pull on their coats, a gust of wind slipping past the open door before they close it firmly on our grieving family.

Aunt Marjatta and Uncle Timo stay the longest. She moves around the room, collecting dishes and tidying, but Uncle Timo sits in silence with my father. "Dishes done, and food put away. Anything else?" Aunt Marjatta asks.

"We'll be okay," I answer.

"Give her time. Your mother will come around. She's suffered more than most." Aunt Marjatta embraces me, and I pat her back gently until she lets me go. She is kind, my aunt, but she does not know what we're going through. My mother's grief is bigger than anything I can imagine, a whole ocean of sorrow that she can't release. I can't allow myself to feel my grief fully yet, let alone hers.

Aunt Marjatta and Uncle Timo speak in quiet tones to my father as they move to the door. He watches their automobile back away from the house, leaving us alone together.

In the small entrance, Hanna's wool sweater hangs on a peg. I bring it to my face and breathe in, hoping to catch her scent, before pulling it over my black dress. Fredi will be back soon to bring me to town, to my empty room. With only a short time left, I sneak upstairs to our shared bedroom in the loft. It's just as we left it. My little writing desk is still under the window overlooking the fields. So many stories written here, so many journal entries. And above Hanna's bed, a collage of pictures carefully cut out of newspapers and magazines displaying all the things she aspired to. A handsome husband, a beautiful house with a picket fence, pretty clothes and shoes. A bigger life, more glamorous than the one she had here. In our own ways, we both longed for escape.

With my little bag packed, I take one last glance around the house and step outside. My father is pacing the driveway, smoking a cigarette. His back is hunched from hard work and age. I wish I had the right words to comfort him.

"You're going now?" He exhales a long stream of smoke.

I nod and glance at my mother's bedroom window. "I wish I could be of use to you. To her."

My father says nothing, just continues to inhale and exhale, slowly and methodically, as though in deep thought. "She needs time."

Ten years? Twenty years? A lifetime? How much time before I am forgiven? I've always tried to do the right thing, for her, and for our family. As a child, I only tried to please her, paying close attention to everything she taught me, never causing problems that might upset her. But I could never do enough to please her. If only I could bring her justice.

The sound of Fredi's truck draws our attention. My father drops his cigarette and stubs it out with his shoe.

"I'm sorry." I don't know what else to say. My father's embrace is awkward, but his arms around me are comforting. Although he is frailer than before, he is not broken. I draw strength from him, from the fact that he is still standing. He has not given up on my mother. I must not give up on her either. Or Hanna. We need the truth.

Chapter Six
April 1933

By the time I get in Fredi's truck, I'm exhausted. My body aches, but it's more than that. My head, my face, my eyes are heavy. The steady rumble of the truck as it makes its way back to Sudbury puts me to sleep. Fredi wakes me when we arrive at the boarding house.

"Will you find a new place to live now?" Fredi asks, glancing at the two-storey building. "You know your mother would have a fit if she knew you lived here."

We've had this conversation a few times, and I'm in no mood to discuss it again. "If I can find something I can afford on my own, then I'll consider it. But I don't think this is the right time to go hunting for a new place, do you? Besides, Borgia Street is no better."

Fredi looks sheepish. "It's not so bad," he says. "The rent is cheap. Lots of good people there. When you're ready, I can help you."

I feel remorse about my tone. He doesn't deserve it. "Sorry, Fredi. I haven't been sleeping and ... It's a kind offer and I'll take you up on it when the time comes." Fredi nods, and I push his cranky old door open with all my might. "Get your door fixed." He smiles. I wave as he pulls away, turning toward Mackenzie Street, his truck rumbling along the partly snow-covered road.

Billy is shovelling the porch steps, his jacket open despite the cold air. He smiles and opens the door with a flourish, giving me a deep bow, which makes me smile. I stamp my feet on the mat before stepping over the threshold.

As I remove my hat and gloves, I listen for voices, but it's early enough and there aren't any guests here yet. Good thing, too. I can't bear seeing Rouva Ruusa or anyone else right now. I savour this quiet time during the day, and today, more than any other, I'm relieved to be alone.

"Essi, Essi, viens ici." Come here, Yvonne says. From the top of the staircase, she motions for me with an urgency I've rarely seen from her. She's one of Rouva Ruusa's newest, and youngest girls, but over the months she's been here, I've come to appreciate her positive energy and good-natured gossiping. I wonder what brought her to this place, but I don't ask questions. Maybe she wonders the same about me.

"What's going on? Is everything okay?" I follow her down the dark corridor to her room at the back corner of the house.

I've never been in any of the girls' private rooms before. Yvonne's is small, but filled with lacy, feminine things. It reminds me of her: dainty with fine features. A silk kimono-style robe hangs beside the door, and a flowery bedspread drapes her bed. My room is plain and utilitarian by comparison, with only our handmade quilts and a woven rag rug providing a little colour. The scent of Yvonne's floral perfume hangs in the air, along with the faint smell of old tobacco and whisky, although I've never seen Yvonne smoke or touch alcohol.

"I was so sorry to hear about Hanna. I didn't know her well, but she was always kind, like you." Yvonne flashes a shy smile. "And I want to help you. Madame Rose says you think it's ... how you say ... foul play."

Why would Rouva Ruusa tell Yvonne about my theory? It feels like a betrayal of my confidence. But then again, she feels responsible for the women in her care and may be worried about them. I must look confused because Yvonne reaches for my hand.

"Someone knows something. What if he is after Madame Rose's girls? We must stick together."

Is someone targeting prostitutes or other women in the Donovan neighbourhood? There are immigrants of all nationalities living here, and crime is rising. I'd read some newspaper articles about those kinds of evil men and scary stories about crime in *True Detective*. What if living here made Hanna a target? I shiver. If someone hurt my sister, on purpose or otherwise, he is still out there.

"Do you know something?" My cheeks feel hot, but my mind is racing with this new possibility.

"I don't know what happened to Hanna," Yvonne says, making the sign of the cross, "but I meet many men. They drink. They talk. They tell me things. Secrets, sometimes. I listen. They think I don't pay attention, but I do." She taps her temple and winks.

Yvonne's right. Someone might know something about what happened that night. "Are you saying you can—"

"Spy? Oui, I spy on the men and learn secrets. I like you. And Hanna. If the person, le meutrier, targets girls around here, we need to protect each other. So, I'll help." Yvonne's smile spreads across her face, and she nods with vigour. "Oui?"

"Anything you find out would be helpful," I say. "The police don't care about a girl like Hanna. They don't even believe she was murdered. They think I should just let it go." Thinking about my interactions with the police makes me angry. If they won't help, I'll have to do it on my own. It's the only way to get justice for our family.

"Oh, Officer O'Rourke, he's got lots of work to do, for sure. He's a married man with three kids. Always working. He's my client sometimes. I ask him questions. I tell him I'm scared someone will come after me, too." Yvonne winks and places a finger to her lips. "Tell no one. It's my little secret."

I'm shocked. "O'Rourke is a client? What about Cane?" I can't imagine the young police officer doing anything illicit, but I wouldn't have believed it of O'Rourke either. Are all police officers just criminals in uniforms?

"The young one. Non. I never see him with one of our girls. He's cute, eh?"

"I guess." She's right. He is good-looking, but I don't have time to think about these things. "Is there anyone else who might know something about Hanna? One of the other girls, maybe?"

Yvonne lowers her voice and leans in. "Ah, oui. A man named Pekka Peltonen. He's not old, but very, how you say, sullen." Yvonne's face contorts until she looks like a sad clown. "You know him?"

"Only to see him," I say. I picture Pekka, a Finnish miner who rarely speaks to anyone and always has a scowl on his face. Drinks too much. I'd heard a rumour last month that he'd been jailed overnight for being disorderly downtown. Started a fight with a man at a bar. Well, finished it, at least. "What makes you think of him?"

Yvonne's big, dark eyes reveal her worry. "Two reasons. One, I introduced Hanna to Pekka a few months ago."

Puzzled, I wait for Yvonne to continue. Why would Yvonne introduce Hanna to a miner who frequents a brothel? Neither of us is interested in the kinds of men who come here.

"Hanna ask me to find someone to help her. Someone strong. How you say? Discreet. I introduced her to Pekka, and they talked in the parlour. Sorry ... I forgot 'til today. I thought you should know ... just in case it's important."

"It's certainly unusual," I say. "What did they discuss?" Had Hanna ever mentioned Pekka to me before? I didn't think so.

"I don't know, but she needed him to help her. She feared someone, I think." Yvonne pauses and covers her mouth. "Non ... not what you think, Essi. She wanted Pekka to warn him, not hurt him. It was ... just in case. She made us promise not to tell you, but now I believe I should have told you sooner."

My head is spinning with this new information. "It's okay. You did the right thing by respecting her wishes, even if I'm desperate to know. You said there were two things you wanted to tell me?"

"Oui, mon amie. I forgot. There are many rumours. People say Pekka had a wife named Sofia. She just, whoosh, disappeared three or four months ago. He never talks about it." Yvonne crosses her arms.

I try to make sense of the information, but I'm so tired my head hurts. "His wife disappeared. Did Hanna know about Sofia?" Why would Hanna need to talk to this man with a sordid past?

"I don't know." Yvonne shrugs.

"What are people saying about her?"

Yvonne shakes her head. "Some say she ran away. Went home to her parents in Thunder Bay. Pekka drank too much, and she had enough. She could have a lover. Or he hurt her. No one knows the real story."

"Do *you* think Pekka killed his wife?" It's hard to think of a man hurting his spouse, and I shake the image away.

"Don't know. Never know what people will do," Yvonne says. "Maybe muetre." Yvonne motions as if to cut her throat with her hand, a wild look in her eyes, but then her gentle smile returns. "Or maybe not. Who knows?" She shrugs again.

"You don't think Pekka had something to do with Hanna's death, do you? If he did it once, he could do it again."

Yvonne's shoulders droop, and she touches my arm. "I do not know who hurt your sister. And if Pekka had something to do with it, I'm sorry I introduced them." Yvonne grips my hands, tears forming.

"It's not your fault. Warn the other girls. We don't know who hurt Hanna, but whoever did it is still out there. We all need to be careful." This isn't just about my family anymore. I need to protect these girls, too.

Yvonne nods and gives me a powerful hug. When she finally releases me, she gives me a fresh smile and says, "You are good people. I knew I should tell you."

Why would Hanna want to meet him? Who was she so afraid of that she needed to hire someone to rough him up, just in case? I thank Yvonne and slip out of her room, running our conversation through my mind as I return to my room down the hall.

It's not late, but my body is so exhausted that I climb under my quilt and tuck my knees towards my chest. Yet sleep eludes me. I toss and turn as the wind wails through the pines, and the branches scratch at the window. Hard snow pummels the glass. Visions of Hanna submerged in water haunt my dreams. One moment it is my sister, and the next, the ice is a mirror, and I see myself below the surface, screaming to break free.

Chapter Seven

April 1933

The small mirror in my room makes it difficult to see how Hanna's navy-blue dress with the tidy white collar looks on me. I do my chin-length hair like Hanna had done for me sometimes, finger waves at my temples, smooth and rolling, but my fingers are clumsy, and my hair looks a mousy brown. From Hanna's drawer, I find some raspberry cream rouge and her favourite red lipstick. I attempt to apply it without making myself look like a clown. I certainly don't look glamorous like a Hollywood starlet, an air Hanna could easily achieve, but I also don't appear like one of Rouva Ruusa's girls whose outfits are a tad too tight and low-cut for my taste. It will have to do. If anyone asks why I'm dressed up, I can tell them I'm going out for the evening, and they won't suspect a thing.

I sidle into the dim parlour and sit at a small table away from the patrons. The scent of old liquor and smoke clings to the dark wood furniture. No one glances my way. I scan the room for Pekka Peltonen.

Across the room, two men talk over one another in a heated debate. Their Finnish vowels slur and I catch only a few words: Socialists, Karelia, opportunities, scam. It's an argument I've heard many times before. When my father left Finland after the Civil War, he hoped to leave behind the tensions between the Socialist Reds and the White Finns in the old country, but that didn't happen. People just couldn't let their differences go, not even in Sudbury, or even little Wanup.

Once, when Hanna and I wanted to go to a dance at the town hall, my father got visibly angry. "Red Finns organized that dance. They'll spout out nonsense to you before the band even plays. I will not have my daughters attend such an event. Absolutely not."

"But Isä, it's just a dance. It's not like we're going to marry one of them. We just want a fun night out. We don't care about politics," Hanna complained. "And Fredi's driving us. He'll keep us safe." She doesn't mention Fredi refuses to go to the dance.

"You should care about politics. Why do you think we came to Canada?" He grimaces. "Why do Finns come to North America for a better life only to turn around for the Soviet Union when things get tough here? A socialist society in Karelia? Do they think it will be better? They'll be lucky if they get any bread, let alone work."

Hanna rolled her eyes and stomped up the stairs to our room. I sat by my father, letting him ramble on about the war and the evils of Karelia before I, too, excused myself and headed upstairs, knowing I would have to comfort Hanna, too.

Since moving to Sudbury, Hanna and I have gone to several dances, some of them organized by socialists. The music was always lively, and young couples whirled around the dance floor. It was harmless and fun. Why had he been so angry?

Now, feeling heartsick for my father, I strain to hear the conversation between the two men. Is one or the other planning to move to Karelia? It's not a simple decision, uprooting your life and moving across the world for the dream of more prosperity. An immigrant's desires and hopes can outweigh the risks and challenges of leaving their home country, or this, their adopted one.

To the right of the squabbling men, a group of miners is playing cards, their meager earnings scattered across the table. Yvonne crosses the room and pauses by their table, chatting and pouring drinks before she looks up and winks at me, nodding toward the man I'm looking for, sitting in a dark corner. Nonchalantly, she slinks over to my table.

"Do you want me to come with you?" she asks, glancing toward Pekka Peltonen.

I hesitate a moment, trying to decide what would be best.

"Thanks, Yvonne, but I'd like to talk to him myself."

Pekka Peltonen is leaning back in a deep armchair, gazing out the window, with a bottle of whisky beside him. Ashes cling to the tip of his cigarette. He is so deep in thought that he doesn't notice me staring at him across the room. His facial features say nothing, but I'm not surprised. It's an expression I've seen repeatedly and often sported myself. He is Finnish after all, and we Finns know how to hide our emotions.

I study his features: the strong jawline, hooded eyelids over blue eyes, high cheekbones, and blond hair. Judging by the crow's feet around his eyes, and a few strands of grey in his hair, he looks to be in his late forties or fifties.

If Hanna were here, he'd have noticed her even before she came his way, put out the cigarette, and sat up straight, eyeing her from head to toe. She'd have sauntered right up, thrown back her blond locks, and shone her wide smile. He would have invited her to sit and have a drink. She'd have laughed at his jokes and touched his sleeve. Hanna would have known exactly how to get him talking. I always worried her flirtations might get her in trouble someday. Now, I wish I could flirt, even just a little.

Smoothing the wrinkles from my skirt and tucking my hair behind my ear, I rise and take a deep breath. This is it. What does this man know about my sister? I stride across the floor like a schoolmistress ready to enact punishment, but with less confidence. Pekka glances up with a quizzical look.

"Kivi, Essi," I say in Finnish, and pull out a chair to sit down. "May I?"

Pekka's brows knit together, but he nods. "Peltonen, Pekka." His words slur slightly, and he looks irritated. "What can I do for you?"

"Can we have a chat?" I grip the arms of my chair to stop my hands from shaking. "You knew my sister, Hanna Kivi?"

"Hanna ... Hanna ... The girl who drowned in Nolin Creek?" His eyes are bloodshot, and the circles under his eyes are bloated.

"Yes, Hanna." His expression shifts so slightly, I almost don't register it. Is it guilt? Does he notice how my voice quivers?

Pekka empties his glass and pours another. "Want one?" he asks, tilting the bottle. "I haven't seen your sister in a long time. Weeks, even."

I take a sip. "Her funeral was yesterday."

Pekka stares at the bottom of his glass, swirling the liquid. "I'm sorry for your loss."

His tone disarms me, and for a moment I forget why I'm here. I thank him for his kindness. Silence lingers on the table between us, as the chatter of the card players, the clinking of glasses, and the laughter of the girls fade into the background.

"Can I ask you a few questions?" I ask. "About her?"

"I barely knew the girl." Pekka pushes back his chair, about to stand.

I reach out and grip his sleeve. "Please. I need to know what happened."

Pekka slumps back into his chair and brings his palm to his forehead, squeezing it with his fingers. "What do you want to know?"

"The thing is, she didn't drown. At least, I don't believe so." I keep my voice low. I don't want to spook him.

"They say it was an accident. It could happen to anyone."

"It wasn't an accident. That's why I'm here. I hope you can help me." I let the sentence hang in the air and watch for a reaction. A twitch in the corner of his eye is almost imperceptible. He takes a swig from his glass and puts it down too roughly. The contents splash onto his hand. "Perkele." Goddamn, he mutters and wipes his hand on his shirt.

The argument I'd overheard earlier erupts again, and we both turn to see what is happening. One man is leaning toward the other, his hands planted on the table. Rouva Ruusa appears out of nowhere and tells the man to sit down or get out. He takes a sip of his drink and sits back in his chair. As usual, Rouva Ruusa has everything under control. I turn my attention back to Pekka, who shakes his head and mutters something incoherently.

"I know you spoke with my sister right here in this very room. Who was she afraid of?" I try to keep my voice steady, but Pekka's eyes have a wild look.

"Look here. I talked to her once. She was nice to me, but we weren't friends. I don't know what you're trying to get at, lady." Pekka shoves the small table, and the half-empty bottle teeters.

"Listen, I'm not accusing you of anything, but I need to know who killed my sister. What did you discuss?"

Pekka surveys the room and wipes his forehead with a handkerchief. "Miss Kivi, I don't know what happened to your sister."

My frustration rises. This conversation is going nowhere. Yvonne may have thought Pekka would tell me what happened to Hanna, but he isn't sharing any of it with me. I bolster my courage. "Where were you that night?"

"You police now? Are you accusing me of something?" Pekka glares at me, his face red from drink or anger or both. "Do you think I had something to do with this?" I catch my breath as he rises, hovering over me. He is a big man, tall and muscular. His fists clench and unclench, his forehead glistening in the low light. "I've had enough trouble with the police lately, and I have done nothing wrong."

The rest of the room is silent. All eyes are on Pekka. One of the card players looks like he's about to intervene, and I feel safe among these strangers. Pekka wouldn't dare harm me here, and if he tried, one of these burly men would surely come to my rescue. At least I've learned one thing: this man has a temper.

Rouva Ruusa appears at Pekka's side. "Time to go, soldier," she says. Pekka sighs and hangs his head.

I touch Rouva Ruusa's sleeve. "No, wait. I just need a moment. Please?"

She pokes him in the chest. "I won't have any trouble from you or any of these men, you hear?"

Pekka grunts and plops down again. "Yeah, I had a conversation with her. She was having some trouble. I'm not supposed to talk to you."

"Why not?" I'm confused.

Pekka shifts uncomfortably in his chair. "I made a promise. To her. I may not be a pillar of society, but I always keep my promises. I agreed not to discuss our arrangement with anyone. Especially you."

That hurts. Something about his tone makes me believe him. He is struggling with what to reveal and what to keep secret. "She's gone, Pekka. You can tell me now. What kind of trouble was she in?"

Pekka stares past me. He hesitates. "She was having problems with a man, but she wouldn't tell me who he was. When the time came, she said she would send me a message through Yvonne."

"Are you saying someone was pursuing my sister? That she was in danger?" Who would want to harm sweet, innocent Hanna?

"I'm saying your sister was unhappy, and scared. She thought something bad might happen."

"Who was she afraid of?" I need answers from this man. He knows more than he's saying.

"She wouldn't say. She just asked me ... if she got into trouble, could I help her out? I swear." Pekka looks sober now, his composure regained.

"How could you help her? What kind of trouble was she in?"

Pekka looks me squarely in the face. "I don't know you and you don't know me, see? You don't know the things I've done. I'm not proud of it, but I have a reputation, you could say. She needed a man who could do the job. Someone who would be discreet."

"What did she ask you to do?" I'm afraid to ask, but I must know the truth, even if it changes everything I know about my sister.

"Rough the guy up a bit. Scare him enough to leave her alone. She thought he was gonna harm her." Pekka crosses his arms.

If Hanna wanted a man to put fear into someone, she couldn't do much better than Pekka Peltonen. The man is intimidating, even when he is almost incoherent.

"Look, I'm not a bad guy. I don't go around trying to hurt people. Your sister got wind of my, um, history and asked for help. Said she'd give me a few dollars. I'm ashamed to admit it, but I needed the money."

"And you agreed?" I already know the answer, but I want him to say it.

"Not at first. I didn't want any trouble." It is Pekka who looks scared now. I want to believe him, but I don't know if I can trust him.

I lean toward him. "Okay, but you still haven't answered my question. Where were you on the night my sister died?"

Pekka picks up his bottle and pours another glass. "I wasn't in Sudbury that night. I was dealing with a personal problem." Pekka knocks the glass back and places it on the table. He leans in, his noxious breath filling my nostrils. "You want to know about your sister? You'd better ask someone else. I have nothing to do with it. And if you mention any of this to the police, I swear I'll—"

"You'll what?" I ask, defiance in my voice.

Pekka scowls as he pushes away from the table and stumbles out of the room, leaving me to stare at the empty bottle.

I slump back in my chair, staring out the darkened window, exhausted by our interaction and the stress of the last few days. The branches scratch against the panes, and a cold draft makes me shiver. Who were you afraid of, Hanna? I take a last sip of whisky. Every part of me is weary, and I don't know what to believe. All I know is Pekka Peltonen knew things about my sister that she'd kept secret from me.

Chapter Eight
July 1931

Hanna pins one end of the sheet to the line as I hold up the other, popping a few wooden pins from my apron pocket between my lips. I wipe the sweat from my forehead and wish for a cool breeze.

"Have you decided?" she asks, glancing at me as she fishes out a skirt from the laundry basket, shakes it, and pins it to the line.

"No," I say, mumbling through the pins.

"No? What do you mean? You won't go with me?" As usual, she sounds like I have no right to make my own decisions, that I exist to support her choices, her dreams. Does she even care what I want? Maybe that's unfair. I don't really know what I want myself.

I take the pins out of my mouth and hold up Isä's shirt. "I didn't say, 'no I won't go,' I said, 'no I haven't decided yet.' How can we leave them alone to do all the work here? Äiti would have a fit." Hanna's problem is that she rarely thinks about anyone else. She's always chasing something shiny and new, without regard to how the rest of us feel. Besides, what's wrong with living in Wanup?

Hanna shrugs. "Let her. We need our own lives, and there's nothing here except more work. You think I'll find a husband living out here? We know every boy within twenty kilometres, and I'll be darned if I'll marry any of them and become a farm wife."

She's so perturbed I can't help but laugh. "It's not so bad. Sure, there are the animals to feed and crops to pull in, but it's nice too. I enjoy knowing our neighbours. It's peaceful. What's so great about the city?"

"Well, there are more people for one. And theatres and restaurants and corner stores and, well, all kinds of things. You're such a bookworm; if you have a book to read or a journal to write in, you're happy. That's not enough for me. I don't want this life. And somewhere out there is my very own Gary Cooper who will swoop me off my feet. I just have to go out and find him."

"I don't know. I'm not sure it's the life for me. Äiti needs help, and Isä isn't getting any younger. Besides, what would I do? How would we live?"

"We'll get jobs, silly. Lots of rich women need servants to do their chores or take care of their children. You could waitress. Personally, I'd love to work at Silverman's, selling perfume or scarves. But I'm happy to work as a domestic, for now." Hanna takes my hand in hers. The sheet we've hung shields us from our mother's prying eyes in the farmhouse. "Listen, Essi. Come with me and see how you feel. If you don't like it, you can come back to the farm, take care of the old folks, and be buried here along with all the other people who couldn't take a risk and never left. I won't hold you back, I promise."

Hanna's eyes plead with me the way they always have since we were kids. She could always persuade me. If I let her go alone, what might happen to her? She needs someone to rein her in, to remind her we live on earth. At least I could keep her safe.

"You promise? I mean, if I come with you, you'll let me make my own decisions about whether I stay?" I'm skeptical, but Hanna has never broken a promise to me before.

"Three months. Give me three months in Sudbury, and then you can decide what to do. Stay or go. Your decision. What do you say?" Hanna's pleading expression deepens.

I nod, and then nod again, watching Hanna's smile beam. She jumps up and down and wraps her arms around me. "Thank you, Essi. Thank you," she repeats.

When she finally releases me, I ask, "What do we tell them?"

"Leave it to me," Hanna says. "I've already worked it out. We're both going to work in Sudbury, so we'll send money home to help them, a portion of our wages. Plus, Fredi already lives there, and they'll like that we know someone. He delivers to Wanup regularly, so we can visit whenever we want. It will be impossible for them to object. And I have a secret. I've already applied for a job, and I got an interview set up. It's not Silverman's, but it'll do for now. Everything's going to work out."

A cool breeze rustles the faded curtains, and I shiver before crossing the small, rented room I share with Hanna to close the sash window. At the sound, a black crow perched on the maple tilts its head as if to ask what we're going to do now.

"I'm sorry," Mr. Uutinen says. Behind him, his wife wrings her hands in her apron. She won't meet my eyes. The Uutinens own the boarding house and have been very kind ever since we moved in two months earlier.

"But I don't understand," Hanna says. "We paid the rent. We've been good tenants, haven't we?"

Mr. Uutinen nods and frowns. "You've been the best tenants, believe me. But the last few years have been very difficult. Not everyone pays their rent on time—or at all—and we've tried to be understanding. It means we're behind on our house payments. We hoped it would get better, but ..."

"Is there anything we can do?" I ask. What would happen to this lovely couple? What would happen to us?

Mr. Uutinen shakes his head. "I'm afraid there's nothing anyone can do. We need to vacate the property. I'm so sorry."

A sob slips from Mrs. Uutinen. Her eyes well with tears, and she covers her face with her apron, turning away before we can say anything more.

Hanna takes my hand, and I feel it shaking, but her voice is calm. "Don't worry about us. You have your own troubles. Thank you for everything you've done for us. We won't forget your kindness."

I mumble my thanks, and the Uutinens move to the next room to deliver the same news again to our neighbours, Mr. and Mrs. Rossi and their two daughters. It will be a hard day for everyone in the building. On our floor, there are four rooms with one shared bathroom. Mr. and Mrs. Uutinen's quarters are on the first floor, along with a bathroom, kitchen, and common area. It has been the ideal place to live, if somewhat cramped for the number of tenants.

"What are we going to do now?" Hanna plops herself onto a chair and pulls her knees up while I pace back and forth across the floorboards.

"Let me think," I say. "Mr. Uutinen says we have the week. Surely something will come up. You ask around, and I'll do the same. It's going to work out."

Hanna rocks herself back and forth, biting her lower lip. "I'm sorry, Essi. I thought moving into town was the right thing to do, but maybe I was wrong. I dragged you away from home, and now look at us—practically homeless."

"We're not homeless yet, and you didn't drag me. It was time to strike out on our own. This is just a minor stumbling block. You'll see." I want to sound optimistic for my sister, but my mind is ticking over the many things we'd need to do before the week's end. "Have faith. Besides, we can always go home if we need to."

Hanna glares and shakes her head. "No, we're not going back. There's nothing for us there."

Maybe Hanna is right, but it doesn't seem like such a bad idea to me. I miss the farm, the horses, and the barn cats. I miss our parents and even our loft bedroom—despite it being too cold in the winter and too hot in the summer.

A few days later, footsteps bound up the stairs and our door flies open. Breathless, Hanna stands in the doorway holding up a piece of paper, with a wide smile across her face.

"I got it!"

"Got what?" I ask, rising from the desk where I've been revising a story. I wipe the ink from my fingers.

Hanna hands me the slip of paper, and I read its contents: an address on Kathleen Street, only a few blocks away. "A room in a boarding house? How?"

"Millie was prying, and I told her we were looking for a place. She said they sometimes have a few empty rooms. Listen, Essi. You need to have an open mind about this one. It's close by, so it will be easy to move—besides, we don't have too many things—and it's even closer to work for me. And it won't add more than a few minutes' walk to Mrs. Johnson's for you. Plus, Millie says the rent is cheaper than this place. Can you believe it?"

"So far, it all sounds too good to be true. What's the catch?" Her expression is enthusiastic, but I can tell she's holding something back.

Hanna takes a deep breath. "You'll be happy to know the owner is a Finnish woman. They call her Rouva Ruusa—Madame Rose—and she rents out rooms in her boarding house, but most of her female tenants also work for her."

I peer at my sister's face and try to comprehend what she is saying. "Rouva Ruusa? Who is she? What kind of business does she own?"

"Well, Millie didn't give me many details, but she hinted that she serves bootlegged liquor."

"And you want to live there?" I'm shocked Hanna would even consider it.

"We just need a room to sleep in; we don't need to have anything to do with her business."

Hanna sits on her hands, and her leg shakes up and down. I perch on the edge of the bed. "Is there something you're not telling me?"

"Just one little thing. It's no big deal. Like I said, it has nothing to do with our renting a room. Her girls, the ones who work for her, are ... ladies of the night."

I gasp. "They're prostitutes? Rouva Ruusa is a madame?" I couldn't imagine us living in such a place.

"Our parents never need to know. What does it matter? We have respectable jobs, and it will be temporary, plus the rent is so cheap. On my way home, I visited the house, and Rouva Ruusa seems nice. She showed me the room we'd be renting on the second floor. It's not big, but it's bigger than this one."

"You've already gone there? What if someone saw you?"

"Don't worry. We have a place to go on Friday, and I've already paid for the upcoming week." Hanna takes off her coat and drops it on her bed.

"What! You've paid? How could you do this without asking me?" Sometimes Hanna makes me so mad. She decides without consulting me, as if I'll follow her to the ends of the earth with no questions asked.

Hanna crosses her arms. "This is the only place we can afford. It's not forever, Essi. We'll just rent for a week, maybe two ... until we find something better."

I slump onto the bed and study my sister's face. "Okay. One week and then we get out of there. We don't tell anyone where we're living. Got it?"

Hanna nods, and a smile returns to her face. "You won't regret it. It's going to work out just fine."

"I hope you're right," I say, sitting back at the desk, wanting to concentrate on my fictional world instead of the one I'm living in. If our parents knew what was happening, they'd insist we move back to the farm. But this little taste of freedom has been enough for me to know I love my parents but don't really want to live with them again.

Chapter Nine

April 1933

The dark clouds have rolled by, and I take advantage of the warm afternoon to walk in the neighbourhood, but I avoid the creek. I need to clear my head and make plans. I have devoted so much time to finding out what happened to Hanna I haven't even looked for a new job or a way to earn money. Can't rely on Hanna's money anymore, either. The reality of my situation is becoming more critical. The rent is almost due.

I turn onto Eva Street and step into the corner store. The owner's wife is organizing products on a shelf behind the counter. She's short and round and barely reaches the top shelf.

"Good afternoon, Mrs. Shevchenko," I say, trying not to startle her. I reach for a newspaper, wondering if there's been anything written about Hanna's death or any other related news that might give me some information.

"Oh, Essi," she says in her Ukrainian accent. Before I know it, Mrs. Shevchenko has squeezed around the counter and engulfed me in a fierce hug. When she lets me go, her eyes cloud over.

A young boy calls from the room beyond the store. "Mama, where's my baseball bat?" Judging by the voice, it's Ivan, the oldest son. A moment later, his head appears around the corner.

Mrs. Shevchenko waves him away. "Not now, Ivan. I'm talking to Essi. Ask your sister."

"Hi Essi," Ivan says and waves a hand. He smiles broadly. "How's school?" I ask. Sometimes, I spend a few hours helping him with his homework. He's a smart kid, but he has no interest in school.

"It's fine," he says, and shrugs. "But I can't wait for baseball season. Will you come see me play?" I agree, and he disappears again, calling out to his sister.

"He's a smart boy," Mrs. Shevchenko says, "but he only wants to play sports. Hockey in the winter. Baseball in the summer." She shakes her head. "What about you? How are you doing?" Her tone is full of sympathy, but I don't know how to respond.

I step away, feigning interest in the playing cards on display as I fight back my tears, surprised that our interaction is affecting me so much. "I'm okay. Just stopping by. I'm wondering if you have any work?"

The bells on the door rattle, and we both look up. Mr. Chen appears and says hello.

Mrs. Shevchenko greets him. "Essi is looking for a job," she says.

Mr. Chen pauses and nods. "I'll keep an eye out for you." He takes a newspaper from the stand and pays Mrs. Shevchenko with the exact change, giving her a quick bob of his head before looking at me. "Sorry for your loss," he says, before turning to leave with his paper tucked under his arm.

"Nice man, Mr. Chen. He doesn't say much, but he is very kind. He gave me a gift when Maksym was born, you know. So, you need a job, eh?" Mrs. Shevchenko leans against the counter.

"Yes, I lost my job with the Johnsons and now, well, I need work."

"Oh darling Essi. Of course, her husband died ... so sad ... I sent Ivan over with some borscht." She shakes her head and sighs. "I wish I had something for you, but I'll spread the word. We'll find you work."

I thank her for her kindness and pay for my newspaper, but my heart sinks. How can I expect the neighbours to give me work when everyone is struggling right now?

In the corner behind the counter, I spy Ivan's baseball bat. "Isn't Ivan looking for this?" I ask.

Mrs. Shevchenko grins. "You're very observant. I hadn't even noticed it."

The bells jingle as I close the door behind me. Defeated, I turn toward the boarding house, wondering what to do next. Fredi says he might get me work at the Borgia Market. I'll have to ask him more about it. On my way, I see Mr. and Mrs. Rossi walking arm in arm. He tips his hat and smiles at me, but Mrs. Rossi doesn't look up from the sidewalk. Whenever I encountered her in our old boarding house, she was always polite, but now when she sees me in the neighbourhood, she avoids interacting. She must know where I live and think I work there, too. I wonder if she prays for my soul. I say hello but keep walking.

There was a time I looked around me before approaching the house, worried someone might see me. Now, I don't even care. I walk on up to the door and take my time. Let them judge me.

With a last, deep breath of fresh air, I wipe my shoes on the porch mat and step inside, closing the door softly behind me. Although it's afternoon, the girls might still be asleep. To my surprise, Yvonne is sitting on the bench in the narrow hallway, tying her shoes.

"You look terrible, my friend." Yvonne pulls on her hat. "What's wrong? You look like you saw a ghost."

"I'm okay, Yvonne. Thought a walk might do me some good. I've been having trouble sleeping lately." I'm not being entirely honest, but it's true sleep eludes me, and when I drift off, strange dreams infiltrate my brain.

Yvonne pats my arm and looks at me with her dark brown eyes. "It must be so hard for you, especially with Hanna's bed empty now."

I nod and change the subject. "Are you on your way out?" She's dressed in her Sunday best: a green day dress with pink flowers, pleats on the sleeves, small buttons done up to the rounded collar. Neatly tied back hair and no makeup except some lipstick. She reminds me of the silent movie star Mary Pickford.

"Going to visit Mama and my sister Marie on Borgia Street."

I raise my eyebrows. "Is it safe to go alone?"

"Oui, it's rough, but I can handle myself, to be sure. Every month I bring my mother some money. She's not well and can't work. Marie helps, but she still goes to school."

"What about your father, Yvonne? What does he do?" I've never asked her about her family before, but now I'm curious.

Yvonne shrugs. "It's only me, Mama, and Marie. We need each other." Yvonne takes her coat from a hook.

"I'm sorry, Yvonne. I shouldn't have asked." It's strange how little I know about her, and she seems to know everything about what's happening in my life. I've been so wrapped up, I'd forgotten to ask about her well-being.

"Non, non. It's okay. I'm happy to help. They are my family, oui? Just like you and Hanna. You do everything for each other." A shadow passes over her face. "Ma mère think I work in office downtown. I did, too, but the boss was too handsy. She would not like me working here. Always looks down on the girls on Borgia Street and spit in their direction." Yvonne sighs.

"I wouldn't breathe it to anyone. I'm sure she's proud of you. You do so much for them." I imagine my mother shut up in her dark bedroom, and my father caring for her the best he can.

Yvonne's smile brightens. "I'm not ashamed of my work. I'm in control, and Madame Rose takes care of any trouble. Earn more than in that office. But I am not a Borgia Street hussy."

Yvonne twists a light scarf around her neck. Spring sunshine falls across the floor.

"Do you have any leads? About your sister?" Yvonne's question sounds tentative, but she has every right to be curious.

"I don't know. It's going nowhere, to be honest. Every time I think I have an idea, I'm filled with doubts. There's no hard evidence, as Officer O'Rourke would say. And there are all these things I can't figure out, like who Hanna needed protection from."

"You think you should stop now? Maybe it's better to let it go. You look so tired, ma chère." Yvonne tucks her gloves into her pockets and adjusts her hat in the hall mirror.

"I can't stop. And I am worried about how to pay my rent. Since I lost my job and Hanna ... well, the little we had saved is almost gone."

Yvonne puts her hands on her hips and looks me over from the top of my head to my toes. A little smile curls up from her thin lips. "I know how you can earn extra money."

At first, I don't catch her meaning. "Oh, no. No way. I'll find some other way to pay my rent." My cheeks burn at the thought of it.

"You're a little plain, but pretty in your own way. Your sister, she was a beauty, but there's something lovely about you. Fresh farm girl. Many of Madame Rose's men like a girl like you." Yvonne is always one to say things as she sees them, but I'm not offended. Hanna was always the beauty in the family, while I was the plain bookworm, always reading a book or writing in my journal.

"No offense, but I couldn't work here. I'm not judging the girls, though." Before moving to Sudbury, I had different ideas, but now I see how difficult it is for women in this world.

"You'd be surprised what a girl can do when she needs money," Yvonne says. "No shame in taking care of yourself. Think about it." Her laughter tinkles through the door on her way out.

The question of my rent is weighing heavily, though I'd rather be searching for clues about Hanna's death. We don't have many possessions, but it's worth going through them to see if I can pawn something. Despite Yvonne's cheery attitude and her income, I can't bring myself to see it as a possibility for me. What am I going to do? The rent is due in a week. If I don't get a job, I'll have to move back to Wanup, and then I'll never find out what happened.

What will I do? How will I continue to look for Hanna's murderer if I'm forced to go back to my parents, back to the farm? All the information I have will be for nothing. I'll have to start again. By then, nobody will care about my sister or even remember what happened to her. The police dismiss my ideas, except Officer Cane. He could be helpful to me. My frustration is bubbling to the surface, and I'm ready to plead my case with Rouva Ruusa.

Chapter Ten

April 1933

There's no more delaying. The rent is due, and I don't have it. I've never been to Rouva Ruusa's private rooms before. The rest of us are on the second floor, but her rooms are tucked at the back of the house, away from the noise of the parlour and the activity of the kitchen. Navigating down the long, narrow hallway, I listen for any activity suggesting this is not a good time to call on her.

At the end of the hall, two steps down and a sharp corner lead to a heavy door. It's an awkward space and must have been part of an extension to the original house. Hers are the only private rooms in the house with its own door leading to the backyard. On this side of the house, in the evening, the faint scent of cigarette smoke rises from her small porch where she sits at dusk before the parlour invites its rowdy guests. All the girls know not to intrude on those quiet moments unless there is an emergency, or the police are at the door.

Now, as I stand outside her door, I'm intimidated. I'm not sure if it's the idea of entering her private sanctuary, or the fact I can't come up with the rent this week, but my hands feel clammy, and my breath is shallow. I take a few deep breaths, clasping my right hand over my left wrist, feeling Martta's button against my skin, and knock.

From within, Rouva Ruusa invites me in. She's dressed neatly with her hair coiled up in a fashion from another decade, kohl-lined eyes like a fortune teller, and her signature red lips. At the sight of me, her eyes widen, but her surprised expression is replaced by a neutral look, one that is harder to read but is more like my mother's than even I care to admit.

"Essi? Is everything okay?" She puts on an earring as she speaks and steps back to allow me into her space. "Why don't you come in?"

The room is in semidarkness. Heavy curtains almost pulled across the window let in a slim shaft of natural light. Smoke lingers in the air, swirling and catching a ray of sun. Its source, a partially smoked cigarette balancing on the edge of a glass cigarette holder, is ringed with lipstick.

Rouva Ruusa turns away from me, takes up the cigarette, and motions for me to sit.

"How can I help you, Essi?" She takes a drag and smooths her hair with the other hand.

She settles herself on the chaise lounge. The room is well-furnished but not opulent. She's taken care to make it feel like a nicer version of home than most of her clients can afford.

Behind Rouva Ruusa, a photograph of a young woman who looks like a starlet on the cover of *Vogue* hangs on the wall. The figure looks vaguely familiar, but I can't place her face. Is she someone famous?

Rouva Ruusa follows my gaze to the photograph. "I was around your age. The photographer was young then, too, but later became quite famous. He promised me the stars but abandoned me for Hollywood. Never heard from him again. But he left me this little gift—for services rendered." She seems to have slipped away from me into a time in her past. I am still, not wanting to disrupt her reflections.

"You were so beautiful ... are so beautiful," I say, trying not to compare the photograph with the aged version in front of me.

"Well, that was then." Rouva Ruusa takes a deep drag of her cigarette and turns away to exhale. "What brings you here?" Her deep voice sounds concerned, but I know she'll want the straight facts, not an emotional plea, something she must get all the time.

"I don't have the rent this week." I spit out the words before I hesitate.

A tap on the door startles me, and we both look toward the door. Ruby, Ruusa's long-time employee, enters carrying a tray with a silver teapot and a cup and saucer embellished with a rose pattern and gold trim, and places it on the coffee table.

"Would you like some tea?" Ruby asks me.

"No, thank you," I say, giving Ruby a weak smile. Yvonne says Ruby and Rouva Ruusa are as thick as thieves. Ruby has been the main housekeeper for Rouva Ruusa since the beginning and is her closest confidante.

"Thank you, Ruby," Rouva Ruusa says. "I'll take my meal in my room this evening. Please join me if you can spare the time. I have some business to discuss with you." Ruby nods and leaves the room.

Rouva Ruusa's look is intense. She takes a sip of tea. "What do you intend to do about your rent?"

She surprises me with this response. "I'm looking for a new position. I'm hoping to get employed somewhere soon. It's been difficult. You see, news of my sister's death has travelled through the community of domestics and their employers, and anytime I apply for a job I'm politely declined. I'm an excellent worker, but I think I'm—"

"Tainted? Yes, I see it's possible. Death and murder fascinate folks, and they want to know everything. Either that, or they're repulsed and fear anything connected to it. What about your parents? Can they help?"

"Their farm sustains them most of the time, and they do some trading with the neighbours for some things. But my mother is unwell. I don't want to ask them for anything if I can help it." I survey the room, pausing on the thick drapes, and the candles on the fireplace mantel.

"Well, no work and no money. I don't know what I can do for you. I'm not running a shelter or a charity here, Essi. And I could use your room. Unless ..." When Rouva Ruusa pauses, I feel uneasy about what she's going to say. "You can work for me." Rouva Ruusa beams at the idea. "Yes, that would be good," she says, as if she has decided.

"With respect, I can't work for you. Maybe it's my Lutheran upbringing, or my mother's voice in my head, but I won't use my body to earn a living." My tone is harsher than I mean it to be.

Rouva Ruusa laughs. "That's not what I mean. You made that very clear. Although if you ever change your mind ..."

"I won't." I understand why some women decide to work at a place like this, but I'm determined to find another way.

"I've sacked Ruby's assistant Agatha for stealing from me. Ruby's been complaining about that girl for months. She was a terrible housekeeper and couldn't boil a potato to save her life. A deceptive little bitch, that one. I gave the girl a chance, but I knew from the minute I met her I'd need to keep an eye on her. You don't expect that from the Poles, do you? But you're an honest girl, and trust me, I know people when I meet them. You can take over Agatha's kitchen duties. Maybe help with the laundry. It's not regular work, but it will cover your rent and give you a little extra. What do you think?"

I am so grateful that I am practically in tears. "Yes. That suits me perfectly. Thank you." It means I can stay, and my search for Hanna's murderer can continue. The idea lifts my spirits, and I'm excited to tell Yvonne all about it.

"Go on then. Ruby will be in the kitchen first thing in the morning. She's been a little cranky for the last few weeks, and I'm sure she'll be pleased to give you a list of duties. You get your work done for Ruby, and you can come and go as you please. And Essi?"

"Yes?" Anything this woman asks, I will do. Within reason.

"Find the devil of a man who killed your sister. We don't need these lowlifes in this town, and we don't want them anywhere near our girls."

"Yes, ma'am." Finding Hanna's murderer isn't just important to me. All the girls in the boarding house have been extra cautious since Hanna's death, rarely leaving except in twos. Yvonne says she's watching for suspicious behaviour. They're all worried. What if the killer thought Hanna was a prostitute because she lived here? What if the murderer is going to strike again? My mind goes wild with possibilities as I leave Rouva Ruusa's room, dreading my room that is so vacant now, yet filled with memories of my sister.

Chapter Eleven

April 1933

I make my bed with neat hospital corners, the way our mother taught us. I hated doing it as a kid, but since leaving home, I do it every day. Hanna preferred her bedsheets rumpled, her pillow on the floor, her nightgown strewn across the bed. Was it her little way of rebelling against our parents and the life we'd left behind? I get dressed and comb my hair, no longer wavy.

Was Hanna so unhappy about her job? I smooth the quilt on her vacant bed and plump her unused pillow.

I yearn for answers. I think back to the loft bedroom we shared in Wanup. The wooden beds our father made for us and the small desk under the window. As kids, we argued about the lack of space, but we got used to negotiating our way around each other.

Back then, Hanna used to tell me everything. But before she died, I sensed she was holding something back. Or maybe I just wasn't listening? About a month before her death, on a crisp winter morning, Hanna was lying in bed while I dressed and readied myself to go down for breakfast before heading to work. I asked if she wanted to come down with me.

Hanna shook her head. "I'm not hungry. Listen, before you go, can we talk?"

"Sure. What's wrong?" I said, curious about what bothered her. I sat on the wooden desk chair below our window with my writing.

"Nothing's wrong. I just ..." Hanna had something to tell me, but she would take her own time about it. She played with the edge of her quilt, avoiding my eyes. "I've been thinking about it for quite a while now. I want to give my notice and look for another job." Her voice wavered.

"Another job? I don't understand. Dr. Wright pays you handsomely. Why would you want to leave?"

"I feel like I could do well somewhere else," Hanna said. "It's hard to explain, but I think it's time for me to go."

"Don't you like it there?" I pictured the stately house, the elaborate meals, and all the guests coming and going from dinner parties, clothed in their elegant dresses and suits. Sure, Hanna complained about working with Millie and grumbled about Dr. Wright and his wife, but wasn't that normal? "Who else will pay you so well?"

"It's true; the pay is good, and there are perks I probably wouldn't get from another family. But ..." Hanna frowned.

"What will we do if you quit? How will we pay for this room, let alone something better?" I looked around at the cramped, shabby space we called our own. We hadn't earned enough to leave Rouva Ruusa's boarding house, and Hanna leaving her job meant we might be here for who knew how long.

"I'll get another job. Besides, you'll get paid soon, too." She looked up with those blue eyes, hopeful and pleading at the same time.

I shook my head. "No, I'm afraid not. Mrs. Johnson is finding it too hard to pay my wages. I've been meaning to tell you—she's letting me go soon. A week at most. Things are so bad for them since her husband died. I feel terrible that I can't do more to help them."

"I'm sorry to hear that." Hanna's shoulders slumped, and her skin was paler than usual. The glow in her skin and eyes was gone.

"Don't worry, Hanna. I'll find something else soon, but if you leave your job, we'll run out of money in no time. And then we'll have to—"

"Go back to Wanup. I know, I know. It's just I don't know how much longer I can stay there."

"Why? Has something happened? Is it Millie? She's such a harlot." I blushed, and Hanna raised her eyebrow. "What? I don't like that girl." I pass a brush through my hair, crouching to see myself reflected in the mirror.

"Millie's the same. Harmless, really." Hanna gave me a weak smile, but it wasn't convincing. "I can handle her."

"What is it then? Why do you want to leave?" The exasperation in my voice was clear, even to me. None of it made sense to me. Was Hanna getting spoiled? Did she think she was too good for her job? Just like her to turn her back on a good thing, because she wanted something more.

"I don't know what to tell you, Essi. It just doesn't feel right."

"Feel right? What doesn't *feel right* is not having food in our bellies. What doesn't *feel right* is not having money to pay our rent. What doesn't *feel right* is not being able to pay our own way and running back to our parents, who don't have anything extra to give us. Stop being so selfish, Hanna."

"I'm not. I just can't do it anymore." Tears brimmed in her eyes and stained her cheeks.

I hadn't meant to make her cry. Nothing seemed to go well for us, but the last thing either of us wanted was to go back to Wanup, to a dark house with an unpredictable mother and an overworked father. "If we can't earn our way, I don't know what to tell you. We might as well go home. We should just go home."

Hanna wiped her eyes with the back of her hand and sniffled. She pulled a pillow onto her lap and hugged it to her belly. We sat in silence for a while, listening to the growing sounds of the household and our own breathing. We used to play that game when we were little—see if we could read each other's minds. Sometimes, I believed we could.

"What if I stay until you find another place to work? Once you find a new job, I'll give my notice. This way we'll have an income to pay the rent, and we won't have to worry about going home with our tails between our legs. We'll make this work. You'll see. I'm sorry I upset you." The enthusiasm seeped back into her voice.

It meant a lot to her to live in town, and to have me by her side. How could I say no? "I'm sorry, too. I should have told you, but I thought I had a lead on another position. It didn't work out. So many women are looking for work that the openings fill before you know they exist. At least we can pay the rent for now. And who knows? Mrs. Johnson may keep me on."

Hanna's eyes brightened. "You're right. Rouva Ruusa wouldn't throw us out right away, I don't think. But still. It's better this way. I can handle working at the Wrights for a little while longer."

I got up from my chair and tucked it under the desk. "We're going to make this work, aren't we? Together." I paused. "Do you want some coffee?"

"Please." Hanna's gentle smile let me know our argument was over and we were back to being friends again.

My head ached, but it could have been the changing weather or the stress of the situation, making my head feel as swollen as a weather balloon. Either way, coffee would do us both good. I closed the door behind me and plodded down the hall to the stairs.

Thinking of that time, I realize I hadn't really heard her. Her problems had been creeping below the surface, like frost inching up a window. There was more to what was happening to Hanna, and I just didn't see it. I need to visit her workplace and find out.

Chapter Twelve

April 1933

The stately brick house seems empty from the street, its upper gabled windows glaring down at my shabby coat and worn boots. I straighten my hat and summon my courage.

Instead of climbing the steps to the front door, I tramp through the slushy snow to the servants' entrance, where I'd picked Hanna up many times before. When was the last time she met me at the gate, a smile beaming across her face, or an irritated expression inevitably leading to a story about Millie or the doctor's wife? We'd stroll home together, gossiping about our day, complaining about the weather, laughing about something someone had said. How many times would Hanna have made this journey back and forth from our rented room to the Wrights' house? The last time she left was after that dinner party. The night she never returned home.

A bitter gust of wind slams across my face, bringing with it a sharp sting as I ring the doorbell.

"Yes? May I help you?" A petite, dark-haired young woman with sharp features asks in a British accent. She's just as Hanna had described her.

"Are you Millie?" I feel awkward standing on the doorstep, unsure about what to do with my hands. Should I reach out to shake hers? Instead, I clasp them in front of me.

Millie scans me from head to toe. "What's it to you?" Her tone isn't as polite now.

"I'm Hanna's sister."

Millie's eyes widen. "I'm sorry for your loss," she says, "but if you're here to ask questions, I don't know what happened to her. I barely knew the girl." Millie moves to close the door.

I kick my foot into the space between the door and frame. "You know her a little better than that. Just a few questions. You might have been one of the last people to have seen her before ..." Millie releases her grip on the door and moves into the house, although she doesn't invite me in.

I cross the threshold of the Wrights' house for the first time. The scent of baking bread greets me as I follow Millie's quick footsteps down a narrow hallway to the back kitchen. Even in this, the servants' domain, the house appears grander than anything I've ever seen. Hanna loved the scale of this house, imagining she might live in one just like it someday. I can't imagine this much space for just two people. It seems indecent, what with all the folks homeless and starving these days.

The kitchen table is a mess of baking utensils covered in flour. Millie drops herself onto a stool. "I do everything myself now. Don't know how I'm expected to keep up." She sounds as if I were to blame for my sister's death.

I stand across the table with my coat heavy around my shoulders in the warm kitchen. Will she offer me a seat? She doesn't. Millie picks up a knife and a large potato, removing the peel with her expert fingers in one long curl.

"What do you want to know?" Millie finally asks. "I just worked with her. We weren't friends, you know."

"I gathered as much. But you worked together all those months. You probably know more than you realize." I pause. I'm convinced Millie knows more than she lets on. "That night, the Wrights were having a dinner party."

Millie stops mid-peel to look at me. "That's right. They had over some of their doctor friends and their wives. Very posh. We cleaned all the silver the day before. Such a lot of work, you know." Millie places the peeled potato in a large pot and pulls another from the basket.

"Who was here that night?" A list of guests may help me. It could have been someone at the party.

"What are you getting on about?" Millie says, pausing with her peeler raised. "Why do you want to know all this? It has nothing to do with your sister's accident."

Didn't Millie understand anything? "I don't think it was an accident. That's why I'm here. Something happened to Hanna that night, and someone is responsible."

A flash of surprise crosses Millie's face before she resumes peeling. "Well, Dr. and Mrs. Wright, of course. The Cartwells, Doctor and Mrs., and Allen Young, the fine-looking young doctor. His wife didn't come, though. She's quite sick, they say. It should have been six, but there were only five in the end. I had to take away a place setting at the last minute while they were having hors d'oeuvres. Hanna served the meal. It's hard to make the table look fine with uneven numbers, you know."

I nod as if I knew, but I've never been to a fancy dinner. "Before Hanna left, she told me she might have to work late, depending on the dinner party. Do you remember what happened?"

"I don't rightly know. It was the usual do the doctor and his wife put on now and again, everyone dressed in their fanciest outfits and furs, trinkets on their fingers and their throats. The missus was in a foul mood, and she came in a few times to cuss at us about being too slow with the trays or some such thing. She had it in for Hanna. I didn't mind that Hanna was getting it. It was me she usually bawled at."

"Why was she upset with Hanna?" My sister had never found Mrs. Wright particularly pleasant, but she hadn't complained of any aggressive behaviour.

"Not sure. Mrs. Wright rails at me for no reason, but she knows there's no one better than me at my job. She ain't fired me yet. But she had it in for Hanna. Not at first, mind you. But something happened. I'm not saying Hanna was perfect, but Mrs. Wright kept finding fault with her. And there were the rumours, of course."

"Rumours? About what?" The knot in my stomach tightens. What secrets had Hanna kept from me?

Millie cocks her head and narrows her eyes. "You don't know?"

"Know what?" I shift uncomfortably on the hard floor and feel a tingle of sweat at the base of my neck.

Millie glances at the closed door and back at me. "I ain't no snitch, see, but if the rumours are true, Mrs. Wright had every reason to be furious with your sister, and it had nothing to do with her ability to clean a toilet."

"What are people saying?" I tug at my scarf to release its grip on my neck.

A smirk flashes across Millie's face. "Why, Mr. Wright fancied your pretty sister, and Mrs. Wright found out there were some no-good goings on under her roof."

My heart drops, and I shake my head. "Oh no, that can't be true. Hanna wasn't that kind of girl." Wouldn't Hanna have told me if she were in love with her employer?

"What kind of girl was she?" Millie asks, batting her eyes innocently. "All's I know is a few weeks before the party I was putting clean linens in the cupboard near the doctor's bedroom and I could hear them, Dr. Wright and the missus, arguing. She said she wanted the girl fired. At first, I thought she meant me—she's always after me about something or other—so I crept closer to the door to have a listen. The doctor said he'd take care of everything. That's how I knew. Your sister wasn't such a good girl, after all." Millie puts another peeled potato in the pot with a wry smile.

My mind swarms with images of my sister. I can't believe she would have had anything to do with Dr. Wright, and Millie certainly isn't the most trustworthy confidante. "Hanna once mentioned you were, how should I say, close to Dr. Wright?"

Millie's eyes flash with anger. "So I am. I'm his favourite. He might stray from time to time to some pretty new thing, but he always finds his way back to me. Hanna was a looker, I'll grant her that, but she had nothing on me. I know how to make him happy. His prude of a wife is all to keep up appearances with his high society friends, and little Hanna was just a temporary plaything. I'm the one he really loves."

None of this makes sense. Hanna would not have fooled around with her employer. She was too smart for that. And she felt bad for the girls who worked for Rouva Ruusa. "It's out of necessity," she'd said. "We shouldn't judge them for what they do to survive."

I thank Millie for the information and slip into my boots at the side door, eager to remove myself from the enclosed house and breathe fresh air. Millie has trudged along behind me.

"There's one more thing I just remembered," Millie says, before I can open the door. "I don't know if it's helpful, but you might want to know."

With my hand on the doorknob, I turn to face Millie. She seems a petty little creature who only cares about herself. My sister's complaints about her make sense now.

"A few weeks before that night, a stranger came to the side entrance, the one you're at—that's why I remember it just now. Thought he was a hobo at first, but too clean-cut. A real Clark Gable type. Asked for Hanna in a heavy accent, European of some sort, and he wasn't here to deliver anything that I could make out. Hanna was upset after that, but she wouldn't tell me what he wanted or who he was. They argued.

Hanna told him to go away and never return to the house. Said she might get fired. Never saw him again."

"Hanna never told you who the man was?" Was it Pekka Peltonen? Would he have come to the house? Had she asked him to fulfill his promise?

"She didn't seem like she was an admirer of his, that's for sure." Millie gives me a smile, with no trace of friendliness in it. She turns on her heel and strides down the hall to the kitchen without so much as a goodbye.

Can I trust Millie or anything she says about my sister? Everything Hanna told me about her suggests I should be cautious. Did Mrs. Wright want Hanna fired? If so, why? I can't believe Hanna ever had an affair with her employer. It's just not possible. I file Millie's words away for now, hoping I can get information to corroborate or refute her statements.

A gust of wind swirls around me in the side yard. For a moment, I stand with my eyes closed and feel the sun straining to shine through the grey clouds and onto my face. Above, a murder of crows circles before settling into a nearby tree. My head is as mottled as the sky.

Chapter Thirteen
April 1933

The headache I've been fostering has intensified, but Yvonne insists I need to go downstairs with her. We peek around the corner from the hallway toward the parlour—tidy compared to their last visit—where O'Rourke and Cane sit on the worn couch with their backs to us, facing Rouva Ruusa.

"Are they looking for me?" I whisper.

Yvonne shrugs. "I'll ask Madame Rose if she wants you." Yvonne slips in and whispers in Rouva Ruusa's ear. A moment later, she is at my side.

"Not this time," Yvonne says. "They're looking for information about a regular. Vanished." Yvonne's hands gesture as if something has gone up in smoke.

"Who?" I can't help but wonder if it has something to do with Hanna.

"She didn't say, but I'm very curious." Yvonne glances back into the room.

"Do they think it's more than a disappearance?" Hanna's face flashes before my eyes. How things have changed since my sister's death. Everything seems tainted now.

"Madame Rose will handle it. I'm sure she'll tell us if we need to worry." Yvonne touches my arm and gives me a look of sympathy, a gesture all too familiar. When will people stop treating me with kid gloves, like I'm a fragile porcelain doll needing protection from harsh realities? Yvonne means well, and she's my only friend these days.

Yvonne glances at the clock and apologizes for leaving me. She goes up the stairs, but I stay in the hallway, listening to the conversation in the parlour. Rouva Ruusa glances up and catches my eye, but she doesn't mention my presence.

"Why do you want to talk to me?" Rouva Ruusa asks. "I don't keep tabs on my guests once they leave here." If I didn't know better, I'd think she was a so-called upstanding citizen, tidy and well-dressed. A woman of importance.

I wish I could see O'Rourke's face. Of course, he keeps opinions close to his chest. "Have you seen him lately?" O'Rourke asks in his Irish lilt. He passes Rouva Ruusa a photograph and points at it. "This is the man. He's a miner, but he hasn't shown up to work for the past few days. According to his supervisor, he's not one to miss a shift, he's never late, and he's a good worker. It's suspicious, and none of his co-workers know where he is. We're hoping you or one of your ... employees ... knows something."

I lean against the wall, hoping not to make a sound. Someone is missing. It seems too coincidental.

Rouva Ruusa examines the photograph. "Hard to tell," she says. "We get lots of visitors here. What's his name?"

"He's a Finlander: Pekka Peltonen. Goes by Peter."

I gasp at the name but quickly cover my mouth. Pekka is missing, so he must have fled knowing I suspect him.

Rouva Ruusa nods. "Quiet fellow. A real loner. Sits in the back corner. Doesn't play cards. Doesn't get involved with the girls."

"Likes his whisky?" O'Rourke asks.

"Now, Officer, you know we don't serve whisky here."

The sun streams through the gaps in the curtains, but the room seems dull and a little depressing. That night in the parlour, the night I met Pekka Peltonen, the space was alive with the sounds of men talking and glasses clinking, cigarette smoke hanging in the air, the powerful aroma of whisky filling my nostrils.

Rouva Ruusa's eyes find me. She nods, letting me know to come in. O'Rourke and Cane turn in their seats. O'Rourke frowns. Cane smiles, and I nod politely.

"Gentlemen, you know Essi Kivi. You might recall you refused to investigate her sister's death."

"Now, strictly speaking, that's not entirely true," O'Rourke says. Cane smirks but lowers his head to hide his reaction.

"These officers are searching for a lost lamb ... a miner. Do you know anything about him?" Rouva Ruusa asks. "I'm always so surprised at how quickly they investigate some people, while others are just left to their own devices."

"No, but I met him once." I glance from O'Rourke to Cane.

O'Rourke flicks his notepad open, pencil ready. "How do you know him?"

"I wouldn't say I know him exactly. We talked about Hanna one night after she ..." I choose my words carefully. "I wasn't sure if I could trust him."

"What made you think so?" O'Rourke asks.

"What he said about Hanna didn't make sense. And I'd heard some rumours." Pekka is not who he claims to be. If he's in trouble with the police again, he may have done more than he's said.

Rouva Ruusa motions to a chair. "Why don't you sit down, Essi?" I take a chair from one of the card tables and place it beside Rouva Ruusa, folding my sweaty hands in my lap.

I have so many questions. "Do you know anything about him? Do you think he would murder a girl, try to cover it up, and then run off without a trace?" Martta's button digs into my wrist.

Rouva Ruusa interjects. "We've all heard Pekka Peltonen can't seem to keep out of trouble. Listen, if there is someone out there targeting girls, I need to know about it. It won't look good if you let another girl die on your watch."

O'Rourke's ruddy cheeks redden, and he clears his throat. "Yes, ma'am. I have no intention of letting that happen."

I look directly at O'Rourke. "Do you think he may have done something to his wife? There are rumours he did it ... he murdered her." Chills pass through me, and I wonder if he's been the one the whole time, amusing himself with the fact that he's gotten away with it, even after everything he's done. Or might have done.

O'Rourke hesitates. A look passes over his face, but I can't read it. "I don't have the answer for you. Plus, there's no body. If there's no body, there's no crime."

Rouva Ruusa raises an eyebrow. "Is that so? What about Hanna? Wasn't there a crime there?"

O'Rourke shifts uncomfortably.

I turn to him. "You're right. If they haven't found his wife's body, then she may not be dead. She ran away, or he has her trapped somewhere." Why would Pekka disappear now? He has a decent job. He's been picked up on minor things, but no significant crime. And then he just disappears?

"It looks suspicious," Robert Cane admits. O'Rourke throws him a look, but Cane ignores it.

Rouva Ruusa places her hands on her lap and looks past me. Her eyebrows cinch. "His wife disappears. He gets drunk and ends up in jail. Charged with assault for the bar incident. He has drinking problems and anger issues."

I pick up the thread where she leaves off. "And then my sister meets him. He makes up a story about her, like they were friendly or something. She was having trouble with a man. Thought Pekka could threaten him and might even be violent."

O'Rourke and Cane look from me to Rouva Ruusa. She says, "But Pekka was lying. Pekka was the man threatening Hanna.

They weren't friends at all. She wasn't coming to ask Pekka for help. She was warning him to stay away from her." Her eyes are animated with the story we are concocting. "And then Hanna's body was found down the street in Nolin Creek. Pekka was absent that night, despite his usual presence on Saturdays. Highly unusual for him. If he doesn't have an alibi, I say he's a suspect."

"Except now he's disappeared. He knows I'm looking into Hanna's murder. I've asked him questions. He might think I'm getting closer. Homing in on him and his crimes."

O'Rourke holds up his hand in exasperation. "Now hold on, ladies. This is a fascinating tale straight out of one of those true crime stories. But a missing man doesn't mean he's a murderer. He might have gone fishing for a few days. Let's not jump to any conclusions." O'Rourke's face is one of amusement, but I can't help but notice he took notes as we spoke.

I have goosebumps. Pekka was acting suspiciously the night I spoke to him. He may have been lying the whole time. But why would he want to kill my sister? I've heard of men who kill for jealousy or rage. Did Pekka kill his wife and my sister because he could? Because he derived some sick pleasure from seeing them die? One missing woman, possibly dead. A second dead woman. Both knew Pekka Peltonen. After everyone I've spoken to, I feel like I have a new lead. The police think a miner is missing, but I think he's fled, afraid I'm getting too close to the truth.

I'm both anxious and terrified to find out what O'Rourke and Cane discover about Pekka. Will they confirm our suspicions? The police don't want to investigate the murder of a girl of no real consequence. In O'Rourke's eyes, she's just another domestic. A dime a dozen. And yet they lost no time in following up on a missing miner. The inequity of it hits me in my heart. Is his life somehow more valuable than hers? If he's taken two lives, he needs to be stopped before another girl disappears. My stomach turns.

"You okay, Essi?" Rouva Ruusa asks. "You look awfully pale."

I nod. "Yes, I will be. I just hope the two of you can get some answers." I grip the arm of the chair, feeling a little faint.

O'Rourke stands and thanks us. "Just don't let your imaginations run wild. We need solid facts, ladies."

We follow them out of the parlour to the front door, and O'Rourke exits, his footsteps heavy on the front porch. Cane pauses at the top of the steps. "Goodbye, Miss Kivi. I hope we can discuss this in more detail later."

"I'd like that," I say, and close the door behind them. Without warning, my confidence disappears.

Rouva Ruusa holds me at arm's length, concern crossing her face. "You're shaking like a leaf. Come with me. I'll get Ruby to make you some strong coffee." She grips my hand and leads me down the hall to the kitchen.

There is strength in her fingers and determination in her eyes. I see her inner strength, her sisu, feel it pass to me through her fingertips. She doesn't need to say anything more. I won't give up.

Chapter Fourteen

April 1933

Although we should be safely in front of winter now, I can still feel the remnants of those cold, dark days, and it's getting more difficult to keep my hope alive. The sun makes a valiant effort to shine through the thick grey haze as I walk toward the tracks at Nolin Creek. I stop to watch the flowing water jostle against the rocks, slamming and twisting, rising and falling, clamouring to move forward with such power that I am envious.

The ice has disappeared from where my sister's body was found, but a ribbon of snow still clings to the sides of the bank as if desperate to stay, willing itself not to melt away and be gone forever. I shudder. Her last moments were alone in the dark, in the icy water, under the steel girders of the bridge.

The vision of my sister lying in Nolin Creek brings back another memory, this one more vivid and more terrifying. It's an image in my nightmares and one I can't shake, even as I try to remember only her beautiful, smiling face. The picture of her dead body on a slab, draped in pristine white. Her pale, swollen skin, her matted hair, her lifeless eyes. Will I ever be free from this distorted version of her?

I push away this image, trying to remember her on a happier day, wearing her favourite dress, her stylish hat and leather gloves. I picture the pin she used to secure her hat, the earrings she wore, and the pendant given to her on her birthday. Hanna loved that necklace and wore it every day. She used to draw the looping square of the cross in her notebook and trace the symbol in the sand. I once asked her why she did it, and she just shrugged. "For luck," she said. "For protection."

What did she need protection from? Did she somehow glean that her life would be cut short? Did the necklace remind her of Martta, who lost her life on the day Hanna received it? Our mother said it would ward off evil. Hanna believed it would bring her luck. I don't think it did either. Evil found its way to Hanna. Her luck had run out.

The pendant was missing from her body on the day I identified her. I remember everything about the room, the stark walls and bare floor, the cold seeping into me, and my deceased sister so pale and swollen. The pendant is the only thing I can't see. It might lead the way to some answers I'm desperate to uncover.

I look to the sky before closing my eyes, the sun a faint warmth on my face, then focus on the road leading me to the Wrights' house. The answer I've been searching for is elusive. Hanna didn't want to stay employed by them, but why? Her plea to leave her work was a desperate one, if only I'd understood that. How I wish I'd paid more attention to her as the older sister. But I was too quick to judge. It breaks my heart. Had I behaved differently, more compassionately, she might still be alive.

The house beckons in the distance. When I reach the servants' door, I pause before knocking and glance at the still garden, not yet in bloom, although hints of green are fighting the soil to push to the surface. The breeze picks up, bringing with it the scent of rotting earth, dormant over many frozen months beneath the snow. Its decay will fuel the new buds and help them bloom. Death comes to all, but life prevails. It's difficult to accept that right now.

I knock on the door, recalling that night. Hanna dressed for work, paying particular attention to her golden locks and worrying about her last pair of stockings, the only ones without a run. She'd been too busy to talk, having only a few hours between her workday and the dinner party where she and Millie would serve the guests. Her dark red lipstick, the perfect wave in her hair, her polished Mary Janes, and the pendant under her white blouse. Was the pendant taken off at the morgue and forgotten about? The coroner said he had never seen it. Lost in a struggle by the creek? I shudder to imagine the scene of desperation and violence. Where did it go? Had she lost it at work?

"Oh, it's you again," Millie says, and steps aside to let me in. I follow her into the kitchen. No courtesies for guests like me. "What do you want now? I thought you had all your answers and more, I might add."

"I have one more important question to ask you, Millie."

Millie takes an overflowing basket of white linens and places it beside an ironing board. I can smell the heat coming from the iron and watch as she tests it by touching a fingertip to her tongue and then the iron. Stroke by stroke, she presses out the wrinkles until the linen is smooth. "Look, sweetie. As I mentioned before, I had little to do with your sister. We worked together, okay? That's all. I don't want to get involved."

"I'm not asking you to get involved. I'm interested in something belonging to Hanna."

Millie folds a napkin and sets it on the table before placing a tablecloth across the board. Her iron moves purposefully across the fabric. Steam rises from the damp material. She is stalling. Finally, she pauses. "Whatever do you mean?"

"Hanna had a pendant in the shape of a square with loops. Did you notice it?"

"Of course. I remember it hung on a chain, and I admired the ring with the pretty stone in it, too," Millie says as she moves the tablecloth down to tackle the next section.

"No, there was no gemstone." I'm puzzled. Is Millie thinking of another piece of jewellery, something belonging to Mrs. Wright?

"Yes, there was—on a rose gold ring. I can tell you I wondered where she got it from. Pricey, if you know what I mean. Not something servants can afford. She may have lifted it from the Missus." Millie gives me a wink.

"I think you've remembered wrong. Hanna didn't own a ring. She wasn't in the business of stealing from her employers, either." Does my voice reveal my rising frustration?

"I don't mean no offence," Millie says. She stops ironing and holds the heavy iron above the linen. "But you got something wrong. There was a ring. I seen it with my own two eyes. She tucked it under her apron, but she liked to play with it, especially when she was staring into the distance, probably mooning over some boy when she should have been working. I had to snap her out of it on more than one occasion, I can tell you. I think it was something new, maybe a few months before her passing."

"Do you have any idea where the necklace is? Or the ring?" My heart is quivering, and I am trying to keep my rapid breathing calm. I don't want Millie to have the satisfaction of thinking she knows something I don't or believing my sister had been up to no good.

"Not since the last time I saw your sister. Hey, you accusing me of something? I never stole a thing from your sister."

"No, I'm not blaming you for anything." Her sharp tone makes me wary, and I turn to leave.

"I asked her about the ring once, but she just blushed and tucked it back under her blouse. She wouldn't say a thing about it. I got my suspicions, though." I'm drawn back toward her. Millie knows more about what happens in this house than she lets on. "She started earning some extra income around the time she got that ring."

Millie has my full attention now. Hanna never told me about any extra earnings. She always paid her portion of the rent and other expenses. We kept a little aside each month for savings, but it wasn't much, even between us. "Do you know what she did to earn it?"

Millie laughs and looks mischievous. "She claimed she was filing papers and whatnot for Dr. Wright. If you ask me, she was doing other things for Dr. Wright that earned her cash, if you know what I mean."

"I certainly don't," I say, a little too sharply.

"She earned enough money to buy her pretty little ring. Or he gave it to her for her services, eh? The good ol' doctor gave her a gift. He's got the dough and can spend it however he likes. He might have wanted to reward her. I don't know. Maybe your sister had a thing for the doctor. Dr. Wright likes the girls, especially the pretty ones."

I feel my skin flush. I can't imagine Hanna wanting to get involved with her employer, especially an older married man. "Do you have any proof of this accusation, Millie?"

"Oh, I'm not making any accusations. I have my own ideas about things. I'm not saying they're right or wrong. When I was Dr. Wright's new little thing, he gave me a bracelet. A fine little gold chain, so delicate you'd think it was spun from the hair of angels. I ain't got it no more. Hocked it for cash long time ago. He rewards the ones he likes. If your Hanna was involved with the doctor, I imagine she was a treat for him, such a naïve girl. Not so innocent after all, I guess." Millie laughs again. "And it's fine by me. I have myself a new man. He's good to me and makes a good living. Not a doctor's wage, no ma'am, but steady. He means to make an honest woman of me."

"Congratulations," I say, trying to digest what Millie's said about my sister. "If you remember anything about the necklace with the pendant ... or the ring... please let me know."

It's hard to believe Hanna might have been involved with Dr. Wright. Maybe that's why she wanted to leave her job. If he had seduced her, she might have felt compelled to keep it a secret from me. Was she in love with her married employer? Was she ashamed? I have a strong desire to confront Dr. Wright, but he could just deny the whole thing. I need more evidence.

I leave through the servants' door and head for Beatty Street, feeling the spring sunshine, finally free of the mist, on my face. I have more questions than answers now. As I reach the creek, the anxious feeling in the pit of my stomach grows. If only I could find her pendant.

In the distance, the railroad tracks guard the creek like sentinels, immovable and implacable. I step my way through the mud and snow patches to the edge of the creek and eye the water. If Millie doesn't know where the ring is and I don't remember seeing it on her body, it could be here, by the creek. A deep inhale and exhale before I lock my eyes to the ground and imagine the route Hanna may have taken.

The water moves rapidly at this time of year. The risk of flooding is real, but it hasn't happened yet. I venture as close as I can to the water's edge, trudging up and down the bank, looking for any hint of something shiny. If the ring came off during a struggle, it might show up now that most of the snow has melted. Before long, I'm on my hands and knees searching the ground and the embankment, but I find nothing. Occasionally I see something stuck between the rocks, but it is only rubbish, discarded items revealed in the spring thaw.

Something touches my shoulder, and I jump out of my skin, teetering off balance. If it weren't for the hand grabbing my arm, I'd be in the creek myself, floating downstream like Ophelia, like my sister.

"Officer Cane," I say, the surprise in my voice clear even to me.

Cane holds out his hand to help me up. "I'm sorry to startle you, but it looks like I came at the right time."

On my feet again, I brush the snow and dirt off my clothes. My shoes are covered in mud. "What are you doing here?"

"Funny you should ask. I was about to ask you the same." He looks at me from crown to toe and frowns.

"I'm searching for something that belonged to Hanna."

"I can assure you we surveyed this area carefully. What are you hoping to find?" Cane seems genuinely interested.

"A necklace with a charm she used to wear. It must have fallen off when ..." My eyes fill with tears, and I fight to hold them back.

"As far as I'm aware, it wasn't with her personal effects. You're sure she didn't leave it in your room? Took it off before going to work?"

"I've just spoken to her co-worker. Millie says Hanna wore it at work along with a rose gold ring I've never seen. It would mean a lot to me to find them."

Cane takes out his notebook and jots down some details about Hanna's Hannunvaakuna pendant and the ring. "I can't guarantee anything, but if someone stole it, at least we have a description. Someone will try to hock it, and I'll get some leads."

"What if Pekka Peltonen took it?" I ask.

"It's possible, but we don't have any evidence yet," Cane says. "When we find him, we'll get some answers."

"I'm grateful. And thanks for keeping me out of the drink." I nod toward the flowing creek. "What brings you around here?"

Cane's colour rises. "I was coming to see you. I went to the boarding house, but you were out. No one could say where, but I noticed someone around the creek and then I saw it was you."

"Is this police business?"

"No. Well, yes. I wanted to check on you and see if you've learned anything new. This is not an official visit. In fact, I'm off duty."

I nod, curious now. "So, this is a social call?"

"Yes. Well, no. I wanted to ask you about another case I'm working on. But if O'Rourke knew I was disobeying his order, he'd take my badge." Cane stuffs his hands into his pockets like a shy schoolboy.

"I understand. I won't tell a soul."

"O'Rourke is the senior officer. I want to help you—I really do—but O'Rourke calls the shots. Right now, we're investigating a socialist recruiter." Cane pauses. "A Finnish fellow. We think he's taking a kickback, so we're looking into it. Do you know anyone who might be involved?" Cane searches my face for answers.

I shake my head. "I've read about it in the Finnish newspaper. My father is fiercely anti-socialist. He has nothing good to say about the society they're trying to create in Karelia. But if I hear anything, I'll let you know."

"I appreciate that," Cane says. "You've probably noticed O'Rourke likes to take charge of investigations. He's not so keen on my looking into this guy, but anything I can bring to the table would be most useful."

"Another good reason for you to help me," I say. "Making progress on this case will show O'Rourke how competent you are as an investigator."

I've struck a chord. I don't know Cane well, but he seems like an intelligent man. Working with O'Rourke must be frustrating.

"There's one more thing. I got a list of folks the recruiter has been in contact with. O'Rourke hasn't even seen it yet." Cane pauses, removing a paper from his pocket. "Hanna is on the list. Listen, it might be nothing."

My surprise is audible. I lean towards Cane, scanning the list for Hanna's name. There it is with a check mark beside it. What does that mean? "May I keep this?"

Cane gives me a copy. "Like I said, it could be nothing. I just thought you should know."

"Thank you, Officer Cane. I really appreciate it," I say, and mean it. "What's his name? The recruiter?"

"Matti Korhonen. He sometimes works at the *Vapaus* newspaper building. And please call me Robert."

I smile. He's on my side, even if O'Rourke isn't. "Thank you, Robert. That's useful information."

"Let me walk you home, Miss Kivi."

"Essi, please." I take the arm he offers, letting him guide me around the mud and puddles.

Why was Hanna involved with a recruiter? None of it makes sense, but at least I know what I have to do next. We cross the tracks together, headed toward Kathleen Street. The sun breaks from the clouds above, and for the first time in ages, I remember what spring feels like.

Chapter Fifteen

April 1933

The mid-afternoon sun streams into the parlour, particles of dust dancing in its beam. The boarding house is quiet. Fredi sits on the edge of the chesterfield across from me, his winter coat still on and his wool hat on the table between us. I never imagined he'd enter this building, what with the way he feels about the goings on here. Yvonne and Annie pass by the parlour, checking on me, I'm sure, but Fredi averts his eyes and scowls.

He looks as though he might bolt out the door at any moment. "What's going on, Fredi?" I ask, trying to be gentle. "Why have you come?"

"I guess I should have called first. There's a telephone here?" He glances around the room.

I nod. "It's in the hallway. If you ever need to reach me, someone will get me. Or leave a message." I wish he'd get to the point.

Fredi clears his throat. "I'm here to see if there is anything I can do to help. I promised your father I'd check in on you, keep you safe and all." Fredi frowns. "I guess I should have checked on you more often."

"He shouldn't have asked you. You're not responsible for us. For me. You're not to blame for what happened to Hanna. Listen, I appreciate everything you've done for us, and for me since …" My voice falters. "There's nothing you can do, Fredi, but I appreciate you asking."

"You'll let me know if I can help?" Fredi's eyes are glassy.

I search his face. "Are you okay? I'm sorry I didn't ask you before."

Fredi nods and straightens up, staring at the table between us. "Police say anything more?"

I hesitate to tell him about the recruiter. Fredi sometimes loses his temper—like his father—and that's the last thing either of us needs right now.

"The police are pretty silent about the whole thing. In fact, I don't know if you can even call it an official investigation. Officer Cane agreed to help me unofficially, but the search moves as quickly as maple syrup on snow. It's so frustrating."

"Has he learned anything new?" Fredi leans forward.

"Not really, just a list of names from a recruiter. Hanna's name was there. I don't know what to make of it." Fredi is as desperate to know what happened to Hanna as I am. I need to tell him something.

Fredi's eyes widen. "What do you mean?"

"Don't worry, Fredi. It might mean nothing." I reach over and touch Fredi's arm to reassure him, but he startles. Everyone's on edge right now.

"You need to let it go, Es. You don't know who you're dealing with. What if something happens to you?" Tears well in Fredi's eyes, but it might just be the usual redness and lack of sleep. He's complained of sleeplessness for years, and nothing seems to help.

"Go on now. No one is out to get me." I try to sound reassuring, but I can't help but feel a slight quiver in my throat. Someone killed her. Would they kill me, too? "Besides, I might have a lead. The police are investigating the disappearance of one of Rouva Ruusa's regulars, a fellow called Pekka Peltonen. The timing is suspicious, don't you think? Plus, there's this fishy recruiter who's helping Finns go to Karelia. You heard about him?"

"Yeah, I know who you mean. Matti Korhonen. Calls himself Comrade Korhonen. He goes all over the country, talking up Karelia. I heard him speak at a meeting once. The number of people who showed up surprised me. Shady fellow," Fredi says. "Before the meeting, he was circulating around the room. He stopped by our group and tried to get me to sign up. I told him I didn't have the dough, thinking it would shut him up, but he said he could organize my passage, and we could make some kind of deal for payment. He wouldn't say what exactly. Not legal, I'd bet."

"You wanted to go to Karelia?" This is news to me. Fredi has never mentioned it, and I'd always believed he was against the Red Finns' socialist ideas.

"Nah, not me. I was trying to put him off. Some fellows dragged me to hear him talk. I don't get it. Do they think life will be better in the Soviet Union?"

Yvonne walks in with a tray. "You want some coffee?" I look at her gratefully, and Fredi manages a tight smile. He takes a cup and thanks her but won't look at her. Yvonne has a twinkle in her eye and gives me a smile. "Let me know if you need anything, honey," she says over her shoulder.

Fredi brings the coffee to his lips, the steam rising. "Essi?" He glances at the door. "I saw Hanna."

"What do you mean?" I want to glance around the room as if my sister has magically appeared but resist the urge.

"Hanna was there. I saw her talking to Korhonen that night." Fredi speaks in a whisper, as if someone in the house might be listening.

"What were they saying? Could you hear them?" Hanna had never mentioned an interest in Karelia before. In fact, it was practically a forbidden topic in our house. Our father wouldn't hear one word about it.

"I was too far to hear anything, but when Hanna turned away from him, he grabbed her arm and leaned in."

I put my coffee cup down, ignoring the spill it made on the table. "You didn't talk to her?"

Fredi hangs his head. "Hanna rushed out of the hall before I could make my way through the crowd. I should have gone after her."

"It's not your fault." I gently remove his hand from his face. "How could you have known? I just wonder what she was doing at the meeting. When was this, Fredi?"

"Let's see now. It was early in the new year. I remember because we had a big snowstorm that night. The snow started falling while we were in the meeting. Truck nearly skidded into the ditch."

For several moments, Fredi and I sit in silence. Yvonne comes in and slides a hand across Fredi's back. "You two alright here? More coffee?" She smiles slyly at Fredi but shoots me a look of concern.

I smile reassuringly at Yvonne. "We're just fine."

Yvonne nods and leaves us, swaying as she walks. Fredi watches her leave, his cheeks and throat bright red. "She's a …"

"One of Rouva Ruusa's girls, yes. She's a good person. And a friend."

"What would your mother say if she knew your boarding house was a brothel?" Fredi does not look impressed.

"I can't do anything she approves of lately, so why worry about it? They're good people, just trying to make a living." Just because Fredi can't understand, it doesn't mean he's right.

Fredi purses his lips. "If you say so. You'd just think they would want to be decent girls, get a husband, have a house, and children."

"I don't see you with a wife and kids, Fredi." I'm tired of these old conversations. Fredi's parents don't have an ideal marriage, but he certainly holds on to the idea that a man needs a wife, and a wife should stay home to raise kids. Fredi looks embarrassed. I've hurt his feelings. "I didn't mean it. Times are tough. We're all just trying to get along."

Fredi pushes his chair back and straightens his coat. "The recruiter ... he's a dangerous guy. I don't like the look of him one bit. I wouldn't try to see him on your own. If you decide to meet him, I'll bring you."

Good old Fredi could be just the muscle I'll need when I confront him. "Thanks, I appreciate it. There is one thing."

"Anything, just name it."

"Can you bring me home this weekend? I need to check on my folks." I wish I had more to tell them, but too much time has passed, and I need to see for myself that they're okay.

Fredi nods. "They'll want to see you."

I follow him to the front door, standing in the entrance while he strides toward his truck and wrestles with the door handle. When the truck finally comes alive, I watch it rumble down the street until it disappears into the distance.

I cross my arms and lean against the doorframe, relieved Fredi has time to bring me to Wanup, but the anxious knot in my belly returns. My father will want to see me, but I'm not so sure about my mother.

Chapter Sixteen
May 1933

A few days later, Fredi drops me off at the farm and I make dinner for my parents. Afterwards, Father sits in his favourite chair by the window, staring at the fields. He looks tired. The grooves across his face, like tributaries from ancient rivers, are deeper than I remember, and his hands have a slight tremor.

I've cleared the dinner dishes and tidied the kitchen. "Coffee?" I ask.

He nods. Father was once a giant of a man, stronger than anyone else I knew. He towered over us and could swoop all three of us into his arms at once. Now, he struggles to raise himself from his chair.

"You should get some help around here," I suggest. "I'm sure there's a young kid who can do some of the work." I glance around the small space, with its weathered curtains, faded furniture, and snagged rag rug. Dust is building up on the windowsills and the mantel, and a fine layer of dirt covers the floor.

Father shrugs. "No money to pay help. I'll manage. It's just the two of us now, and we don't need much." He stares at the fields. He does not smile. It isn't his way to show emotion, and yet his life is written on the wrinkles on his thin-skinned hands, the greying of his hair, the sadness in his eyes. I haven't seen him since the funeral. He has changed. But then, haven't we all?

I pour two cups of coffee—leaving a third empty in case my mother emerges from her room—and search the cupboard for something to offer my father. A piece of cake, a cookie or two. The food the neighbours provided is gone, and they can't be expected to continue cooking for my parents. The cupboard is almost bare, and I know my mother has not been baking, let alone making meals for my father. What she has on hand was likely from a trade with her neighbours. Some home-churned butter for a bit of sugar, some milk or eggs for jars of jam. In some ways, they are faring better on the farm than some folks in town, many of whom rely on the soup kitchen. At least here they have good neighbours who take care of one another and barter for what they need. But it's clear she hasn't been up to much these days. I make a mental list of the items I'll purchase and the baking I can get done tomorrow morning. At least the cow has been milked, and the eggs collected.

"Do you have any information about Hanna?" His tired eyes search mine, and I wish I had better news to make him smile again.

"Nothing I can say for certain." I glance toward my mother's room and turn the bracelet with Martta's button around my wrist. My mother's door is slightly ajar, and I see the curve of her body as she lies on her side under the weight of the Hudson's Bay blanket. She breathes evenly. She must be asleep.

My father follows my gaze. "She doesn't talk much," he says. "Not since ..."

"Give her time." I'm not sure I'm telling the truth. How can she be okay? Two daughters gone. And an unborn child, lost at sea. "Do you remember sailing to Canada? The four of us walked together along the promenade every day. Äiti's belly was as big as a ship, so I couldn't wrap my arms around her. Water was the only thing you could see in all directions."

My father nods. "It was a difficult passage. Your mother ... she wanted that baby."

I take a sip of my coffee. One dark night, the ship had rocked back and forth so violently in enormous waves. "When the storm hit, I was so scared. Äiti was in so much pain. Hanna and I curled up beside each other on our bunk. From the port window, we watched the high waves and lightning strike in the distance. Every time the thunder roared, Hanna and I gripped each other and hid our heads."

"I barely remember the storm. I was so worried about your mother. And the baby."

"And then the doctor arrived with two women. One wanted us to come down from the bunk, but we didn't understand what she was saying, and you told us to go with her. After that, she didn't leave her bed. The weather cleared, and the sea calmed, but from then on Hanna and I walked the promenade without her."

"Losing that baby broke your mother. She couldn't forgive herself."

I never talked to my mother about her miscarriage and never considered how crushed it had left her. "But it wasn't her fault. There's nothing anyone could have done."

My father turns his attention back to the fields. "She's not been the same since losing Martta. I don't know if she'll ever recover after Hanna." He wipes his sleeve across his eyes, and I pick at the crocheted doily on the table, so he doesn't know I notice the tears streaming down his face. He's not a man who cries, but these days tears come unbidden.

The snow is gone now, leaving room for fresh stalks of rye and the distant memory of what was here before.

"I remember Äiti in the days before Martta died. She seemed happier." My mother worked beside my father in the fields, milked the cow, collected the eggs, and always had something delicious on the stovetop or in the oven. In the evening, she darned socks by the light of the kerosene lantern or repaired our few items of clothing, sometimes humming a song.

"Even in the old country, when we were first married, I saw the signs. She would go to a dark place. Sometimes for hours. Sometimes for days. I hoped that moving to Canada would give her a fresh start. But the dark place followed her." My father shakes his head and frowns.

His words surprise me. "Has Äiti had this illness her whole life? I always thought it was because of Martta. Because of me." I place my coffee on the table, shaken by my mother's frailties. I know so little about her. She's never been one to let me in. Mostly, I craved her affection or feared her reprimands. But I didn't understand her. Only now do I want to understand who my mother really is.

"It was never your fault. Never. Your mother struggled for many years. This time is different. She just can't get herself out of it." My father's voice catches, and I think he may cry again, but he pulls his shoulders back and takes a sip of coffee like we are talking about the weather or next season's crops. I've never seen my father cry, not even when Martta died. But those lines. They aren't just on the surface of his skin. I think they're seeping into his frail body and threatening to break him apart.

"I'm here for as long as you need," I say, knowing that time away from work might jeopardize my life in town, my ability to search for Hanna's murderer.

My father nods. "You've always been here to help. I could always depend on you, even when you were just a child."

My heart swells. I didn't think anyone noticed, but his recognition makes me feel good. "Thank you, Isä. There's something I've been meaning to tell you. After Mr. Johnson died, the family couldn't afford to pay me anymore."

Father raises his eyebrows and then nods. "It's a hard time for everyone. Especially if her man is gone. What do you do for money? You can always move home."

I shake my head. "I'm working for my landlady—in the kitchen and laundry, anything that needs tending—until I find something more permanent." I don't mention it's in a brothel. He wouldn't understand. "I learned something interesting," I say, hoping to change the subject from my living situation, but not sure talking about Hanna's murder is helpful right now.

He looks at me expectantly. He wants answers. I want answers.

"A man with a history of drinking issues, who knew Hanna, has disappeared. The police are looking for him." I run through my conversation with Pekka. "He told me what he thought I wanted to hear, but I think it was all lies. Why would Hanna need to protect herself?" Should I tell him about the strange man who visited Hanna at Dr. Wright's? Or about the recruiter Korhonen? It might upset Father to think Hanna was involved with the socialists.

"What did the police say? Is he a suspect?" My father leans his forearms against the table.

"They still say Hanna's drowning was accidental, but I don't believe it. Why would Hanna cross a partially frozen creek in early spring when she knows the waters are treacherous? There's no way Hanna would have taken the chance. Besides, crossing it wouldn't have saved her any time. She would've had to crawl up the bank on the other side. Nothing about it makes any sense."

My father nods. "Good."

"Good? But I don't know anything yet. The police aren't very helpful." I want to tell him more, give him a real reason to hope, but everything I know is so flimsy.

"You're doing the right thing, thinking through why this man might be a suspect and asking the right questions. You'll find the answers."

"I hope you're right. If we catch the man, Äiti will feel better. At least she'll know what happened." I can't help but glance toward her room again.

"Do it for Hanna. Your sister deserves to rest in peace. Your mother will be okay. I'll take care of her."

Now that spring is here, the workload will increase. I won't be here to help.

"I have good neighbours," he says, as if reading my mind. "You can't take care of everyone, Esteri."

I look away, hoping he doesn't see the tears forming in my eyes. I don't have my father's sisu. He's taken care of all of us these many years. In some ways, I'm still his little girl, seeking his approval, but more than ever, I feel the weight of responsibility I've carried since I was a child.

Chapter Seventeen
May 1933

The rain hasn't stopped since Fredi picked me up at the farm. Now, a heavy downpour obscures the road, and Fredi pulls over near the creek. We sit in silence for several minutes, listening to the rain bullet down on the roof of the truck. Like a train, the powerful sound diminishes as it moves into the distance.

I pick up the conversation. "I don't remember Hanna ever talking about Karelia or Korhonen. But now that I think of it, she started reading *Vapaus*, but only because she wanted to read Finnish articles. I thought nothing of it."

"Did your sister associate with communists?" Fredi turns to face me, his eyes squinting like he's trying to bore into my brain. I feel like someone on trial.

I shake my head. "We went to dances together, but we weren't there to discuss politics. She was interested in the boys. I liked the music."

Fredi frowns. "Yeah, I've heard about those dances. Filled with sympathizers. Nothing good could come of it."

"Of dances? Fredi, you really need to have more fun. There's nothing wrong with having a good time, getting together with friends. A few spins around the dance floor. Just keep politics out of it."

"That's what you think, but in the middle of the polka they're convincing you to ditch the church, make free love, and before you know it, you're unmarried, with child, and living with some man who is ready to whisk you off to the Soviet Union."

I can't help but laugh at Fredi's description. "You've obviously thought about this too much, Fredi. Besides, why can't women enjoy themselves just as much as men? Seems unfair that no one judges the men who go to Rouva Ruusa's and yet all of society thinks her girls are dirty good-for-nothings, ruined for life."

"Those girls should get decent jobs. They shouldn't be selling themselves to men." Fredi shakes his head and scowls.

"You're saying I'm disreputable because I live in a boarding house where those things happen, plus I'm unmarried and go to dances with boys who have political ideals, regardless of whether I agree with them?" I cross my arms and glare at him. The rain taps on the roof and streams down the windshield. He's more like his father than he wants to admit. "You sound old-fashioned, Fredi."

"I know you're a good person and you're living there because it's all you and Hanna could afford, but that doesn't make what's happening there okay. You should distance yourself from those women." Fredi taps the steering wheel with his fingertips.

"I'll have you know I like *those* women." I'm getting perturbed now and a little defensive. Yvonne has been as kind to me as a sister, and Annie has only ever been friendly. Rouva Ruusa has been more of a mother figure than my mother has been in recent times, and Ruby has been nothing but kind. I sigh and shake my head. "What does this have to do with anything?"

Fredi shrugs. "If Hanna was involved with Red Finns, who knows what mess she might have gotten into."

"It doesn't sound like Hanna. I think she would have told me." Most of Hanna's conversations revolved around her workplace and featured Dr. Wright or his wife Glenda, and their sneaky little servant Millie, but otherwise Hanna talked about the usual things: clothes, food, and films. We rarely had money for any of those pleasures, but Hanna knew exactly how she'd spend it.

"I'm going to find out how he knew her. Go to the newspaper, try to see Korhonen, and get answers." My mind is turning over the possibilities. Hanna attracted a lot of attention. Who knows who she met at a dance? They might have worked at the *Vapaus* or written for it. Is that how she met Korhonen?

"It's worth pursuing," Fredi says, watching a stray drop of rain zigzag down the windshield. "Rain's stopped. Should we get going?"

The sun is desperately trying to peer from behind the thick clouds. "No, I need to walk. Clear my head a bit, but thanks for the ride."

It's quieter now. I push the creaky door open and step into the cool air, suddenly realizing how stifled I'd felt in Fredi's truck.

Fredi leans towards the passenger seat. "Essi, I didn't mean to offend you. I don't always think before I speak."

"I know. It's okay." I close the door with a bang. A startled crow caws and swoops to a nearby tree.

The truck's engine revs up, and it lumbers away through the muddy street. I stand at the edge of the embankment for a while, watching the water play against the rocks before joining the foray downriver toward Junction Creek. If I could, I'd blame my soaking cheeks on the rain. Chills pass through me as I watch the ripples. There's a murderer out there, and no one cares to stop him. I think about my sisters. It should be my fate, too. Would anyone miss me if I let the water drag me away?

Chapter Eighteen
May 1933

Yvonne blocks the front door while I pull on my coat. "You can't go alone, Essi. It not safe. A killer is out there. Annie, you tell her. I'm right, non?"

Annie crosses her arms, and she leans against the door frame, a slight frown across her face. "I think you're tougher than Yvonne gives you credit for."

"I appreciate your concern, but I'll be fine." Sometimes, I overhear the girls talking about a murderer, someone who targets young women, but when I come closer, they always change the subject. The gossip about Hanna's death has put everyone on edge.

Yvonne shakes her head. "It *is* a bad part of town. Crooks and bad guys on the street corners. Prostitutes."

I tilt my head and smile at Yvonne. "Really?"

Annie emits one of her spontaneous laughs. "Yvonne, what the hell do you think you do here, girl?"

"I mean the not-so-good kinds. The ones with diseases," Yvonne whispers. I'm surprised that even among the girls there are social classes and hierarchies.

The sound of Rouva Ruusa's footsteps approaching from the back of the house precedes her. "On your way out, Essi?" she asks, pausing at the entrance to the parlour.

"Essi is going to see a bad man. Someone who sends those Finns to Karelia to live with the Reds. Maybe *he* murdered Hanna." Yvonne's tone is dramatic. She could have been an actress, a star of the stage or screen, but she is here, struggling to make a living.

"What bad man?" Rouva Ruusa asks, eying Annie and then me. "Does this man have a name?"

"Matti Korhonen. He works for the Karelian Technical Aid Committee and helps people arrange their paperwork and passage to Karelia. We don't know if he's a bad person, and just because he's helping people get to the Soviet Union doesn't make him one." I shoot Yvonne a look, and she shrugs. "I believe he knew my sister." I don't want to tell Rouva Ruusa I suspect him, at least not until I have more evidence.

Annie shakes her head. "This girl is just looking for trouble."

"I know you want to do right by Hanna, but you need to protect yourself. Why don't you send the police? Officer Cane took a real shine to you. I'm sure he would be happy to help you out." Rouva Ruusa smiles knowingly and crosses her arms.

I feel the heat prickle on my neck and cheeks. "Officer Cane told me about Korhonen, something to do with an investigation of illegal dealings that O'Rourke is looking into. I don't think they see any connection with Hanna's death—they don't care about that—but I need to explore it."

Yvonne touches my arm and looks at Rouva Ruusa. "It's my day off. I will go with Essi. I might look small, but I'm as tough as nails." She raises a thin arm and flexes.

Annie grins. "She's right. Yvonne may look like a little thing, but don't cross her."

Rouva Ruusa nods. "Yvonne's got a mouth on her that can scare a grown man out of his boots. If you two get into any trouble, you get yourselves out of there as fast as you can."

"Yes, ma'am," I say. Truthfully, it's a relief to have someone with me.

Yvonne and I trudge arm-in-arm through the mud, down Kathleen toward Mackenzie and then onto Elm Street. Cane said Korhonen sometimes used an office in the *Vapaus* newspaper building. Our strides slow as we approach the entrance.

"You nervous?" Yvonne asks, scanning the building.

"I should be. I'm just worried he won't tell me anything and this will be for nothing."

A sign in the window says they're looking for a reporter. One who speaks Finnish. It crosses my mind that it would be a good job, but they might not hire a female reporter with no experience. I pull open the door, and we walk in with a gust of spring air.

I expected to find a hive of activity, but the place is quiet. "Are we in the right place?" I whisper to Yvonne. "It looks deserted."

"Why don't you ask that lady?" Yvonne gestures to a young woman behind a large oak desk.

The woman is typing, her spectacles balanced on her nose. She is so focussed on her work, I don't want to disturb her. I glance around the office.

At the end of the line, she flicks the carriage return and raises her eyebrows. "Are you here about the job posting?" She asks her question in Finnish. She removes a pencil from behind her ear and wiggles it between her fingers as she waits.

"No, I'm not. I'm looking for Matti Korhonen." I respond in Finnish.

"Korhonen!" The woman yells without taking her eyes off me. She looks me up and down. "Another one for you."

Yvonne and I glance at one another. "I'll explain later," I say in English.

Before long, a man emerges from the back. He grins as he approaches us and holds out his hand. "Korhonen, here. Lucky you found me. My office is a little out of the way. What can I do for you lovely ladies?"

"I'm wondering if you can give us some information. We hear you're the person to talk to about Karelia."

Korhonen's eyes light up. "Yes, I'm your man. Please follow me."

"I hope so," I reply. Korhonen pulls open a wooden gate and ushers us past a few desks piled high with papers. Other than the woman who greeted us, only one other person is working, tucked away in the back of the office. He types with two fingers, each key clacking against the keys with far less grace than the woman we met. We follow Korhonen to the back and down a set of narrow stairs.

"My apologies. This was the only space they could spare me. I rarely bring clients down here to the dungeon," he says, shooting us a sparkling grin. "I'm only in Sudbury for a short time. Off to Toronto in a few days."

At the bottom of the stairs, we enter a long, dark hallway, and he directs us to a small office. There's not much here. Boxes stacked on the floor, paperwork strewn across the desk, a narrow window that hasn't been cleaned in decades. It smells of damp and dust and old cigarette smoke. On the corner of the desk are two small flags: one Finnish and one from the Soviet Union.

Korhonen motions for us to sit with a gallant sweep of his hand, stands behind his cluttered desk, and picks up a cigarette he's left smouldering in an ashtray. He takes a drag of the cigarette and exhales slowly, stubbing it out before sitting down.

"First, let me welcome you." He speaks Finnish. Yvonne's eyes widen.

I glance at Yvonne and take a deep breath. "This is my friend, Yvonne. She doesn't speak Finnish."

Korhonen looks confused but switches to English. "I can see you are just the type of healthy young woman who will prosper in Karelia. They need plenty of skilled workers to help them modernize, and the best thing is you keep your Finnish language and culture. Eventually you might find yourself a husband there, and you'll want the best education and health care to raise your children in the Finnish way. We're always looking for hardworking, devoted socialists who will help this new society thrive. What do you say? Should we start the paperwork?" Korhonen reaches inside a drawer and pulls out some papers.

"I'm Esteri Kivi." I let this sink in, watching Korhonen's face closely. His expression doesn't change, except for a slight twitch at the corner of his mouth.

"Kivi ... Kivi ... The name is familiar. Are you related to someone who has already gone to Karelia? You plan to join them?"

"No, she's gone, but not to Karelia. I was hoping you could tell me how you knew her. Hanna Kivi." I wait, gripping the gloves folded in my lap, but trying to betray nothing on my face.

"I read in the paper about a girl named Kivi. A tragic end to a young life. Drowning, wasn't it?" He shakes his head and reaches for his silver cigarette case and lighter. "The rivers and creeks are so hazardous in the spring. Junction Creek has overflowed so many times, and the flooding can be quite dangerous." He shakes his head as though he's spent too much time contemplating the rise and fall of the city's water systems.

I can't read anything on this man's face, but I know the answer. "Did you know Hanna?"

"No ... no, I can't recall. I meet so many people, especially through my travels." Korhonen lights his cigarette and shifts in his seat. He leans back, unable to sit still, but his discomfort is clear in his fidgeting fingers and his inability to sit still.

"Let me refresh your memory." I pull out the list Robert Cane gave me, smooth the creases against the desk, and point to my sister's name. "She spoke to you at one of your recruitment meetings on the night of the snowstorm in January."

"Let me get this straight. You're the sister of the girl who drowned in Nolin Creek? Am I right?"

Korhonen is trying to buy time. I nod.

He clears his throat. "Right. I remember now. I wanted nothing to do with your sister. She came to me. She needed my help."

"Why? What did she want from you?" I can't remember her referring to Korhonen. She'd once asked me, as we were walking home from a dance, if I knew anyone who'd gone to Karelia. I told her about Mrs. Johnson's cousin, who went to work in the lumber camps and later sent for his wife and young daughter. They never returned, but Mrs. Johnson received a letter from them once. Hanna had said nothing more on the subject. I should have listened to her. Asked more questions.

"She wanted what they all want: the dream. She had Karelian fever." Korhonen sounds like an actor on a stage, impressed with the notion of what he is selling to the audience, although he's delivered the line so many times before.

A heavy silence hangs in the air between us. "Are you sure it was Hanna who spoke to you about going to Karelia? My sister? She said nothing of it to me."

"She was concerned about her man. She hadn't heard from him for many weeks and was worried something might have happened to him. I reassured her, of course. The post isn't always so reliable coming from overseas, and things get lost. But she was insistent. Karelia is a new society. Not everything is in tip-top shape yet."

"Her man?" Hanna had never mentioned a boyfriend.

"Jussi Kallio. John. Don't you know about him either?" Korhonen flicks his ashes into the tray and gives me a look dripping with judgement. I am supposed to be interrogating him, and here I feel like the criminal.

"You *did* know her." My voice warbles, and Yvonne reaches over and squeezes my hand.

"I'll admit I knew Hanna. To be frank, I don't need anymore attention on me, what with the police asking questions right now. I had nothing to do with Hanna's death, but you can understand it doesn't look good. People come to me because they want to go to Karelia, or they want to donate to the cause. I'm here to help them. Like her fiancé. Jussi Kallio paid his fare and said he would send your sister the funds for her passage as soon as he earned them. He left, let me see, late last summer, or early September, excited about the prospect of starting anew. He wanted her to join him within the year."

I'm stunned by Korhonen's words. I've never heard of Jussi Kallio, and Hanna never said she had a boyfriend, let alone a fiancé. All those nights she said she was working for Dr. Wright, was she meeting with Jussi? "What happened? Didn't he send her the money?"

Korhonen shakes his head. "Hanna told me he sent her a little, but after a few months, he never sent a dime. Making your way at the beginning in any new job, let alone a new country, takes time. I believe he kept writing to her. Hanna showed me one of his letters herself. She was getting worried after not hearing from him for a while. Of course, he may have changed his mind. Found a nice Soviet girl. Who knows?"

"You argued with Hanna. Why?" I struggle to focus.

"You got it all wrong, dollface. We weren't arguing. Hanna wanted answers about Jussi and asked me to help her get to Karelia. She didn't have the funds to travel, and I said I could get her some extra work to help her pay her way. Nothing unusual."

Yvonne speaks up. "What did you make her do?" Her voice betrays her concern.

Korhonen grins. "She did nothing she didn't want to do."

"What did she do?" I ask.

"Nothing illegal, if that's what you're thinking. She came willingly to every meeting I organized." Korhonen reaches for another cigarette and pulls a lighter from his breast pocket. He inhales deeply.

"Meetings?" I'm puzzled. "What did Hanna do at these meetings?"

"Gave information to the women, mostly housewives, about the benefits of moving. If they weren't interested, she'd ask for donations. She was an excellent recruiter. I even offered to pay her way if she'd travel around the country with me, but she refused. I didn't realize she was—"

"Dead?" I ask. Korhonen's eyes widen, and he looks away. "And where were you that night?"

"At a meeting on Borgia Street. Hanna called to say she was working at a dinner party and couldn't get away in time. She never showed." Smoke curls from his cigarette. I watch it disappear.

"So, you came after her that night as she was walking home from Dr. Wright's house? You drowned her in the creek?"

"What? You're crazy. I had nothing to do with her death. I was trying to help her get to Jussi, and I needed an assistant to recruit the women. That's all there is to it." Korhonen stands up, his features tense. "Is there anything else?"

"I'm guessing the police will have more to say about your activities, Mr. Korhonen," I say, as Yvonne and I rise to leave.

"If you change your mind about Karelia, let me know. I'm sure you could get yourself a husband in no time if you moved there, Miss Kivi." I look behind me and scowl at this man who knows my sister's secrets.

Korhonen doesn't follow us up the stairs, but his cigarette smoke lingers in the air and sticks to my clothes. We pass through the newsroom where a group of men is now gathered, looking at a set of photographs on a desk and arguing. They pause and turn to watch us leave, but I ignore them.

"He's guilty," Yvonne whispers. "I don't trust that man."

"I don't either," I say. Something about his attitude, the way he exudes confidence but takes no responsibility, rubs me the wrong way.

As Yvonne and I pass the woman's desk, she drops her pencil, and it rolls across the desk onto the floor. The whole place makes me question everything I know.

Chapter Nineteen
May 1933

The next day, there are so many conflicting ideas swirling in my head about my conversations with Hanna. How many secrets has she kept from me? I don't know whether it's the rain soaking through my clothes or the chill that's seeping into my bones, but all I want to do is get back to Rouva Ruusa's boarding house, slip under my covers, and sleep. Even the small bag of items from Mrs. Shevchenko's corner store feels heavy in my arms. As I climb the few stairs to the stoop, my breath hovers around me. I heave the door open with my body and sink onto the bench in the foyer.

For a moment, I close my eyes and lean my head against the wall. The room is suffocating, and I struggle to take off my coat. The foyer is vacant, and the place is as silent as a tomb. It's still early afternoon, and there are no signs of clients in the parlour. But who knows? Some girls could be entertaining in their rooms.

"Essi? Is that you?" Yvonne's light feet scamper on the stairwell. "I've been waiting."

There's an edge to her voice I can't quite interpret, and her expression concerns me. "Are you okay?"

Yvonne bites her lip. "Oui, oui. Fine," she says, a tremor in her voice.

"You're scaring me. Is someone hurt?"

Yvonne sighs. "I'm afraid it's not good news. I found this letter addressed to you." Yvonne pulls a folded note from a pocket in her dress. Her hand quivers as she passes it to me.

"No envelope. I'm sorry I opened it. I should not have read it before you. But—"

"It's okay, Yvonne. I don't mind." She looks scared. Yvonne might be the youngest of the girls, but she has tenacity. I've never known her to be afraid of anything. I take the note from her shaking hand.

"Oh, Essi. You must stop this business. I know you want to help Hanna, but it's not worth your safety."

No information about the sender on the outside. I unfold the note and stare at the brief text:

Stop your search or lie with your sister.

Someone typed the letter, so I can't even recognize the handwriting, and it is unsigned, but it's something.

"A death threat?" I read it again, turning it over to look for clues. Any doubts Officer O'Rourke had planted in my mind vanish. My sister *was* murdered. "You know what this means, don't you? It's someone Hanna knew."

"Non, it means someone wants to kill you. Let your sister rest in peace and forget this terrible business." Yvonne makes the sign of the cross.

"This is proof, Yvonne. Someone is threatening me because they're worried that I'll figure out what happened. My sister's death was no accidental drowning. It was murder."

"Do you think it was Peter—I mean, Pekka Peltonen? Maybe you scared him. Or that awful recruiter Korhonen." Yvonne shivers. She holds the cross she wears between her fingers and strokes it with her thumb.

"I don't know. Pekka was certainly a threatening character, but if he wanted to hurt someone, would he send a note first?"

"He wanted to throw you off, to make you think it was someone else. To scare you."

I pull my boots back on and retrieve my coat. "Would you mind putting that bag in my room?"

"Of course, but where are you going? The storm is getting worse." A flash of lightning lights up the entrance followed by a clap of thunder.

"The police will be interested in this little gem. Now, they'll have to help me." I smile at Yvonne and pull my hood over my head, grabbing an umbrella from the stand.

On the stoop, I look down the street toward Nolin Creek, watching the rain pour down. I can't face the creek today, so I'll go the long way. Taking a deep breath and exhaling slowly. The rain pummels my face.

By the time I walk from the Donovan, past Sudbury High, all the way to Elm and down to the police station, the rain has tapered, and the sun is bravely trying to shine through the dark clouds. My chills have subsided with the exertion of my walk and my newfound determination. Yvonne might be right. I should be worried about the threat to my life, but this is a clue—a real clue—and it can help me.

The police station is quiet. When I enquire about O'Rourke, the man at the desk tells me he is on a call. Disappointed, I turn to leave.

"Miss Kivi?" A familiar voice calls from down the corridor. I turn to see Officer Cane striding toward me, a puzzled expression on his face.

"Officer Cane," I say, perhaps with too much excitement. "I have proof." I pull the note from my coat pocket and wave it in front of him.

Cane's eyes widen, and he glances up and down the hallway, grabbing my arm at my elbow. "Come with me." He leads me to a sparse room with a long table and chairs.

"Is this where you question criminals?" A chill passes through me. How many guilty men have sat in this room?

Cane nods. "Sometimes." He shows me a chair, and I take a seat across from him. "Okay, let's see what you have." His voice is steady, but the flush rising from beneath his shirt collar toward his jaw makes him look younger than his years, which I guess at mid-twenties, not much older than myself.

I slide the note across the table. His fingertips touch mine as he reaches for it, but maybe he doesn't notice. His expression shifts as he reads the contents. "This is a death threat."

I nod more enthusiastically than I mean to. "It proves someone hurt my sister. Hanna's death was not an accident, and it wasn't a random act by a stranger."

Cane folds the note and places it on the table between us. His expression is not encouraging. Enthusiasm seeps out of me.

I lean forward, my palms on the table between us. "It's solid proof, right? You'll investigate now?"

"Do you have any idea who might have typed this note?" Cane asks, and I shake my head. "Did anyone see it delivered?" Again, no. "I'm afraid it doesn't tell us much. Listen, step back from digging into all of this. Leave it with us."

Clenching my hands in my lap, I voice the anger erupting within me. "I wanted to leave it to the police. I asked for your help. Now, here you are telling me to forget it, just like O'Rourke did. I thought you were different. Are you, or are you not, going to help me find my sister's murderer, Officer Cane?"

"Miss Kivi, I mean, Essi, you need to be careful. I've had strict orders from O'Rourke not to pursue this case." Cane speaks quietly, and he looks genuinely concerned. I want to believe him. To trust him. I need someone on my side.

"I don't understand. I have proof now. Tell O'Rourke."

Cane shakes his head. "I wish I could tell you more, but O'Rourke will not be any help to you. Trust me." He leans back in his chair and sighs.

"There's something else," I say. "I met with Matti Korhonen in his office. He admitted knowing Hanna and employing her to recruit women for Karelia." I explain everything Korhonen told me about Jussi Kallio and Hanna's engagement. And then I fill him in on what I learned from Millie.

Officer Cane jots notes in his notebook. "Listen, you did good work here. I'm going to do some more digging, but it's not official. Do you get me? Don't breathe a word to O'Rourke or he'll have my head. But it's better for everyone if you let me do my job now. It's safer for you."

"Thank you, Officer. I can't tell you how relieved I am," I say, offering my hand. He takes it and holds it for a second too long. I feel the heat rise in my cheeks, but it must be the warm room after my cold walk. "You'll let me know what you learn?"

Cane agrees and escorts me to the main door. "Just in case, let's take this note seriously. It's better to be overly cautious. I wouldn't want anything to happen to you. Be aware of your surroundings. And whenever you can, don't go anywhere alone. Just out of an abundance of caution. And please stay away from Korhonen."

I nod and thank him. If it is truly a death threat, I need to figure out who wrote it and why. But Cane is right. I need to be more careful.

The storm has abated, and the sun is trying to shine through the dull grey sky. I pause on the steps of the police station, feeling the cool air on my warm cheeks. Now I can learn the truth. Cane will help me, and I'll have answers. I'll be able to go home to my parents and tell them what really happened. My sister will be at peace, and, I hope, my mother will forgive me.

Chapter Twenty
May 1933

From our table near the window of the Kuluttajat Restaurant, Elm Street has a steady stream of pedestrians. It is quiet, just before the lunch hour rush, so Fredi and I practically have the place to ourselves. Fredi sits across from me, holding his coffee, its contents nearly spilling on the shaking table because of the bouncing of his knees, a restless habit he's had since we were kids. I try to ignore it and examine the nail I've chewed to the quick.

An old man is sitting alone reading a newspaper, and a young couple are laughing together across the room, holding hands, and making eyes at each other.

I take a sip of my coffee and lean toward Fredi. "Korhonen said she had a man, a fiancé even. Can you believe it?" I keep my voice low, but glance around at the other patrons. The waitress is pouring coffee for the old man, and they're chatting in Finnish. The young couple doesn't even glance up.

Fredi stares at his coffee as though a big mystery is about to be revealed there.

"It's unbelievable, right? There's no way Hanna was planning on going to Karelia. She would have told me." I'm looking for confirmation, reassurance. I want someone to tell me Korhonen was wrong. Even though Yvonne didn't trust Korhonen, she seems to have bought his story about Hanna wanting to go to Karelia.

"I knew." Fredi's voice is so quiet I'm unsure I heard him.

"You did?" My chest hurts, and my voice catches in my throat. "Fredi, what are you talking about? What did you know?"

"She was hanging around a boy. I saw them together downtown, walking arm-in-arm. When she noticed me, she dropped his arm and pretended she didn't know me. They walked right past me as though I were a ghost."

"This boy, do you know who he was?"

Fredi twists a napkin between his fingers. His knuckles whiten. "Not at first. But after that, I paid more attention. I saw them together at least three or four more times. They were always very cozy. It was like I was a stranger. You'd think she'd at least say hello. Introduce me, even."

I try to picture the young men Hanna and I had encountered since moving to Sudbury. She'd dismissed them one by one. "What did he look like?"

Fredi describes Hanna's suitor, down to his shoes and hat. An image of the young man we briefly met at the movie theatre—a handsome, well-dressed young man, if a little shabby at the edge of his trousers and the wear of his shoes—comes to mind.

"Was his name Jussi? Jussi Kallio?" First Hanna, and now Fredi. Doesn't anyone tell the truth anymore?

Fredi looks startled. "Yes, I think so. I asked around about him. Goes by John." Fredi hangs his head. "I'm sorry, Essi. I should have told you sooner."

I shake my head and reach over for Fredi's hand, gripping it in my own. "Why didn't you tell me? You don't need to be sorry. You were just looking out for her. If anyone should have told me, it was Hanna." My sister had every opportunity to share news about a new beau, but she never did. Was I closed to the idea of someone courting her? Had I talked too much about myself? I hadn't paid enough attention to her.

Fredi pulls his hand away and makes a fist. He looks so much like his little boy self in this moment.

"What is it?" All my attention is on him now. Hanna's passing has hit us both hard.

Fredi clenches his jaw. "I should have told you sooner," he says again. "You could have helped her."

"You didn't know what was going to happen to her. Neither of us could have known." Perhaps I'm trying to spare his feelings, but I'm not sure I'm telling the truth now.

"But telling you might have—I don't know—saved her."

Could I have saved her? What could I have done? The string of "if onlys" is like an endless film reel running through my head. If only I'd asked her more about her life. If only I'd picked her up from work that night. If only she had stayed overnight in the servants' quarters instead of trudging through the snow after the party. If only I'd gone looking for her instead of sleeping right through, as though my entire world hadn't just been turned upside down.

I lean in across the table. "What do you think happened? She was engaged to Jussi Kallio, but he's in Karelia. It couldn't have been him. Plus, she was in love with him, or at least that's what Korhonen says. She wanted to be with him. But what about Jussi's recruiter? Korhonen says Hanna worked for him so she could go to Jussi in Karelia. Was she being coerced? Did she trust him? Could it have been Matti Korhonen?" My voice is a whisper. The last thing I want is to draw attention from the restaurant patrons.

Fredi shakes his head, his eyes on the napkin between his fingers. It's so tightly coiled now as to be unrecognizable. "I know Kallio was going to take her away to Karelia and Korhonen was going to make it happen. We would never have seen her again if she had gone away." Fredi's eyes cloud over. "I can't understand why she didn't tell you about her plans or ask us for help."

"I've asked myself the same thing." Fredi never had many friends; we were like sisters to him. I should have been more aware of his feelings. I'm hurting, but so is he.

"But there's just one more thing." Fredi's eyes flash with anger, and his nostrils flare. "If I ever see either of those sons-of-bitches I'm going to kill them."

I want to make him feel better, but his anger is contagious. Jussi Kallio convinced my sister to move across the ocean to an untamed country. He manipulated his way into her life. Made her love him. Taught her to lie to her sister, her parents, her family. Part of me wants Fredi to take care of him the way Hanna was so casually disposed of. The other part of me doesn't want to see anyone else hurt.

Before I can respond, Fredi charges out the door. He's angry with Jussi for what he's done. I even understand why he's upset with Hanna. But I don't understand why he'd leave me here alone, as though his grief is greater than my own.

Chapter Twenty-One
May 1933

The nights are long, and the shadows in my room taunt me. I try to sleep but my mind races, images of Hanna as a child playing in the fields at home, a girl whirling around the dance floor with abandon and admired by all the young men, and more recently, a tired young woman with worries that I, her closest confidante, hadn't noticed. Why hadn't she told me about Jussi Kallio? Would it have made any difference? Flashes of her eyes staring up at me through a thin veil of ice, pleading with me to save her. It's not the way I want to remember my sister. I turn on my narrow bed, trying to find comfort, but when I open my eyes, I see only the empty bed where Hanna should be.

The sounds of music and the tinkle of laughter drift up from Rouva Ruusa's parlour. Only a few visitors are here tonight, and I didn't recognize the men's faces as I slipped past the parlour on my way up the stairs earlier in the evening. Maybe Fredi is right. It's time I found a new place to live where her empty bed doesn't haunt me every night and the voices below don't make me question their every intent.

I must have fallen asleep because loud voices jolt me awake. I open my bedroom door a crack so hear what's happening.

Yvonne opens her door and inches into the hallway, her eyes wide. "Get dressed, Essi. It's a police raid," she whispers. Yvonne is dressed up for the evening, with her face made up and jewellery shining. She listens at the top of the stairs. "I don't recognize the voices. They aren't the usual coppers," she says. Her small features are pinched tight as she looks from me to the stairs.

I follow her gaze, but no one appears. "Won't Rouva Ruusa deal with them?" In the past, she's been able to pay them off, and it's been business as usual.

Yvonne's eyes plead with me. "It's better to get out of here if we can. Be quick. I'll meet you at the back stairwell."

I close my door, careful not to make a sound, and pull on the dress I'd worn earlier in the day, grab the thick sweater—Hanna's sweater from home—and throw on some shoes. My coat is still hanging in the front entrance. From the back stairwell, we can gain access to the back lane and escape down the narrow road. But why do I feel a need to flee? I've done nothing wrong. I just live here.

I venture into the hallway. The sound of Rouva Ruusa's deep voice reaches me. "How can I assist you, officers?"

"Take her in," an unfamiliar voice says. Boots clomp against the floorboards in every direction. How many are there?

Several footsteps resound on the stairs and down the hall. I retreat to my room, clasping my hands in my lap and waiting silently. I'd pray, but I don't know who would be listening. The steps approach my door and pause.

Yvonne shrieks, and the footsteps move in her direction. Now's my chance. I open the door, look down the corridor and the stairwell. The passage is clear. There is arguing below.

"You're all going to the station," a commanding voice says. "Get in the paddy wagon."

One girl is crying, but I can't tell who it is. Others are talking back at the police officers, hurling threats and insults.

"Take your hands off me!" Annie's distinctive voice booms.

I creep down the stairs, trying to stay in the shadows. My heart pounds. I feel like a caged bird. I fear for the girls and Rouva Ruusa. What will happen to them?

I'm about to bolt toward the back hall when an officer appears from the parlour. I turn to fly up the stairs, but another one stands at the top of the stairs, blocking my way.

"Time to go," the officer from the parlour says, taking me by the arm in a rough grip. I say nothing and let him lead me to the paddy wagon, where Rouva Ruusa and her girls huddle close together. Despite the scant light, their eyes are wide.

Yvonne sits close to Rouva Ruusa, and I cram myself beside her. She scuttles over a little to make room. Annie is across from me, looking furious. Ruby is sitting in a corner, her arms crossed tight and a scowl on her face.

"Essi? You okay? Did they hurt you?" Yvonne whispers.

I can tell she is afraid. Sitting here with them, I am too. "I'm fine," I say. "What about you?" Her petite body is shaking despite the warmth our collective bodies are generating in the small space. The paddy wagon pulls away from the boarding house with a jolt.

Yvonne tries to smile. "They shouldn't take you." Her usual cheerful manner has disappeared, and left behind a fragile little girl.

Annie scowls. "They don't care who they take. They have all the power, and they'll use it against us. People came and took my little brothers and sisters away to residential school. No one asked our parents. No one cared."

Annie has never shared anything about her family with me before. I'd always assumed she had no family. I reach over and hold her hand. She squeezes back.

Yvonne shakes her head. "That's so terrible, Annie. I'm so sorry." She directs her attention to me next. "You are not one of us. I mean, you are one of us, but they should not have arrested you. You did nothing wrong." She pauses for a moment, then looks me in the eye. "I did nothing wrong, either. None of us. We just try to put food in our mouths and help our families."

Yvonne's determination makes me think she can make things happen. If only someone believes her.

"Thank you, Yvonne. Don't worry about me." I reach over with my other hand. She grips it as if her life depends on it. I glance at Rouva Ruusa, who sits coolly on the hard bench seat as the paddy wagon jostles over the bumpy road. She looks straight ahead, her chin held high, and her shoulders relaxed as though she is simply taking a drive on a Sunday afternoon. An example to her girls. I breathe deeply, trying to calm my quaking.

The truck stops, and I hear the bolt unlock from the outside. An officer helps us down one by one. When it is my turn, I refuse the man's hand and try to leave the truck as gracefully as possible. I glance left and right, hoping no one has witnessed my descent. A vision of my mother's face flashes before me, wearing a look of grave disappointment.

A police officer marches us into the station, past the front desk, to what must be the women's section of the jail. The door closes with a bang.

"What do you think you're going to do?" Annie's voice is calm.

The officer ignores her question. "Keep walking." He nudges her back down the long corridor.

Annie throws him a look but glances over her shoulder to grin. She won't let them push her around. I suspect they're going to process us, ask us questions, and Annie is first.

One by one, the girls leave and return. When it is my turn, I muster my courage. Surely logic and calmness will prevail. I will tell them the truth. It must be enough.

I'm delivered to a big man sitting at an enormous desk, his glasses propped in the middle of his wide forehead while he's writing. He gestures for me to sit across from him, so I do. He lowers his glasses to look at me but pushes them back up on his forehead as he sorts out his paperwork.

"There's been a mistake," I say. I cross my arms and look directly at him, hoping he has some compassion for my situation.

The man raises his eyebrows, looking at me over his spectacles. I wonder how long he's been doing this kind of work. He must be as old as my father, older even. His hair is white and very thin, and he's bald on top.

"Sure, lady. That's what they all say. Name?"

"Kivi, Esteri." I lean forward. "Listen, I just live at the boarding house."

"Sure. Don't you all live there? Age and date of birth?"

"I'm twenty-two; twenty-three next month. Born June 17, 1910. I mean, I rent a room. I don't work there."

"Right. Everyone's giving it away for free. Address?" He reaches for a handkerchief in his pocket, blows his nose loudly and wipes it twice, before stuffing the handkerchief away.

I give him the address of the boarding house. "But my family lives in Wanup," I say, giving him the address of my parents' farm. "I worked as a domestic for the Johnson family until recently. Took care of the children, some housekeeping duties."

"Until you took work at the boarding house?"

"Yes, but it's not what you think." I'm flustered and can't seem to sort out my thoughts into words.

He grunts and keeps writing. Everything he writes is going to follow me for the rest of my life. This man cares nothing about me, about the girls from Rouva Ruusa's brothel. Are the police only here to serve the rich and powerful? He waves another officer over. "Get the next one," he says.

The police officer takes my arm and pulls me toward the door. "I clean and do odd jobs. I don't … you know, do other things," I say, looking over my shoulder

"Sure," the officer says, looking down at his work again. He doesn't care. I'm just an immigrant girl of no value. Like Hanna. Not even worth his time.

The police officer doesn't look at me or even know I exist, except for the grip on my arm. It hurts where his fingers dig into my skin. I'm not resisting him, so why does he need to be so rough? The hallway feels longer, and when we approach the cell, I'm relieved to be back with the girls, but nothing about that interaction was satisfying. The guard unlocks the cell and releases my arm. It throbs.

"What happened?" Yvonne asks. "I was sure they'd let you go." She's still waiting her turn, but her usual buoyancy has long since disappeared.

"He didn't believe me. I tried to explain, but he wasn't interested."

Yvonne pats my arm. "I'll tell them the truth about you. You'll be out of here in no time."

"You don't need to do that for me. I'll sort it out." My mind races. I can call my parents, but how will I explain where I am and what brought me here? My father will be so disappointed. My mother will say I deserve my fate and should rot here until doomsday.

When Yvonne returns, I can see she's been crying. "What happened, Yvonne?" I ask, but she just shakes her head, wipes her tears with the sleeve of her sweater, and slumps to the floor. I've never seen her look so dejected.

The other girls are leaning against one another, trying to find a comfortable position for what could be a long night. I sit beside Yvonne. Soon, she lays her head on my lap, her legs outstretched on the floor, and closes her eyes and sleeps. Even here, when I should be figuring out how to sort this mess, all I can think about is Hanna. As children, Hanna shared all her secrets with me. What happened to us?

I must have drifted. When I open my eyes again, a sliver of light shines through the barred windows above. I sit up and try to stretch my aching body. Yvonne, like the other girls, has curled herself up in a ball. She is sleeping soundly, and I try not to disturb her. Only Rouva Ruusa sits awake on the bench, watching over her girls, while my thoughts return to Hanna and the man with whom she fell in love.

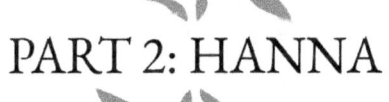

Chapter Twenty-Two

October 1931

The lights of the Regent Theatre draw us closer. Everything about it makes me happy. Seeing motion pictures is an indulgence both Essi and I decided long ago is worth the money from our nearly empty pocketbooks. We both love a film, watching the handsome actors and beautiful actresses singing and dancing across the screen, or getting wrapped up in some dark mystery with its twists and turns. We never went to picture shows when we were kids, but now I want to see them all. It's an escape from our dull, grey, day-to-day existence, a chance to get out of the boarding house and imagine a different life.

"Popcorn?" Essi asks, and I nod.

As my sister lines up at the concession stand, I survey the crowded lobby. Most people dress in their best, though a little worn. A young man leans against the far wall as if he's waiting for someone. He looks like a blond Gary Cooper, with nowhere else to be and not caring about what anyone thinks. He catches my eye and beams a smile. My heart flutters. Essi always comments on how I turn heads, but I ignore her. There are lots of pretty girls. I'm nothing special, but this time I'm the one who can't look away. Before I know what I'm doing, I'm walking over to him, feeling suddenly bold.

"Got a light?" I ask, holding up my cigarette. In the other hand, I cradle the shiny cigarette holder Essi gave me for my last birthday. She must have saved for ages for it, although she let it slip it was secondhand. I'm wearing my second-best dress and know it flatters me, hugging my curves in just the right places. Essi made fun of me as I was getting ready. She didn't think I needed to do my hair or makeup, but I told her you never know who you're going to meet. Boy, was I right.

The man pulls out a lighter and flicks open the lid with his thumb, never taking his eyes off me. His clear blue eyes twinkle, and he brushes a long blond lock from his forehead. He hasn't said a word, and I think I'll have to turn away, but he takes a gentle hold of my arm. His manner doesn't alarm me. I am intrigued.

"You here with friends?" he asks. He speaks English with a slight Finnish accent. I should have known by his appearance, his hair neatly trimmed and swept back with Brylcreem. He casually holds his fedora in one hand, and his suit, a bit worse for wear, is pressed and clean. Only his scuffed Oxfords suggest some imperfections, but at least an effort to look good. More than I can say about most of the Wanup boys I grew up with, like Fredi Virtanen, who looks like he's just come from the fields, dirt under his fingernails, hair unkempt.

"I'm here with my sister Esteri. She's buying snacks." I gesture toward Essi, who is nearly at the front of the line now, her back to us.

"I see." He takes a long drag of his cigarette and surveys the room.

"Are you waiting for someone?" I ask, wondering if this handsome man is already spoken for. Something tells me he is not.

He shakes his head and smiles. "I hear *24 Hours* is a good drama if you like that kind of thing." He doesn't make a move to go into the theatre. "Man accused of murdering his wife makes for a good story, I guess."

"I like a drama as long as it keeps me guessing. Thanks for the light." I glance at Essi and turn away as if I'm not interested. I check my watch, holding the cigarette in one hand, trying to look as alluring as Greta Garbo, and trace the lines of my pendant with my free hand. Essi would say I was flirting, and this time she'd be right. I can feel my heart beating against my chest, but I keep an impartial expression. If he's interested, he'll need to do better than that.

He's standing closer than a stranger should but doesn't show any intention of moving away. "Where are you from? Originally, I mean," I ask, hoping he doesn't think I'm too forward.

"Helsinki," he says, "but I moved here several years ago with my family. I'm the only one left. Jussi Kallio. My English friends call me John." He tucks his fedora under one arm and holds out his hand. The air of formality makes me pay closer attention. His hands are too soft to be a farmhand. I wonder what he does to earn a living.

"Hanna Kivi. It's a pleasure to make your acquaintance. You're the only one left?" I grasp his hand and smile my twinkliest smile. Unexpectedly, he pulls my hand toward him.

"I mean, I still live here, but the rest have left. My father took a job in the States, and so my parents moved there with my three younger siblings. I had other plans. So here we are."

"Yes, here we are." I smile up at him.

Still holding my hand in his, he leans forward, lips close to my ear. "It's my pleasure to meet you, Hanna Kivi. Until we meet again." A chill runs down my spine. He lets go of my hand and disappears into the darkened theatre.

"Who was that?" Essi asks as she joins me, a bag of popcorn in her hands.

"I'm not sure, but I'd like to know more. He's quite a looker." I can still feel the heat of his hand on my skin and hope I'm not blushing.

"Every boy looks good to you," Essi says, a disapproving look crossing her face. "Let's go in before the film starts."

I follow Essi into the theatre, looking down the aisles for Jussi Kallio. I scan the rows, glossing over the art déco interior, and strain my eyes for a figure resembling his.

The lights dim, and the opening credits appear on screen. As we watch the film, I can't help thinking that somewhere in the darkened theatre a pair of blue eyes are searching for mine. I can't suppress a smile as I reach for the popcorn.

This is just the type of film Essi loves, and she'll want to dissect every detail afterward, piecing together the plot as it unfolded. She has a sharp eye and never misses a detail because of all that reading she does, I bet. I prefer musicals, with their costumes and sets. Sometimes, I don't pay much attention to the storyline if the actors are nice to look at.

When the film is done, I follow Essi out of the theatre, watching the people move up the aisles and hoping to glimpse Jussi Kallio.

"I'll use the ladies' room and meet you outside," Essi says, and weaves between the patrons in the lobby. I linger by the double doors, monitoring everyone who exits, but I don't see him.

After several disappointing moments, he appears beside me. "Miss Hanna Kivi. We meet again." His voice is like silk, and he sports a mischievous smile. Utterly charming.

"Mr. Kallio," I say. I try to look nonplussed, but I'm flustered. "Did you enjoy the film?"

"Indeed. There's nothing like a good murder and mistaken identity story. And Kay Francis." Jussi produces a low whistle.

"Is she your type? Hollywood starlets with lots of money and glamour?" Strange to have a tinge of jealousy for a woman I will never meet.

"I prefer girls who are ... real. I like that the husband and wife reunite in the end. Meant to be together, I guess." He grins and winks. "I hope we'll see each other again."

"I'd like that, Mr. Kallio." And I would. I hope our paths cross soon. If it is meant to be, it will happen.

Jussi Kallio tips his hat at me and turns away from the theatre, hands in his pockets. I can hear him whistle even as he turns the corner. Just on cue, Essi exits the theatre, fussing with something in her handbag. "Chewing gum?" she asks as she pops one into her mouth.

I shake my head and glance back down the street where I last saw Jussi Kallio. With all my heart, I hope I see him again.

"You look flushed," Essi says. "Are you okay?" She touches my forehead with the back of her hand, more like a mother might do than a sister. But then, Essi's always been like a mother to me, since our mother, Ida, was often not present for us.

"Couldn't be better," I reply, and link arms with my sister. Essi and I turn down Cedar Street toward Durham Street. "Time for coffee?"

Essi agrees, and we make our way down Elm Street, ducking into the crowded Kuluttajat Restaurant. I expect she'll want to chat about the film. I'm in such a good mood I'll let her talk my ear off.

"Listen," Essi says, pausing while the waitress pours our coffee. "I think it's time we thought about moving. Now, just wait. I've been thinking about it a lot. You have a good job with Dr. Wright, and Mrs. Johnson may not be paying much, but it's steady income."

I take a sip of coffee, letting Essi give all the reasons I've heard before, but my mind wanders, and I look out to the darkened street lit by storefronts and streetlights.

"What do you think, Hanna? You're quiet."

"Why would we want to move now? Our rent is cheap. We're not going to find something better than Rouva Ruusa's place. You know I'm right." It isn't the best place to live, but if we want to save a little money, we'll have to stay where we are.

Essi sighs. "I just hate lying to our parents. Imagine if word got out in Wanup. What would Äiti tell the neighbours? The people at church? Her reputation would be ruined. So would ours. Besides, you said it would be temporary."

Essi's not wrong. I said it would be for a week, maybe two. But I'm tired of living my life for other people. If only Essi could see things the way I do, but she's already sacrificed so much for me by coming here. I probably wouldn't have moved into town without her agreeing to come with me. Our parents would never have allowed it.

"I tell you what. Why don't you keep your eye out for another place, and if we find something we can afford, we'll look into it. A little extra space would be nice." I doubt she'll find a cheaper place, but I'd like a bigger room, or even two rooms.

Essi looks pleased, and a little relieved. "I'm sure I can find something suitable, and it will be such a relief not to hide this from Isä and Äiti." She places her cup back on the saucer. "Ready to go?"

I leave a small tip for the waitress and follow my sister out of the restaurant. She chatters on about the movie, and I nod occasionally, but I'm only half listening. I'm tempted to tell Essi about Jussi Kallio, about the way he looked at me and how it made me shiver. I tell Essi everything—all my secrets, my hopes, my dreams, even my frustrations—but this time I want to keep him to myself, at least for now. Besides, we might never cross paths again.

Chapter Twenty-Three
October 1931

I take one last look in the mirror and apply another layer of deep red lipstick with my fingertip, sweeping a wave of hair behind my ear and adjusting the pendant on my necklace. If only I could afford a new dress, but this one is new-to-me thanks to Yvonne. It fits me like a glove and the Baltic blue sets off my eyes.

The door opens and Essi lumbers in, dropping her purse on a pile of newspapers and flopping down on her bed. I hoped I'd be out of the boarding house by the time she returned from the Johnsons. "You're home early," I say, rolling down the lipstick and placing the case in my purse.

Essi is lying with her forearm draped over her eyes, the other arm limp and hanging off the bed. Another one of her headaches. "Mrs. Johnson let me go a little early this evening. Good thing, too. I'm so exhausted. You have no idea how noisy three children are, and the little one, Henry, seems to have caught a cold again."

Essi hasn't noticed Yvonne's dress or my freshly applied makeup. I may still slip out without her asking questions. "You should go to bed early. You look terrible."

"Henry kept coughing on me. I hope I didn't catch whatever he has." Essi pulls herself up and drapes her legs over the edge of the bed. "You look nice."

My shoes are a little scuffed, so I rub them with a clean cloth, hoping to get the shine back. What am I going to tell Essi? The truth?

"Where are you going? Not back to work, I gather." Essi looks puzzled.

I could lie to her, tell her Dr. and Mrs. Wright are having a party and I'm serving, but I just can't. She'll know right away. "A movie. A girl from work invited me, and I thought it would be nice."

"Really? It's not horrible Millie, is it? I thought you didn't like her."

"Millie? No, I don't want to spend more time with her than I already do. It's one of the temp girls they get in for big events. Lillian. You'd like her. I hope you don't mind if I leave you home alone tonight. I mean, you can come if you want," I say, hoping she'll refuse.

Essi shakes her head. "I have a splitting headache. I'll make some tea and curl up with a book."

"You're a peach," I say. "Feel better." It's just a little lie, but it makes me uncomfortable to fib to my sister. I hesitate at the door. Should I tell her the truth? Surely, she'd be pleased for me.

"Have a good time." Essi gives me a smile and pulls her favourite sweater over her shoulders.

I close the door gently behind me and skip down the stairs, guilt pushed aside by my excitement to see Jussi Kallio again. He's meeting me at the end of the road near Nolin Creek, and we'll walk from the Donovan to downtown, enough time to get to know one another a little better.

As I approach the creek, leaves crunching underfoot, I scan the horizon for his figure. He's not there. He could be late, or maybe he changed his mind. Perhaps he doesn't want to see me after all.

Last week, as I was leaving a shop on Durham, he crossed the street, getting honked at, and rushed toward me. He was just as I remembered him, with his eyes twinkling and a smile brightening his face. It would have been impolite not to stop to say hello. He got right to the point and invited me to dinner, and I said yes. I should have been more hesitant, but he wasted no time, so neither did I. When we parted ways, I could hear him whistling and my face hurt from smiling so much.

Now, I have my doubts. He might not be interested in me at all, and I have been too forward. I pick up the smoothest rock I can find, watching the movement of the water as it trickles between the rocks and laps at the edge. It's so peaceful. If he's not here in three deep breaths, I'll toss the stone into the depths, make a wish, and go home.

One ... I close my eyes. Sunshine kisses my cheeks. Breathe in. Breathe out.

Two ... Birds call to one another. Leaves rustle. Breathe in. Breathe out.

Three ... Footsteps approaching. Whistling. Exhale.

My heart races and my eyes flutter open to find Jussi Kallio a breath away from me, a quizzical smile on his face.

"You're the most serene creature I've ever seen," he says, a hand rising to my temple to push aside a lock of stray hair.

I'm flustered now, delighted he is here, but level my voice. "Late, aren't you?" I glance at my watch. "I wasn't sure you'd come. Was just about to leave, in fact."

Jussi smiles. "Fashionably late, I'd say, and I wouldn't miss this for the world."

He's the most charming man I've ever met, and the most handsome. Does he know it? Is this a game he plays with all the girls? It wouldn't do to fall in love with someone who might break my heart. If Essi were here, she'd advise me to keep my head on straight, think logically, but my heart says something else. It sings in his presence, as if meeting its other half.

"Shall we?" He offers his arm as though he's done it a thousand times, and I let him.

"Hanna Kivi, tell me about yourself," Jussi says. We turn from Kathleen onto Monk. And I do. I tell him about Essi and my parents. I tell him about the farm in Wanup, about our neighbours and our church. I tell him about Dr. Wright and his wife, Glenda. Even about annoying Millie. I tell him about Martta, too. I've never talked about Martta with anyone, especially not to a stranger. But Jussi doesn't feel like a stranger to me.

"I'm sorry," I say, feeling my face blush at the realization I've talked all the way from Nolin Creek to Elm Street. "I've said too much, and you haven't told me anything about yourself."

Jussi just smiles. "Never apologize, Hanna. I want to know everything about you and your life. Every detail." We turn on Elm and head toward downtown, a streetcar clanging past us filled with passengers on their way to Copper Cliff. The evening is crisp and cool, and I sneeze. Jussi offers me his handkerchief.

"There's not much to tell," Jussi says. "I'm renting a room near the courthouse. It's a family my parents knew before they moved, and they've been very kind. Good home-cooked meals and freedom to come and go as I please. I've been nomadic for the past two years. A season at a lumber camp. The money was good, but the work wasn't for me. They hired me at the mine, but I have no interest in being underground. Now I'm doing odd jobs. Working with a carpenter. He's showing me how to make furniture. I have much more freedom to do as I please. Besides, it's only temporary. And I like the work."

I hang on every word, surprised he's sharing as willingly as I did with him. "What are your plans?" It occurs to me he might leave Sudbury, join his family in the States. I wait with bated breath for his response.

"Nothing's official yet, but I'm working on saving enough money to go to Karelia." Jussi's eyes light up. "You know about it? They're building this brand-new society, and I have a chance to be part of it. Make a fresh start, you know? Canada's pretty good, but with this Depression and everything, I think

I can do better. And it's an opportunity to make a real difference, you know?"

"Karelia? The Soviet Union?" I wish I'd paid more attention when my father rambled on about the Red and White Finns, but I left the conversation to my sister, who was more interested or at least pretended to be.

"Lots of Finns going from Canada and the States. Finland, too. You wouldn't believe how many people are unhappy with what's going on in the world, especially since the stock market crash. Karelia has work for everyone who wants it. It's like a mini-Finland in the Soviet Union."

I release my arm from his to place the handkerchief into my handbag. "It sounds interesting." My father would be furious if he knew I was walking with a socialist. I'd never hear the end of it.

Jussi stops and takes both of my hands in his. "You seem disappointed."

"Not at all. I ... I just don't know much about Karelia. Only what my father has told me. He's not in favour of it. He's wholeheartedly against it, in fact. We left Finland, and he hoped to leave those political divides behind."

Jussi's face clouds over. "Why don't I tell you all about it at dinner and you can make up your own mind? I may even convince you," he says, the twinkle returning to his eyes. It's like a challenge he's set himself, and I see already he likes a challenge. "Here we are," he says, opening the door to Kuluttajat Restaurant. "Is this place okay?"

"Perfect," I reply.

Jussi helps me remove my coat, and we find a seat in a quiet corner. He holds the seat for me and helps me tuck it in. He's such a gentleman, like an actor in a film.

The waitress takes our order, and Jussi watches me intensely. When I look up at him, his gaze stays on me, and he smiles more brightly. No one has ever given me such undivided attention.

"So, convince me," I say. "Tell me about Karelia." But in my heart of hearts, I don't need any convincing from this man. I would follow him to the ends of the earth if he asked me to.

Chapter Twenty-Four
May 1932

Essi links her arm into our father's. "How's Äiti doing?" she asks. I pick a daisy from the garden and breathe in its sweet scent as I trail behind them, unable to pay attention to their conversation. My thoughts are with Jussi. Always with him these days. It has been eight months since we met, and we've been inseparable. I wish today I could have brought him with me, but I'm not ready to tell my parents, especially about his plans for Karelia.

At the mention of our mother, Father turns to Essi, a forced smile on his face. "Some days are good and some are not so good. Today is a good day. She's happy to have you both home."

Essi grins and looks relieved. As much as she misses home, she's often anxious at the thought of returning to it, and when she's away, she worries about them. She's always needed to take care of everyone. Our parents, me, Fredi, even.

"I'll be right in. I need to see my old friends first." Essi saunters past the house and barn to where Freya and Inkeri are grazing in the field near the fence. Freya neighs in greeting and pushes on her hand until Essi strokes her. Even the more aloof Inkeri sidles up for attention, and Essi's laughter tinkles through the breeze. She's at home here. It's a wonder I ever convinced her to leave.

My father pauses at the bottom of the steps to the house, pulls a rolling paper from his case, sprinkles tobacco in a long line, and deftly rolls a cigarette on the flat newel post. His hands are calloused with hard work and his jagged nails are accentuated by crescents of dark earth. Should I stay, awkward beside him, or go inside to greet my mother, discovering what state she might be in? Here, I can admire the garden, comment on the house, or enquire about the crop or cows. Our conversation will be more stilted without Essi as our buffer. I just never know what to say to him. And he doesn't know what to say to me. He's always had a deeper connection with Essi somehow. Maybe because she's the oldest, and took on more responsibilities growing up.

The first inhale is deep, and his gaze wanders to his fields, thriving in the warm weather, although the worry about them is always close to the surface. He exhales and turns to me. "No niin." Well then, he says, speaking in Finnish as he did when we were children. "You're faring well in the big city?"

I cross my arms, wondering if the simple question will turn into a barrage of questions.

"Yes, everything is fine."

"You're still working for the doctor and his wife in the big house?"

Essi is chatting with Freya, but Inkeri has wandered off, solitary now under a large oak. "Steady hours and good pay, but I might look for something else soon."

"Why would you leave such a good job? Something happen?"

Has he always been this suspicious, or is it only since we moved away? "Nothing's happened. I just might want a change. Lots of girls change jobs when things become available. Better pay or hours, or different responsibilities. I don't know." I hang my head and gaze at my shoes. I feel like I'm a little girl again. "I might stay." I shrug.

A noncommittal grunt suggests he's not convinced. "Always looking for something better. Maybe settle down." His smile widens as Essi jogs toward us. I'm struck by her bright eyes and fresh face, more relaxed than I've seen her in weeks. The country air agrees with her. "Sorry, I had to have a little chat with Freya."

The door at the top of the steps opens and our mother appears wearing a simple housedress and a clean apron. "Coffee is ready."

We follow our father up the steps and drop our shoes at the front entrance. Judging by the scent of cardamom, she's been baking, always a good sign. The table is set with four places: a cup and saucer, dessert plate, forks and spoons. In the centre, a glass platter, given to her as a wedding gift, is laden with open-faced sandwiches on fresh rye bread, sliced *pulla*, pieces of cardamom cake, and gingerbread cookies in the shape of hearts.

Essi sits down and pulls out a chair for me. "Everything looks delicious, Äiti."

Our mother returns from the kitchen with strawberry shortcake, my favourite. "For your birthday, Hanna."

Essi's eyes widen and her mouth drops. My birthday had passed earlier in the month, but we'd heard nothing from our parents. I didn't care one whit about celebrating, and I had brushed it off then, claiming not to be upset, but Essi knew better. Now, she appears more surprised than I am.

"You didn't have to go to all this trouble," I say. I couldn't help but think about Martta, and I could tell from Essi's expression that she was thinking about her, too.

"No trouble," our mother says. When everyone has eaten sandwiches and been served coffee and cake, she finally sits in her chair across from Essi. For several minutes, we eat and drink in silence.

I search for a topic of conversation. Nothing about the weather, or we'll talk about the crops and how, if they fail, the farm might not survive. Nothing about the water level this year, or our mother might be reminded of Martta, and her good mood will take a turn. Nothing about Sudbury, or we might reveal we live at Rouva Ruusa's boarding house. I take another bite of the sweet strawberries laden with fresh cream and allow the flavours to soothe my nerves.

Our mother wipes her mouth with a napkin and places it beside her plate. "What news do you bring from Sudbury?" She glances from me to Essi and back to me again.

"Pretty well the same. Working lots. Sometimes, Essi and I go to the movies."

Father leans forward to encourage me. "And what films have you seen?" It seems a safe topic.

Essi describes the latest film. Our father nods occasionally between his sips, but our mother tut tuts.

"Sounds like a waste of money," she says. "Read a book instead if you have so much free time on your hands. Why waste your money on such a thing?"

Essi struggles. There's no convincing our mother of anything. "It's nice to go into town, meet people ... you know. And the stories, the films, they're like a brief escape from our day-to-day lives.

"Essi's a regular at the public library. You should see her pile of books," I say. I'm not much of a reader, but sometimes she brings me a good romance or a true crime."

"Why do you need an escape? You chose your life there. Tell me about the people you meet." Her tone is edging on accusatory, but I can't help but wonder if she is genuinely interested in our lives there, so different from her own.

My cheeks burn, and I focus on the bubbles on the surface of my coffee. Don't they mean something? Bubbles moving toward me mean financial gain. Or is it bubbles moving away? I don't look up at my mother.

"I mostly spend time with Mrs. Johnson's three children, to tell the truth," Essi says. "The girls are sweet, but the boy is a handful." Essi prattles on about their antics, and Äiti seems amused by her stories.

"And you, Hanna. How is your work?" she asks.

"It's good," I say. "The doctor pays well, and the house is beautiful, like a mansion." I tell them about one of Mrs. Wright's tea parties with her socialite friends, what they're wearing, and what we served. But I can't tell them about Jussi. Not now. I'll find a way, eventually.

Mother nods as if our stories are acceptable. I reach for a cookie and let it melt in my mouth. If only I could tell my family about Jussi Kallio. I haven't breathed a word, not even to Essi. Our mother would be disappointed, and our father would be furious. Only Essi would understand, but not the part about keeping it from her for so long. That part is unforgivable.

I glance at Essi. She's doing her best to stay positive but shifts in her chair, looking a lot like the little girl who took all our mother's berating after Martta died. I push the image of that horrible day aside. It wasn't anyone's fault. Not hers. Not mine. "We're so busy working, it's hard to meet anyone other than our neighbours and people at work," I say. "We should make a point of doing more social activities. It would be a way to get to know new people."

Essi's eyes widen slightly, as if to tell me to stop my line of reasoning. I take another cookie and chew furiously.

"The cake is delicious," Essi says, taking her last forkful.

The rest of the afternoon is spent in small talk, and I'm relieved when I hear loud footsteps on the steps and a heavy knock on the door. Fredi is here to bring us home. It might be the first time I've ever felt happy to see him.

Fredi's not one for small talk, but he lets our father lead him to the barn to look over some piece of machinery or other while Essi and I tidy the table and clean the kitchen. Fredi's good at fixing things, and my father likes that about him.

"He's an odd duck, isn't he?" I whisper to Essi.

Essi hangs up the damp tea towel. "You want men to be like the actors in the picture shows—handsome, intelligent, strong—but it's not real life. Fredi wasn't even coming home this weekend, and he drove us here because we asked him." Essi gives me a look that tells me she's disappointed in me.

"You're right," I say. "I'll be nicer." But no matter what Essi thinks, I still think he's odd.

By the time we go outside, Fredi and our father are inspecting his truck, and our mother is asking after Fredi's parents. She's wrapped up some baking for him, and he accepts it politely.

Essi nudges me. "Thanks for driving us today, Fredi," I say. "You've been a real pal."

Fredi breaks into a smile. "No problem. Just let me know, and I can drive you home anytime ... or anywhere else you need to go. I'm happy to do it." He rushes around the truck and fiddles with the handle until the passenger door opens for me. I step into the battered truck and glance at Essi as she slides in beside me. Now, I'm wedged between Fredi, who smells like cow manure and sweat, and Essi, who can't stop grinning.

"You've made a friend for life," she whispers, stifling her giggles.

Fredi says goodbye to our parents. I squeeze as close to my sister as I can, trying not to let my leg graze his. If only Jussi had an automobile, he'd drive me to Wanup and be the one chatting with our father and accepting baked treats from our mother. I don't mean to be cross, but I can't help it. It's not fair. My parents would be happier if I were dating Fredi instead of Jussi. For the entire trip home, I ignore Fredi and Essi and think instead about how I'm going to break the news to my parents. Their daughter is in love with a socialist.

Chapter Twenty-Five

August 1932

The summer is flying by, and I yearn to capture every moment. Jussi is waiting for me by the creek. He is leaning on a rail, watching the water move by, and whistling "All of Me." When he finally sees me approaching, his face lights up. He steps toward me with his arms extended. I rush into them.

"Good thing you came," he says, the crinkles at the corners of his eyes opposing his serious tone. "I have news."

"Oh, do tell." I take his hand. We stroll until we find a place to sit on the grass out of sight of any passersby.

"Well, there are two things, really." Jussi pauses.

Curious, I imagine what he might tell me. Perhaps he has a new job, or he's going to visit his parents in the States.

Jussi clears his throat and looks serious. "I know we haven't known each other for very long, but I know you are the one for me. I knew it from the first time I saw you at the theatre, giving me those flirtatious smiles."

I laugh and punch him lightly in the arm. "If I remember correctly, it was you who took my hand and wouldn't let it go."

Jussi laughs. "You're right. What I'm trying to say is, I love you and have always loved you. I want to marry you." Jussi pulls out a rose-gold ring with a gemstone.

I gasp. Of everything I thought he might tell me, a proposal was not on the list. I search his eyes.

"It was my grandmother's ring," he says, as if to fill the silence.

"It's beautiful." I stare at the ring and then into Jussi's eyes. I want so desperately to take the ring, to put it on my finger, to be his wife. I am happier than I have ever been in my entire life. But I hesitate. "What is the other thing you wanted to tell me?"

Jussi lowers his head. "My documents for Karelia are in order and my passage is booked. I'm leaving in a few weeks."

My eyes well with tears. The ring sits in his open palm. All I need to do is say yes. Jussi searches my face, but he is patient. He will not make me rush this decision.

I take a deep breath. "Yes, Jussi Kallio. With all my heart, yes."

Relief floods Jussi's features as he places the ring on my finger. "You won't regret this, Hanna Kivi. I will send for you as soon as I can, and we'll begin the best life you can ever imagine in Karelia. You will be the lady of a fine house, with a fine husband, and raise fine children."

With Jussi, I imagine everything is possible. He will make all our dreams come true, and I will follow him wherever he leads me.

A few weeks later, we are in the Regent Theatre, the very place we met, but this time we hold hands in the dark watching *Love Me Tonight*. Maurice Chevalier plays a tailor, falling in love with Jeanette MacDonald's princess, and my heart swoons. When it's over, we sit in the dark until the lights go up and the theatre is empty. I wipe away my tears. This is our last evening together.

"It's going to be okay, Hanna," Jussi says. "It's not forever."

"I know." But I also know that when he leaves my heart will break. I feel it pulling apart already. A small tear that started when he first told me he was going has grown into a wide chasm with every passing week.

Jussi wraps an arm around me and hums the tune "Isn't It Romantic." We stroll past the closed shops on Cedar Street to Station Street, and Jussi suggests we walk toward the CPR station. He wants to see everything one more time.

People bustle by. Some stop to gaze in the windows of the shops. A poor fellow sits at the corner with his hat out, hoping for spare change. He's quite a young man, dishevelled and unshaven. I wonder how long he's been out of work, so I search for my change purse and drop a coin into his hat. It's not much, but he needs it more than I do. Jussi's decision seems to be the right one. Things are only getting worse here.

Jussi pauses across from the train station, and we look at the transforming sky. The sun is setting, and the clouds absorb the colours, so I feel like I may never see something more beautiful than tonight's sky. Speaking will break the magic of it, bring me back to the real world, where he will be gone and I will be left alone, with no one to tell how I feel.

"When I'm gone, you'll need someone to rely on, Hanna. I don't know your sister except from what you've told me, but she seems like someone you can count on. A good head on her shoulders."

I wrap my arms around Jussi and rest my head on his chest, gazing at the shifting clouds making way for the bright pink and gold hues of the sky. "It just doesn't seem like the right time. When you send for me, I'll tell her everything. Until then, let's keep it between the two of us. No one can talk me out of it if they don't know our plans." Essi would point out all the issues, tell me I am reckless, foolish to make this rash decision. But it's not rash. I've known I would go with him since that first night at the restaurant when he poured out his dreams of Karelia.

Jussi squeezes me tighter, and we stand for a long moment in silence. How can this be the last time I feel his arms around me? Karelia is so far away.

"I'll write to you as soon as I'm settled," Jussi says, as though he has read my mind. "My work will give me enough to live on and save a bit for your ticket. It won't be long before you join me, kulta."

"You don't have to go," I say. "We can create a life here." My heart fills with love for this man, and I know this is his dream.

"This is what I've wanted for a long time," Jussi says. "And when you come to me, my world will be perfect."

I touch the ring on my finger. I know I can't dissuade him from his dream. Karelia will be our new utopia. Life will be better there. I could even convince Essi to come with us. Our parents will do what they've always done on the farm and won't miss us one bit, but I can't bear the idea of leaving Essi behind when I finally have my chance to join Jussi in Karelia.

"The distance is wide, and the heartstrings are already pulling," I say, tilting my head to receive his kiss. "I will never feel whole again until we are together again."

Jussi holds my hand, and we walk at a slow pace, savouring every step. When we reach Rouva Ruusa's boarding house, I look up to the window of the room I share with Essi. A light is visible, but the curtains are closed. She won't have seen us approach, and if she has, I'll tell her this nice young man kindly offered to walk me home. The evening is already dark, the last of the painted sky shaded over, but we duck under the porch of the house to avoid any unwanted eyes. I don't want this moment to end.

The tears well in my eyes again, but I refuse to let them fall. In the distance, a train approaches. I feel it reverberating under my feet. The sound grows louder. Our embrace lasts for a long time, neither of us wanting to let go. When he finally holds me at arm's length, he stares into my eyes. "Until we meet again, my love," he says, and kisses me so I never want him to stop.

This goodbye is not forever. He turns away, and I watch him walk down the street. Several houses down, near the creek, he turns and waves one last time.

Inside the boarding house, someone is playing a violin. The tinkle of glasses greets me. I glance inside the parlour. Billy has his arms wrapped around Yvonne. They are slow dancing, but he can barely hold himself up. I feel sad for them both as they sway in the dim light against a backdrop of hazy cigarette smoke. Neither of them knows about love. Or heartache.

I take off my shoes and pad up the stairs. Essi has left a light on, but she is curled up on her bed, snoring lightly. I place the light quilt over her shoulders and sit on the edge of my bed, tears sliding down my cheeks.

"You're home," she says, her voice muffled as she speaks against her pillow. "Where've you been?"

"I got called into work for another dinner party. Just one couple this time, so not too bad. Go back to sleep," I say.

I can barely see the clasp through my tears as I remove my necklace. Jussi's rose gold ring slides easily from my finger, and I hold it in my palm for just a moment—it is his promise to me—and place it on the necklace beside my pendant. The ring will stay safe by my heart until we can be together again. One for luck and protection, and the other for hope and love.

Chapter Twenty-Six

September 1932

My fingers graze the sharp edges of the letter I tucked safely in my apron, feeling its weight inside the small pocket, its heat through the layers of my clothes. I long to put aside the pile of dirty dishes soaking in the lukewarm water and ignore the unfolded laundry crumpled in its basket and escape to the warm sunshine in Mrs. Wright's garden. There I would find a place to sit alongside the azaleas and read and reread my lover's words, transported to faraway Karelia, to a world that will make my dreams come true.

Millie slams a cupboard closed. "Quit your daydreaming and take the pot off the stove. It's going to bubble over." I pull my hand from my apron pocket and rush to the stove. The boiling water spits and stings. I stir the contents, watching the bubbles pop and subside. "You really are worthless, aren't you? I don't know why the good doctor hires foreign workers. Lazy Finlanders." She shakes her head and turns her back to me.

I cringe at Millie's words. "I work as hard as anyone." Harder than Millie, but I'd never say it aloud.

"Leave it to cool and take up the dough. It wants kneading," she says.

I purse my lips and slap the dough on the table. A cloud of flour dust rises.

Millie was born in Canada, but her parents are from England. Doesn't it make her parents immigrants like me? I shake my head. Is it because our native tongue is Finnish and not English that makes her somehow better than me? My fingers dig into the fleshiness of the dough, the heels of my palms pushing it across the table with more force than needed. Another word from her and I swear I'll—

"Be right back," Millie says, putting her coat on over her apron. She searches in her pocket and takes out her silver cigarette holder and lighter.

I don't know how Millie can afford all her little trinkets. They're probably gifts from the men she keeps telling me about. In the back garden, Millie strikes a pose, her cigarette balanced between the tips of her fingers and her wrist at such an angle you'd think her hand would drop off. For several minutes, she stares off into the distance; her smoke rings float up and away.

I try to ignore her as the heel of my palm presses the dough, pushes it away, pulls it back, repeating the action until the muscles in my forearms strain. Sweat trickles down my back. I wipe my brow with my sleeve and scowl at Millie, but she can't see me through the window. Just as well.

The letter in my apron calls to me. I have just a few minutes to read it before Millie stubs out her cigarette and returns. I wipe the flour from my hands on the front of my apron, carefully pull the letter from its envelope, and bring it to my lips. I close my eyes and inhale the scent.

My darling Hanna,

I've made it! I can't tell you how relieved I am to be off the ship and on to dry land again. The bus ride to Halifax was long. All I wanted was to set sail, but our ship was delayed. We Finns—a family of five from Northern Ontario, two single men from out west, and a newlywed couple from Toronto—pooled our money to pay for accommodation. The couple looked so happy to be together; it made me quite jealous and sad to think of you so far away from me. I know, my love, you will join me soon, and it gives me great hope for our future together.

One problem was where to store all the tools and supplies we'd brought from Canada and the United States. Luckily, Olavi, the father of three, discussed our situation with the port authorities, and they provided a storage area for our goods, which included a small automobile and a large tractor. I'm guessing both will be needed in the Karelian outposts where we'll be assigned. I was wary about leaving my carpentry tools unattended, but very relieved to see everything just as we'd left them when we returned.

The Atlantic sailing was pleasant, with only a brief storm at sea, but the company was even better. Apart from us Canadians, many American Finns had already boarded when we arrived. They greeted us like we were old comrades, and it was like I'd found a new family. There was much eating, drinking, and singing during the journey, as well as games of chess and other entertainments to keep us occupied over the many miles of sea.

When we arrived in Gothenburg, some Swedes entertained us with songs and dances, some in Swedish, and some in the Russian style. A group of small children danced in traditional costumes, and we felt very well taken care of. They fed us a lovely meal and saw us off on a train to Stockholm. From there, we boarded another vessel.

I must admit, I wasn't looking forward to getting back on a ship for the next leg of our journey. We sailed for two days to get to Leningrad, so it was very brief compared to our transatlantic journey, and I had nothing to fear. Someone had a bottle of Russian vodka and I'm afraid I must have partaken of too many sips, because the next day I was quite queasy. It didn't help much when we arrived in Leningrad to what I might call a cool reception, but I suppose the authorities were just trying to be professional and ensure us newcomers got on *the right trains with the right papers. Finally, we were on our way to Petrozavodsk, where the Regional Settlement Agency is located. It was another 400-kilometre journey, but although I was already weary from my travels, I was almost home. Someone started singing, and we all joined in. That buoyed everyone's spirits, I think.*

Petrozavodsk is a curious town that looks medieval. The main street is made of cobblestones, but the rest are just dirt roads. There are many people bustling around and speaking several languages. Russian, of course, and Karelian, but also many Finnish and English speakers, like me, who speak Finglish as though it's their native tongue! I feel quite at home here. The accommodations are simply furnished and I'm sharing a room with two other families, but it is temporary. I believe I will receive my assignment tomorrow and be sent to my new workplace.

Everyone has high hopes for the new world we have entered, and a genuine spirit of optimism and comradeship among us. I hope I'll see my new friends again. Above all else, I keep the image of you in my heart and look forward to the day when you will join me in Karelia.

All my heart,
Jussi

As I read, relief floods over me. He is safe, and he has met friends, and he has not forgotten about me as I had feared he might. When I finally tell my parents, his words will help convince them I am doing the right thing. Mrs. Wright's footsteps become louder as they approach the kitchen door. I fold the letter and tuck it into the envelope, stuffing it back in my apron pocket. I return to kneading the dough.

When I first met Mrs. Wright, she strode into the sitting room with confidence, her hair coiffed in the latest style, a two-piece kelly green suit with a white blouse underneath rising to her neck. She'd looked all business as she'd peered over her reading glasses at me. "Have you worked as a domestic?" She'd asked, eyeing me as if I were some ripe fruit on a market stall.

"Not as a servant, but I can certainly do all the work required. I did much of the housework at home because my mother is unwell. The cooking and cleaning, paying household bills, and some farm chores were left to me and my sister. I can also darn and sew, and whatever else is required." I tried to keep my voice from quivering. Mrs. Wright's stare and her pursed mouth, along with her long, angular nose, gave her face the appearance of a hawk about to swoop down on its prey. I lowered my eyes, the heat spreading in my cheeks. She didn't look impressed with my responses.

"You speak English with no accent," she said, her finely plucked eyebrows arched in curiosity.

The comment surprised me. "I came to Canada as a young child. We speak Finnish at home, but otherwise I spoke English at school and with my friends."

"Humph," Mrs. Wright muttered. "The last one barely spoke English. I couldn't understand a word Danuta said. Polish, I think ... or Ukrainian ... maybe Croatian. Something like that." She shrugged as if it didn't matter.

I didn't respond.

"I hear Finnish girls make the best domestics. Would you agree?"

How could I answer her? "I suppose we have a reputation for being hardworking."

"If I hire you, I'll expect you to live up to that reputation. Understand?"

Although I didn't think our interview had gone well, Mrs. Wright offered me the job. "You'll do well to keep your head down and pay attention to your work and nothing else. Danuta couldn't seem to get it into her head that she was here to work."

"Is that why you let her go?" Surprised by my overstep, I hoped I wasn't about to go from hired to fired.

Mrs. Wright shook her head and scowled. "Never you mind. Do as you're told, and there won't be any trouble. And don't pay any heed to Millie. She's the best cook I've ever had, but she can make trouble."

I wanted to know more, but Mrs. Wright was not forthcoming. She ushered me out the door with instructions about returning through the servants' entrance early the next morning.

Now, Glenda Wright's footsteps move past the kitchen and into the main rooms of the house. I sigh with relief, but the distinct scent of Dr. Wright's Aqua Velva precedes him. Just as he appears in the kitchen, Millie returns, taking her coat off and hanging it behind the door.

"Ladies. I'm sorry to interrupt." Dr. Wright's tall figure fills the doorframe. He doesn't quite step into the kitchen. It is not his domain. I stop my kneading and stand at attention, straightening my apron and pushing a stray hair away from my face with flour-covered hands.

"Oh, Dr. Wright. You could never interrupt us." Millie coos and takes a few steps toward him.

Dr. Wright is a handsome man, not as old as my father, but considerably older than Millie and me. His dark hair is grey at the temples, and he wears spectacles to read, but takes them off when with guests. He's always nicely attired in a suit and a tie. When he smiles, he reveals dimples on both cheeks. I can see why Millie is attracted to him, but he's married and nearly old enough to be her father.

"I wonder if I might have a spot of tea. I'm afraid the first lot has gone deadly cold."

"Right away, doctor," Millie says. "I'd be happy to deliver it myself." She winks conspiratorially. I keep my mouth shut and eyes straight ahead.

"You look busy, Millie. Have the new girl bring it to me in my office." Dr. Wright turns on his heel and strides down the hall.

I've been working for the Wrights for over a year, and he still calls me the new girl. Does he even know my name yet? It's true, we've only had brief interactions, and those are usually at one of Mrs. Wright's dinner parties when I serve drinks or hors d'oeuvres to their fancy guests.

"Well, what do you know?" Millie glares at me across the table. "He's asking for you. And what have you two been up to then? A little hanky-panky? Oh, you might look innocent, but I'm on to you, Hanna."

I bite my tongue and will my lips not to open. My face is, I hope, blank. "The doctor would like some tea, and I will serve it. That's all." I wash my hands of the flour and put the kettle on to boil.

"You'll serve it alright. I see now. You're trying to take him away from me. You don't have to say a word. Just sway your hips and bat those eyelashes at him. He'll be tired of you before long. He always comes back to me." Millie turns her back. "Make the tea, you little tart," she says. "You'll see."

There's no reason to argue with Millie. I don't know if she's telling the truth half the time. If she and Dr. Wright are having a tryst, it's no business of mine. I steep the tea and place the teapot on the tray with a fresh cup and saucer. Beside it, I put some biscuits on a plate as I've seen Millie do. She glares at me from across the room. Without another word, I exit the kitchen and walk down the corridor to the servant's staircase leading to the second floor.

I've never been to the doctor's private office. When I arrive, the door is ajar, and Dr. Wright is sitting at his desk with a pen in one hand and a cigarette in the other.

"Come in," he says, but doesn't look up from his paperwork. I look for a place to put down the tray, but every surface is covered, so I wait for his instructions.

While he reads, I take in the room. One wall has mahogany bookshelves filled with more books than I've ever seen. Essi would be so envious if she could see it. She could write a complete novel in this office. His desk is organized with files in orderly piles at one corner and a writing pad ready for notes. A chesterfield is on one side and a chair against the wall, with a small round table between them.

Dr. Wright looks up. He clears space for the tea tray at the edge of his desk, and I place it down, ready to bolt from the room.

"Hanna?" he asks, as if to verify my name.

"Yes, sir." I cross my hands in front of my apron and feel Jussi's letter hidden within the pocket.

"You've been in my employ for seven or eight months now?"

"About a year, sir."

"And you find it an acceptable place of employment?"

"Yes, sir."

"Is there anything I might do to make your experience here more, hmm, profitable?"

"Sir?" I'm confused. Is Dr. Wright offering me a raise? My savings for Karelia have not grown as fast as I had hoped, and Jussi has sent little yet. I fear I will never get to him.

"Sometimes a young woman from a foreign country finds her wages insufficient for those little extras she might desire. Those things other young women around her might take for granted."

I nod and remember the doctors' wives decked out in their gowns and jewellery at the last party at which I served. No domestic could ever make enough money to dress like that, but even a small increase in my wages would help get the plain articles I'll need to go to the Soviet Union.

Dr. Wright stands up behind his desk and moves toward me. He smiles kindly and reaches to take my hand. I freeze. My hand is limp in his. "You are a very attractive girl, Hanna." The doctor leans closer to me. I hold my breath. "I could make your extra time, your extra attention, worthwhile."

I pull my hand away and step back. "Dr. Wright, I'm not that kind of girl."

Dr. Wright's eyes widen and his mouth gapes open. I imagine he isn't spoken to so plainly. A moment later his eyes crinkle as he breaks into a wide grin.

"You misunderstand me, Hanna. There's so much work to be done here in the office, and I could use a bright young woman like yourself to help with some filing. Of course, you'd need to do your house duties first, but it's an excellent way to earn a little extra. Millie has too much work to do on her own, but I've got too much to do for my medical practice. You're not interested?"

My face flushes with heat, and my hands still tremble from his proposal. Am I mistaken about his intentions? Is it office help he wants or something else? I can usually trust my instincts, and nothing about this feels quite right, but I may be wrong.

The doctor returns to his chair and opens a file. "Don't concern yourself another moment, Hanna. I'm sure I'll find a suitable employee to help me here. I don't want you to feel uncomfortable, not since you have done such excellent work in my house." He doesn't look up from his papers.

I feel Jussi's letter in my apron. How will I get to him if I don't take these opportunities? "I would be grateful to work in the office."

"Good," he says. "You can begin tomorrow after you've completed your duties downstairs."

I thank him, pick up the old tea tray, and leave the room. The doctor's actions confuse me. He was making advances, wasn't he? But when I refused, and I did refuse, he stopped. The work will just be the work and nothing more. I raise my head and straighten my back. Millie must not know what happened, and there must be nothing for either Mrs. Wright or Millie to suspect.

It's uplifting to know Jussi and I will be together sooner than we planned. Everything is going to get better. The excitement wells in me, and I can't wait to go home and tell Essi about my extra duties and Mr. Wright's beautiful library of books. Someday soon, I will come clean—tell her about Jussi, about Karelia—but not yet.

Chapter Twenty-Seven
September 1932

Essi sits at the kitchen table across from me, stirring her bowl of stew, and I watch the heat rise from it. She is lost in thought. She always worries too much.

"Can I get you two anything else?" Ruby asks. "Some fresh bread? Coffee is made, so just help yourself. And leave those dishes. I'll take care of them in the morning."

"Thanks, Ruby. We'll do them," Essi says, taking another slice of bread.

"No need. It's quiet here in the morning. Suits me that the girls like to sleep in late."

"Do you live nearby?" I've never asked her about her personal life and don't want to intrude, but I'm curious.

Ruby nods. "Only a few blocks away. I have a one-bedroom apartment in a house, just big enough for me and my cat. A little balcony, too." Ruby beams with pride.

"Did you always live in Sudbury?" I ask.

Ruby shakes her head. "My sonofabitch husband—God rest his soul—worked on the railroads, and we moved up here from Toronto. Not too many black folks living here in those days."

"How did you meet Rouva Ruusa?" Essi asks, leaning forward.

"At Borgia market. We got to talking, and she offered me a job. It turned out we had a lot in common with our no-good husbands, although she'd left hers years earlier. I should have

About the Author

Liisa Kovala is a Finnish Canadian author, book coach, and podcaster living in Sudbury, Ontario. Her debut historical novel, *Sisu's Winter War* (Latitude 46, 2022) received a Literary Creation Project Grant from the Ontario Arts Council. Liisa's first book, *Surviving Stutthof: My Father's Memories Behind the Death Gate* (Latitude 46, 2017) was shortlisted for a Northern Lit Award and published in Finland by Docendo Publishing (2020). Liisa is a member of The Writers' Union of Canda, Canadian Authors Association, Historical Novel Society, and Historical Writers' Association. She is also past president of the Sudbury Writers' Guild. Liisa earned a Graduate Certificate of Creative Writing with distinction from Humber School for Writers and a Creative Writing Certificate from the University of Toronto. She publishes Women Writing on Substack, hosts the Women Writing podcast, and co-hosts Rekindle Creativity Women's Writing Retreats. She is currently working on the Nordic-inspired Hygge House Cozy Mystery series under the pen name A. L. Jensen. Liisa is inspired by her Finnish heritage and the northern landscape she calls home. Learn more at liisakovala.com and liisakovalawomenwriting.substack.com.

www.ingramcontent.com/pod-product-compliance
Lightning Source LLC
LaVergne TN
LVHW051828200226
832130LV00012B/590

done the same, but in the end, he was killed on the job, an accident."

"And you lived here, in the boarding house?" I ask.

"Yes, for a few years, but as soon as I saved enough, and with a little loan from Rose, I got my own place. She's been good to me. To all of us."

I nod, wanting to ask more questions about Ruby's life and Rouva Ruusa's mysterious history, but Essi interrupts my thoughts. "She takes care of people."

Ruby glances at the clock beside the cupboard. She takes off her apron and hangs it on a hook before putting on her coat. "Time to go. Goodnight, ladies," she says.

"Have a good night, Ruby," I reply. I take another spoonful, savouring the flavours. It reminds me of our mother's stew. Rouva Ruusa's girls are lucky to have Ruby here to cook homemade meals for them. And she's Rouva Ruusa's most trusted friend.

When the door shuts, I turn to Essi. "That's the most I've ever heard Ruby say. And did you know Ruusa had left her husband? There must be an interesting story there. I'd love to know more. You should write this stuff down."

Essi frowns. "It's nothing she's ever mentioned to me. But did you hear Ruby? Even she wanted to move away from here, and she's Rouva Ruusa's best friend."

"About that. I can make some extra money," I say, taking a spoonful of my stew.

"Hmm? What was that?" she says, looking up from her meal. "I'm sorry. I'm just so exhausted. These children are going to be the death of me. What were you saying?"

Essi has complained about her work for Mrs. Johnson before, and I want to be sympathetic, but I have news, and she's so focused on herself.

"I was saying Dr. Wright has offered me a job working in his office. It's just a few extra hours a week doing some filing and typing, but he'll pay well for it." I dip a piece of fresh bread into the stew and stuff it into my mouth.

"That's great, Hanna. More money means we can move out of this place sooner. But I thought you weren't so happy there."

She's right, of course. "I know. Millie is irritating, and Mr. Wright, well, I can't put my finger on it. Just a feeling I have. But I'm happy about it. It will be good for me to do something other than housework, and it gets me away from Millie for a few hours a week." I'm not sure if I'm trying to convince Essi or myself. I haven't told her about the uncomfortable way I feel around Dr. Wright lately, but I'm not sure if it's just my own insecurities. Not every man is after the girls in his employment. He's offered me a job. Nothing more.

Essi scoops the last of the stew from her bowl and wipes her mouth with a napkin. "I'm happy for you. Listen, I was thinking we should go up to see the old folks next weekend. Fredi said he can give us a ride if we don't mind coming back right after church on Sunday. What do you think?"

"I suppose we'd better. We haven't seen Ida and Edvard in a while. I wonder how she's doing these days." I take a sip of coffee and flip through the *Vapaus* newspaper, scanning the headlines for news of Karelia.

"I think we should see how they're getting on. Besides, it's been ages and I'm aching for a long walk in the bush." Essi reaches for my empty bowl and spoon, crossing the kitchen to wash them in the sink. "Why do you insist on using their first names?"

I shrug. "We're adults now. They're our parents, but still."

Essi laughs. "I dare you to say their names to their faces." She puts the dishes in the cupboard and dries her hands on a dish towel.

"What are they going to do? Kick me out of the house? Too late." I laugh.

"Come on, then. I'm worn out, and I have an early day. Let's go before the patrons arrive." Essi leads the way from the kitchen, down the hall, toward the front stairs.

Some girls are milling around the main floor and give us a nod or smile. Yvonne waves as we pass the parlour. Already, a few guests are having drinks and dealing cards. Annie is singing along to a sweet jazz tune I recognize from a movie we once watched at the theatre. I hum along and dance a few steps as we make our way to the stairs. I grab Essi's waist and take her hand, spinning her around in a circle. Essi can't help but laugh. I'm so lucky to have my sister with me. I don't know what I'd do without her.

Chapter Twenty-Eight
November 1932

The kitchen is quiet this midmorning with Millie out fetching some groceries from the Borgia market, giving me time to contemplate. The bread loaves are rising nicely under the tea towels, and I transfer them into the oven to bake until they're golden brown—Millie will have my head if I let them burn again. Even the morning light streaming into the kitchen and across the table does little to cheer me. I reach into my pocket to retrieve Jussi's latest letter and reread it for the hundredth time.

My Dearest Hanna,

It was quite an adventure going from Petrozavodsk to my workplace at a lumber camp in Rutanen, about twenty kilometres from the city. I expected to work in a factory, but this work is fine for the time being. I saw several kulaks—that's what they call the Russian peasants—aboard the train, ghosts of their former selves. Some were no more than bags of bones. The eyes got to me. So large and sad, like puppies that had been struck and were left whimpering in a corner. There were a few other newcomers like me who were going to Rutanen for their first jobs. I struck up a conversation with one of them and, to my amazement, he'd come from Northern Ontario, too. Kalevi was on an earlier ship and worked for a while in Petrozavodsk before being transferred to the lumber camp. We have much in common, I think.

Nothing much to say about the camp at Rutanen. I'm sure it's like many others: a dining hall and kitchen, a laundry hut, a clothes drying room, a horse stall, a pig stall, a sauna, and a blacksmith's building.

I share living quarters with a few other single men, both young and old, and despite the lice and cockroaches, the people are friendly. We have a few makeshift pieces of furniture, but they serve us well. We have one washbasin for us to share, but we don't have electricity, although there are rumours it's coming. For now, we make do with outdoor plumbing. I imagine it will be a little chilly in the winter, after all the comforts I had in Canada. There is no insulation in the barracks, and the windows are single-pane, so the first few nights I had a hard time sleeping with the wind howling through the building. Now that I've been making shingles all day, I fall asleep as soon as my head hits the mattress.

Overall, I can't complain. Well, if I were to complain, it would be about one old gentleman, Arvo, who smokes day in and day out. I like my cigarettes, I'll admit, but even I can't take this much smoke in a small space. I probably should smoke more.

I couldn't have asked for a better workplace to start my new life in Karelia, our new life, because I know you will join me as soon as you can. Here, timber is green gold, and the Canadian lumberjack is prized for cutting 12 cubic feet of wood when the Russians can only manage 3 cubic feet. We are making a difference here, helping to modernize the country and providing our valuable skills. In fact, I've recently heard about work at the ski factory in Petrozavodsk that I think I'm suited for. I'd be making skis and furniture, more interesting than making shingles day in and day out. I hope I can eventually transfer there.

Darling, I think about you every day and dream of the time when you will join me here in Karelia. I'm sending you a little money to set aside for your fees, and I hope you have met with Matti Korhonen to start your application. I can't wait until you are my wife.

All my love,
Jussi

I try to read between the lines. He seems satisfied with his work at the lumber camp, but it doesn't sound too pleasant to me, and not how I pictured it. I imagine him working hard beside his comrades, singing as they toil, laughing over dinner, happy as he lays his head on his pillow. Perhaps if he gets the job at the ski factory, he'll have better living conditions. I place the money and the letter back into my apron pocket, calculating the amount I've saved so far. It's not nearly enough to cover my application fees. I need to meet with Matti Korhonen so I can get my paperwork in order. He'll know what I have to do next. There is still the problem of Essi. Once everything is settled, I'll tell her my plans. My hands shake with both excitement and trepidation at the idea of moving to Karelia as I check the bread loaves in the oven.

Dr. Wright's figure casts a shadow in the doorway. "Hanna? Come to my office." I don't remember the exact moment I became afraid of Dr. Wright's voice. It commands respect without bullying, and its deep tones can even be called melodious, but when he speaks to me, I'm overcome with a feeling of unease. Maybe I'm imagining things. I shake it off.

"Yes, sir. I'll be right there." I take a potholder and pull out the loaf pans, one by one, to cool away from the hot stove. In my rush, I burn my hand and almost drop the loaf pan on the floor. With no time to put my hand in cold water, I hurry up the stairs to his office.

Dr. Wright is seated, not behind his desk, but on the small chesterfield against the wall opposite. He pats the seat beside him. "Sit, won't you?"

I don't move. "Millie's expecting me back in the kitchen, sir," I say, rubbing my hand.

"Have you injured yourself? Let me see." Dr. Wright rises from the chesterfield and takes my hand, gently tracing the red mark. "I'll give you some ointment, and it will heal in no time."

I nod and pull my hand away, my skin crawling at his touch.

"You're distracted lately. Is something bothering you?"

His tone is kind. Had he been a few decades younger, I might have thought him handsome. The grey at his temples and laugh lines in the corner of his eyes give his face a look of wisdom. My eyes well with tears. Jussi is too far away from me. I stare straight ahead, trying to show no emotion.

"Is this about Millie? She's all impatience and little kindness. Has she been treating you well, at least?"

"Well enough, sir." I long to escape back to the warmth of the kitchen, where Millie's outright hostility is more welcome than feigning polite conversation with Dr. Wright.

I avoid his gaze, letting my eyes linger instead on the rows of medical books on the shelves, the photographs of well-dressed men and women, and the medical certificate hanging on the wall. Everything speaks of his great importance and makes me feel insignificant.

"Millie and I have an ... agreement," Dr. Wright says. "It satisfies both of us. She has spoken of it?"

"No, sir." What kind of agreement do they have? I'm afraid to ask.

"She is well provided for. It's the kind of deal you and I could have. It's mutually beneficial. I had a similar arrangement with the girl you replaced."

"I appreciate the extra work." My hand feels for the ring hanging around my neck. It's covered by my uniform, but my fingers find the outline just above my heart.

"But you may have other desires, ones you won't speak to anyone about. You can trust me." Dr. Wright places a warm hand on my arm and gently squeezes. He's so close now I can feel his breath on my face. It smells vaguely of nicotine, stale coffee, and aftershave.

"I wouldn't want to trouble you with my problems, Dr. Wright," I say, moving back and toward the door.

With a quick step, he pushes the heavy door closed and stands between me and the exit. The air is stifling, and the dark wood bookshelves seem to close in. My heart beats faster, and my palms sweat. A photograph of young Glenda Wright, looking like a Hollywood movie star, stares out at me from its ornate frame. She looks wide-eyed and startled. I wish she would interrupt this scene, but I know she never comes to her husband's office for any reason. It is strictly his domain. He says he must protect the privacy of his patients' records.

"I'm a doctor, Hanna. My work is to help those in need. What needs do you have?" He sidles up to me. My breath catches in my throat.

I glance at the window, but it faces the side yard, and no one can see us through the trees. Dr. Wright grins. He enjoys trapping me, like I'm a little bird unable to fly away from his talons. If I try a different tack, he might let me go. Leaning back, I create some distance between us. "In fact, I have something weighing on me. I've received word from a friend who has gone to work in Karelia. He's asked me to contact the local recruiter, but I don't remember his name or how to contact him." I hope my lie sounds like concern for my friend.

Dr. Wright looks at me quizzically. "Karelia? Fascinating. I've heard something about this place. Your friend is already there, you say?"

"Yes. He left in early September." It seems so strange to be telling him about Jussi, especially as I've told no one else.

Dr. Wright folds his arms across his chest and taps his fingers a few times. His brows furrow as they do when he is deep in thought. I wait patiently, moving slightly farther away from him. His eyes brighten, and he grins.

"I may know just the person who can get you information. I had a patient whose family recently moved to Karelia with the help of an agent. He has contacts in Canada, the United States, and the Soviet Union. He can help you find out about your friend."

I let out my breath, barely aware I had been holding it. "Sir, if you can find the agent, I would be grateful to you."

The doctor's smile alters subtly, and his gaze intensifies. "I would be delighted to help you. I expect you'll owe me now. Won't you?" He chuckles. I don't like the suggestive tone in his voice.

I look away, my heart beating against my chest and my hands shaking. He opens the door in a gentlemanly way. As I walk down the hall toward the stairwell, I replay the scene. Have I misinterpreted Dr. Wright's words? His actions, if I were to describe them to someone, would seem unimpeachable. Just a caring man concerned about me. If that's true, then why do I feel such unease with him? Why am I afraid?

Chapter Twenty-Nine
December 1932

The week passes at a snail's pace. I try to avoid encountering the doctor, but it is impossible in this house. If he wants to find me, he knows where I will be. He arrives unexpectedly or calls me into his office. I am not imagining it. He has designs on me, and they are not aboveboard. Even Millie seems to notice his unnecessary attention. As the week draws to a close, I know I must do something, but what? If I tell Essi, she'll insist I leave my job and return to the farm. I can't do that.

I bundle my scarf around my neck as the wind whips around me. The road is slippery as I navigate toward Kathleen Street, eager for the warmth of my room and the comfort of my sister's presence. I haven't told her anything about Dr. Wright's advances and don't dare write to Jussi about him. He'd only worry, just as I worry for him.

The stairs to the boarding house are snow-covered but trampled down by sets of large boots. It's early evening, but the party has already started inside. From the porch, I can hear music playing from the phonograph and laughter emanating from the parlour. At this time of day, it's a house full of men.

That's it. I'll ask Yvonne. She'll know who among these big, burly men would do something for me if my situation with Dr. Wright gets too unwieldy for me to handle on my own. Essi never needs to know, and I'll feel safer, even have something to threaten the doctor with, if it comes to that.

Inside, I remove my scarf, coat, and boots and head upstairs to our room. Essi is sitting at the small table under the window between our beds, writing in her notebook as usual.

"How come you're so late?" she asks without turning around. Her hand keeps scrawling along the page. She once told me she wanted to write a novel. I wonder if that's what she's working on now.

I sigh and change my dress to something more fitting for the atmosphere of the parlour. "Millie had a list a mile long for me today. Plus, Dr. Wright had some extra work for me in the office, too." I slip on my Mary Janes and check my lipstick in the mirror, smoothing out the strands of my hair.

"Going out?" Essi pauses for a moment, looking over her shoulder as I adjust my stockings, a question in her eyes.

I pick up my lipstick and return it to my clutch. "No, I just needed to feel more human again. I'm going down to get a bite. Want to come?" I ask, hoping she'll say no.

"You go ahead. I already ate," Essi says, returning her attention to her notebook.

Thankful her attention is on her writing, and not on me, I tread down the stairs, keeping an eye out for Yvonne. Passing the parlour, I see her pouring a drink for an older man who is chatting with her in French. He's old enough to be her grandfather. I shudder to think what he wants with her.

I catch Yvonne's eye. She puts a hand on the man's shoulder and leans over to say something I can't make out, then laughs and turns toward me. "What do you need, Hanna?"

I'm not sure what to say now that I'm here. This was a terrible idea. "I have a favour to ask, and I'm not exactly sure how to ask it." Glasses clink and Annie's boisterous laugh rings out.

Yvonne takes my arm and guides me down the hall where it is quieter and we're not likely to get interrupted. "My mother would say, 'Spit it out.' Maybe that works for you, too." She grins.

I feel the tension release from my shoulders. Yes, of course. Just ask. "I'm having a few difficulties with a man who is overly ... attentive."

Yvonne's eyes widen, and her jaw drops. "Has he ...?"

"No, no." I shake my head. "But I don't want it to come to that." I was thinking—and maybe this is a bad idea—if one of these men, someone you trust, would help me. Maybe step in if things go south."

Yvonne cocks her head and regards me thoughtfully. Is she about to tell me I'm being ridiculous? As if she is reanimated, Yvonne smiles widely. "I know just the man. He's big and strong and would make any other man feel intimidated. All he would have to say is 'boo' and no one would ever try to bother you again."

I glance toward the parlour where the men are having a pleasant time drinking and chatting up the girls. "Is this a good idea?"

Yvonne nods. "Sometimes you have to put the fear of God in these men."

"There's only one thing. Please don't tell my sister. She'd be so worried about me, and I don't want that." Could Yvonne keep my secret? Only time would tell.

"Mum's the word," Yvonne says. "Come. I'll introduce you to the fellow. He doesn't say much, but he's your man." Yvonne slings her arm through mine and confidently strides toward the parlour. I've never been in there when the girls are working with paying guests. It's a haze of smoke, and I can taste the whisky in the air.

Within seconds, I'm sitting across from Pekka Peltonen and Yvonne is introducing us. She pours us both a glass. I take a quick sip, but Peltonen slams his back.

"What's this about?" he asks in Finnish. His steely eyes bore into mine.

"I have a problem, and I hoped you could help me." My words come out in a stutter. Why does this man make me feel so nervous?

"Yvonne said as much. Be more specific." He leans back in his chair and crosses his arms on his broad chest.

I tell him about how uncomfortable I am with the attention I'm receiving from Dr. Wright, but don't give Pekka any names. "If the problem escalates, I want to know someone can come and tell him to leave me alone. Threaten him, I guess." Do I sound like I'm pleading? Like a helpless girl who can't handle things on her own?

"You want me to rough the guy up?" Pekka says, clearly considering the idea.

"Yes, I mean, I just need him to stop." I'm second-guessing myself now. Even if Pekka agrees, what will happen if we actually go through with this plan?

"But you don't want me to, you know, kill him?" Pekka leans in as he says the words.

"No, of course not." It hadn't even crossed my mind that Pekka might think I wanted to place a hit on Dr. Wright.

"And you won't tell me his name?" Pekka asks.

I shake my head. I am firm on this point. "I'll send you a message through Yvonne when … if the time comes. Otherwise, no names." I'm almost certain I'll never have to ask Pekka for his help, so why risk it?

We discuss a price and shake on it. "This stays between us," I say. "My sister Essi lives here. She can't know anything."

Pekka nods and slugs back another whisky, staring out the window into the dark night. "No concerns there."

I leave the parlour feeling lighter. There is a plan. Father always said it was better to have a plan if you have a problem, but I suspect this isn't what he had in mind. I creep back up the stairs to find Essi on her bed, reading a book. She barely notices my arrival and doesn't ask about why I was gone so long. I put on my nightgown, head to the shared bathroom, and drop into bed. As I drift off to sleep, I imagine Pekka confronting Dr. Wright, and Mrs. Wright astonished in the background. The vision makes me smile.

Chapter Thirty

December 1932

I long to be out in the fresh air, walking home. Fat snowflakes have been falling for hours, gathering like magnets, clinging to the branches of trees like sweet icing sugar piped on gingerbreads. But my work is not done, and now Dr. Wright has summoned me.

"I'll help you finish up here as soon as I'm done," I say, knowing Millie will be upset if she has to do all the work herself.

"He's really taken a shine to you, hasn't he?" Millie stands at the sink with a big pot, her hands dripping soapy liquid into the dirty water.

"Who has?" I ask, feigning indifference.

"I thought you were better than that, Hanna." Her eyes bore into me like little carving knives, twisting under my skin.

Millie is playing with me, I know, but I think I'm better than that, too. I don't respond. I don't want rumours to fly from her mouth, but it doesn't matter what I say. She doesn't believe me.

"Don't you worry, missy," Millie says. He'll tire of you in no time, and he'll be back around to see me. It wouldn't be the first time, that's for certain." Despite the confident way Millie speaks, I can hear a slight tremor in her voice. Can Millie really love a man like him? A married man. A deceptive man.

I empty the dustpan and put the broom in the closet, wipe my hands on my apron, and hang it behind the door. "It's not like that. I have no interest in your doctor. I'm simply trying to earn a few extra dollars, and he's paying me to do some office work. That's the entire story."

Millie runs the dishtowel over a pot. "It's nothing to me. Not really. Just don't get yourself into any trouble, if you know what I mean. Men like him are interested in one thing, but don't think they'll take care of you if you get in trouble. Trust me, I know."

"Are you saying you've been in trouble?" I feel bold asking, but Millie doesn't seem to think any topic is off limits.

"Me? No, I know how to take care of myself. But I've helped plenty of girls in their time of need. Look, I don't recommend it to anyone, but sometimes a girl has to take matters into her own hands."

"You mean, they ... got rid of it?" I don't know how to discuss this. The thought of it makes me squeamish.

"Yeah. Some do it to themselves, but that never turns out well. Infections, or worse. If they're smart, they get a doctor to do the procedure, and they go home. It's not a big deal. More girls get it done than you would expect." Millie shrugs and turns back to her drying. "I'm just saying you better be careful."

"Thanks, but it's unnecessary. Like I said, there's nothing between me and the doctor. I have to go. He's waiting for me." Dr. Wright has not touched me in the past few weeks, but my uneasiness hasn't gone away. I try to schedule my work so he's with patients, but sometimes, like today, the workload in the house has been too much to leave Millie on her own.

I climb the back stairs and plod toward Dr. Wright's office, letting the tips of my fingers graze the ridges of faded wallpaper peeling away in the long hallway. In the main reception areas of the house, the wallpaper is fresh, the floor shines, and the furniture, though old and stately, is perfectly upholstered. The back halls, the servants' quarters, and the family's private rooms tell a much different story. Cracks in the foundation zigzag in the basement, where Millie has her cold storage. The wood floor in the halls is worn and creaks, and baseboards are broken or missing. Damage from ice buildups shows in the patches on the plaster and the sagging ceiling. Like Mrs. Wright, the house wears beautiful outfits and drips in finery, but under it all is the tragic sense of age creeping forward. It was such a grand house when I first arrived, but now I know appearances can be deceptive.

As I approach Dr. Wright's office door, the nausea returns so vehemently I lean against the wall to take a few deep breaths. If there is no answer, I'll let myself in and get to work. I raise my hand to knock, but the creak of a floorboard startles me.

"Ah, Hanna. So lovely to see you, my dear. Are you feeling alright?" Dr. Wright raises his hand to touch my forehead. "You're quite pale and clammy."

I straighten up. "I'm fine, Doctor." I want to step away, but he opens the door and makes a sweeping motion for me to enter.

"Right. I've got some filing for you today. Not very exciting work, but it must be done. I don't need to remind you that everything that happens in this office, anything you see, is strictly confidential." Dr. Wright's brows furrow as he glances around the space, but he adds a smile when his eyes reach me waiting near the door. I do not return his smile. A wooden banker's box is sitting on the floor in front of the couch, and a pile of files is stacked on a side table. Dr. Wright checks his wristwatch. "I have a patient to see, so I'll leave you to it." His tone is kind, yet professional. Is my apprehension unfounded?

As Dr. Wright leaves his office, the tension releases from my shoulders. What was I so worried about? Millie's digs, her petty jealousies, her innuendos of some wrongdoing, have seeped into my consciousness. Thinking back on our few meetings, I can't rightly say Dr. Wright has acted inappropriately toward me. His lingering looks make me feel uneasy, but that's probably more about me than him. He's used to being the important man in the room, taking control of every situation. I've seen him with his guests at dinner parties. The women adore him and his little attentions, while the men revere him. Millie's descriptions of him are quite different and drop him from his high and mighty pillar, in my estimation. I shake off the thought as I sift through the files.

I'm more than an hour into Dr. Wright's paperwork, taking care not to focus on the patients' names or pertinent details about their health. It's none of my business, and I want to respect their privacy. That's why Dr. Wright trusts me instead of Millie with this kind of work. I won't talk about it. Millie would probably read it all and blab it to everyone she knows. I'm discreet. He even teases me because I barely talk and rarely smile.

"You Finns are all the same," he said once. "Impossible to read, but loyal as they come."

My Finnish friends and family are as diverse as any other—talkative, opinionated, and argumentative—but I could see how some might think them, and me, cool at times, and quiet with strangers. I'm often skeptical about meeting new people and choose to keep to myself, at least at first.

I rise from the floor and gather the banker's box into my arms, ready to haul it to Dr. Wright's storage area where it will be neatly labelled and piled alongside the other boxes he's collected over the years, but as I do so, I hear the scrape of the latch as the doorknob turns.

"Ah, I see you're done for today," Dr. Wright says. "And I've seen the last patient, God willing. You're very efficient, Hanna. Why don't I take this heavy box from you?" Dr. Wright's hands cover mine. I pull back and shake my head.

"I'm all right," I say. The box feels heavier in my arms now.

"Hanna?" Dr. Wright steps forward and places a hand at the base of my neck. He lets it linger there for a moment. My mind races. I want to pull away and leave his suffocating office, but he pushes his office door closed. "Put the box on the table," he says. It is a command, not a request. For a moment, I'm frozen, the box a barrier between us.

Trembling, I do as he says. How can I escape to the kitchen and get out of this house? The fresh, wintery wonderland is waiting for me. I want to be away from here more than anything.

"Oh, my dear girl, you look positively afraid of me." The doctor's smile is dripping with feigned kindness. He places his hand on my shoulder, like a father might do to a young child.

"Please, Dr. Wright. Millie is waiting for me in the kitchen. A few more chores to finish this evening." I hope he'll see sense and realize I'll be missed.

"I've seen Millie and sent her home. She won't miss you for even one minute. And Mrs. Wright is playing bridge with her group tonight. She'll be gone for hours," Dr. Wright says. "Besides, it's coming down out there now. We might get snowed in."

His hand slides down from my shoulder, along my arm to my wrist. He encircles it with his large hand, not tightly, but enough so I know I can't pull away without making a fuss. His other arm reaches around my waist and his hand comes to rest on my lower back, his fingers splayed. He pulls me toward him. I gasp and try to move away, but his grip is tight, and I am anchored in place, his body pushing against mine. His breath comes heavy against my neck, and his chest rises and falls as he nestles his face in the space between my shoulder and jaw.

"Dr. Wright ..." I want to scream, but my voice is hoarse. I can't breathe. I can't think. I can't move. I'm held in place by some force wanting to protect me from feeling what is happening in this moment. If I fight, I fear he will hurt me.

"You are so beautiful. Surely no one can resist you." Dr. Wright's hands are strong and urgent. I try to pull away, but his grip tightens. "Don't deceive yourself. You've invited this moment. The way you look at me. The way you stand near me. You want this, too."

"No. No," I say with as much conviction as my small bird-like voice can muster as my little body is caged in his grip. The more I struggle, the more pain I feel grasping my skin and twisting my bones.

"Don't resist, little Hanna," Dr. Wright says, as he reaches over and bolts the door.

The revelation of what will happen next puts my whole body into panic, and I fight with all my might, but he is a big man and only snickers at my feeble attempts to escape. He pins me to the chesterfield and is hovering above, the kindly doctor turned vulture. I turn my head away from the ugly sight and stare out the window at the snowflakes falling fast and furious against the windowpane, willing myself to be away, any place but here, now, this moment, which lasts both a moment and a lifetime.

Chapter Thirty-One
December 1932

That night, when I am released from his grips, I trudge home through the deep snow, wishing the snow could wash away what happened. Tears stream down my face, and I shudder with cold. What will I tell Essi? How can I break it to her? The worst has happened, and she will be devastated. I don't want that for her. Or for me.

By the time I open the door to our room, peeking into the darkness, I still don't know what to do. To my relief, Essi is sound asleep, tucked peacefully under her quilt. I won't wake her. I need time to think.

I haven't stopped shivering since I bolted from his office, tugging at my clothes and grabbing my coat from the kitchen. Now, I tiptoe to the shared bathroom and clean myself as best I can, wanting every trace of that man off me. I'm shocked by my pale face and eyes rimmed red. Bruises on my arms. Pain between my legs.

In our room, I tuck myself under the quilt, willing my eyes to close against the waking nightmare replaying in my mind. It is hours before my body gives in, and I drift off to a restless sleep.

"No!" I bolt upright, my fingers gripping the soaking sheets, sweat streaming down my face. Bookshelves threatening to dismantle and crush me. A chesterfield swallowing me whole. Office walls closing in until my body is crushed. Snowfall covering my body.

My heart pounds against my chest. Dark shadows loom in the corners. Is someone here? I struggle to breathe and clutch at my throat. I am safe in my room.

Focus on breathing, my mother would say if she were with me now. I try to calm myself, not wanting my sobs to wake my sister. I plant my feet on the cold floor and rest my arms on my knees until my heart slows and the shadows retreat. A light snore emits from Essi's side of the room. She mumbles something incoherent and turns over on the bed.

I can't tell Essi what happened to me in that office, or I fear everything—all my lies—will pour out of me and I will never be forgiven. Essi would insist I leave my position immediately, call the police, return to Wanup. More than anyone I know, Essi would want to protect me and seek justice, but I can't bear for anyone else to know. If Jussi got word that I had been violated, perhaps he would reject me, too, now that I am tainted by another man. My mind spins with awful scenarios. I shake them off and focus on a future away from here.

Essi will have to understand. I cannot stay here any longer. Someday, I will tell her the truth, but not now.

Chapter Thirty-Two
January 1933

Christmas passes, and the year ends with a promise of a better year ahead, but every day I struggle to get up for work. I avoid Essi. It would devastate her. I am devastated. I can't just walk away from this job. Not yet. And I can't get to Jussi fast enough. To my surprise, I receive a note from the doctor with one name scrawled across the page: Matti Korhonen. Does he think this is some kind of payment to me? I crumple it up and throw it away.

Now, Essi and I sit with Rouva Ruusa at the kitchen table, but I'm thinking about tonight's meeting with Korhonen. As soon as I read his name, everything Jussi had told me about him came flooding back. Korhonen was a good guy, but a little shady. Jussi didn't entirely trust him, but Korhonen had organized his paperwork and passage. Either way, I need Korhonen to help me the way he helped Jussi.

Essi takes a piece of buttered toast from my plate. "See you tonight?"

I nod. "I shouldn't be too late. There's some filing to do, but not as much as last week."

"The doctor sure has you working a lot of hours these days." She takes a large bite and studies my face. "Are you unwell? You look a little pale. Why don't you take a day off?"

I shake my head. "I'm okay. Besides, there's a lot to do and we need the money." It's true. I haven't been feeling well lately.

Essi kisses me on the top of my forehead and smiles across at Rouva Ruusa. "Don't work too hard," she says, and she bounds down the hall. I may look haggard, but Essi is filled with energy. Working for Mrs. Johnson must agree with her.

I pull out Jussi's last letter, its folds worn and edges softened by my handling.

Dearest Hanna,

I finally have my new job at the ski factory in Petrozavodsk, *and none too soon. An outbreak of typhoid at the lumber camp was quite serious. I was ready to leave that place behind. There are good fellows here, and I even met up with Kalevi again. It turns out he's a fine musician and plays in the orchestra. Too bad I never learned to play an instrument, or I'd join them, too.*

The work suits me fine, but I must confess I miss a few luxuries from home. There is a shortage of coffee, so I've taken to drinking the Russian chai served everywhere. It's something one gets used to. It would be nice to have white bread once in a while, but they say Russian brown bread is better for you, anyway. *No fresh fruit in months, but we "foreigners" receive better rations than the locals, so I shouldn't complain.*

I'm enjoying the Iltamat programs in the evenings. There is a good variety of drama, music, and dancing, and you'll like the kinos, although they mostly show Russian films.

Missing you every day, my dear one.

All my love,
Juusi

I fold the letter and place it back in my pocket, happy that he's settled into his new job at the ski factory. But the letter is so old now. Anything could have happened after he wrote it.

Rouva Ruusa pours herself a coffee. "More?" she asks. I nod, and she tops mine up. "Anything interesting?" She gestures toward the letter.

"Good news from afar. My mother says it's like water for a weary soul."

"I've never heard that expression before," Rouva Ruusa says.

"My mother often recites verses from the Bible. My father says that a weary soul doesn't need water, it needs sisu." I frown. Water has been a mixed blessing for our family. The vast ocean brought us to this new country, but water has also taken a devastating toll. Maybe it's hope that sustains a weary soul. It's all I have right now. "Has the post come yet?"

"Not yet," Rouva Ruusa says. "It's hard not knowing, isn't it?"

I nod and hold my tears back. It's like she knows something that I have not said aloud.

"If you ever need to talk, I'm here," Rouva Ruusa says. She takes a sip of coffee and changes the subject. "Essi's been looking well these days."

"I was just thinking the same thing. She seems to love Mrs. Johnson's children, even though she complains sometimes. She'll make a good mother someday," I reply, happy to focus on someone other than myself.

Rouva Ruusa agrees. "If that's what she wants. What about you? Do you plan to marry and have a family?"

I stare at the bubbles in my coffee cup, hoping to see the future there. "Someday. I'd love to have a husband and a little house with a garden and lots of children. Once upon a time, I imagined marrying a wealthy man and living the high life, but now I want a simpler life." I imagine Jussi at my side, with a baby in my arms. I chuckle at the thought of Essi with children of her own. "You're right about Essi. She's always been more into her books, interested in learning and doing things. She may end up an old spinster."

Rouva Ruusa laughs. "Nothing wrong with that. All the independence you want and none of the trouble."

Annie strolls in with a stack of letters and hands them to Rouva Ruusa. "More bills, I bet. Why don't folks send us money instead?" She laughs as she grabs a slice of toast.

"Anything for me?" I ask, hoping not to sound too anxious. For weeks, I've worried about his letters, or lack thereof. The post from Russia is slow, and he might be too busy to write. As long as he hasn't forgotten about me. Or found a new love.

Rouva Ruusa sifts through the letters until she finds one and pauses on it. "From the Soviet Union?"

I feel a blush rise in my cheeks. "Yes. It's from my friend," I say, as she hands me the long-awaited letter. My senses heighten as I touch the cool, smooth envelope.

"I didn't realize you and Essi have friends in Russia," Rouva Ruusa says. She sounds casual, but her right eyebrow rises.

"Actually, Essi hasn't met him. He's gone to work there." I hesitate as I turn the letter over in my fingers. "Rouva Ruusa, I wonder if you might not mention this to my sister."

Rouva Ruusa looks puzzled, but smiles and says, "Your secret is safe with me."

I feel a wave of relief. If anyone can keep a secret, it's Rouva Ruusa. She values privacy more than anyone I've ever met. If my mother were here, she'd be hammering me with questions until I finally shared everything with her or felt compelled to lie. Either way, she wouldn't allow me to have any secrets. And this one is mine to keep.

Rouva Ruusa takes her coffee and letters and pads down the long corridor to her own private sanctuary where she'll work for the rest of the morning. We know not to disturb her unless something happens that we can't handle on our own.

I take a deep breath and release the sealed flap from the envelope with a long fingernail, trying not to damage the letter. I'll want to keep it bundled safely in my room with the others. They are so rare and infrequent lately. I value every word he writes.

Dearest Hanna,

I have little time to write to you, but know you are always in my heart and uppermost in my mind. I fear my letter won't reach you, and you will be lost to me forever.

If something should happen, I want you to know you were always the one for me, and I would never betray your love and trust. I have done everything so that we could have a better life together. I have done everything in good faith and for the good of our cause in Karelia.

I just learned my neighbour in Petrozavodsk disappeared in the middle of the night. His wife says officials knocked at the door, questioned him, and then took him away, but they didn't say where they were going. She thinks he's been arrested, but she doesn't know what the charges are or what crime they say he has committed. No one seems to know, either. Everyone is fearful at work, but no one wants to talk about it except in whispers in corners where they can't be heard.

I keep my head down and do my best at work not to make any waves. I'm considered a fast and efficient worker and I've become very good at making kick sleds, and I do my best to get along with my comrades, even the Finnish Finns who are sometimes more skeptical about us foreigners and the Russian locals who care little for us.

I miss you and love you and hope you are well.

All my heart,
Jussi

My hands are shaking when I finally put the letter down after reading it a second time. I'm afraid for him. He doesn't make any trouble, but people are starving and paid so little, there's no saying what is happening there. People who have returned from Karelia are sharing disturbing news. The rumours about the place abound. Not a day goes by that I don't worry about him. Despite my fears, it makes me more determined to go to Karelia to be with him.

Chapter Thirty-Three

January 1933

I search the stage and the people milling around it for the recruiter, Matti Korhonen. The hall is filling with people, both young and old. The clatter of their voices and the chime of their laughter fill the room. There are tidy rows in front of the low stage, and tables at the back. Chairs scrape as the audience finds seats. I scan the growing crowd for familiar faces. The small hall makes the turnout look larger than it is, but I'm still surprised at how many people came to hear Korhonen's talk about the promise of Karelia, especially with the threat of a winter storm looming.

A man matching Korhonen's description is adjusting his tie and buttoning his suit coat. By the time I reach him, I am breathless and nervous. It must be him. He is a middle-aged man, possibly in his fifties, hair combed back, and wearing a tidy suit. He looks respectable and wears a welcoming expression. I remember the way Jussi had described him, how supportive he'd been. Fatherly, even.

"Well, hello doll. What can I do for you?" Korhonen gives me his winner's smile. I'm sure it charms many young women.

"Mr. Korhonen, we haven't met, but you helped my fiancé, Jussi Kallio, when he was completing his paperwork for Karelia." I pause and search his face. It has been almost five months since Jussi left.

"Kallio, you say? An eager young man. Very excited to make the journey. He's doing well there, I presume?" Korhonen glances at his watch as he speaks.

"I got a letter from him this morning, but the date is old. I'm worried about him. I'd like to know if he's okay." We have little time, and Korhonen, although feigning interest, is distracted.

"I don't know what to tell you, lady. I don't have information about all the emigrants to Karelia. Once they're on the ship and arrive in the Soviet Union, my job is done."

I thrust the letter at him. "Just read it," I say. "He's not himself. He sounds worried. Even afraid. What's happening over there?"

Korhonen glances at it but doesn't seem to read a word. "He's a grown man. He'll be fine. No one said it was going to be easy. Maybe he's not up to the challenge."

I scowl. "He's up for any challenge. I need to go there myself."

Korhonen sighs. "You can pay?"

"I have some money, but not enough. Mr. Korhonen, this is important. Something's wrong. I can feel it. I must go to him." I don't want to tell Korhonen about my situation with Dr. Wright, and how I need to flee my job. That's none of his business.

Korhonen pulls me away from the stage. "Look, I can't help you if you don't have the money. Passage overseas isn't free."

The stress of the last few weeks bursts from my body, and I grab Korhonen's arm. "You got him there. You must help me now."

He leans in, his voice a whisper near my ear. "I'll get you there on one condition. You work for me now. I'll get you to Karelia. Agreed?" He speaks deliberately, but under his soothing tones, I hear a sinister element. Is he just in it for the money? When he pulls away, he smiles as though nothing is wrong, as though we are old friends having a pleasant conversation.

The announcer calls his name, and Korhonen steps onto the stage, grinning and waving to the crowd.

I'm rattled by our quick exchange. I rush to the nearest exit, wiping my tears with my sleeve, the relief of knowing I'll see Jussi soon flooding my senses. Now I'll get some answers. Korhonen will help me earn my passage. I don't know what this man will make me do, but Jussi is worth it. If only I could tell Essi and convince her to move to Karelia with me.

As I push open the door, I glance back at Matti Korhonen, addressing the crowd with enthusiasm and authority. People seem to hang on his every word. Desperate, hardworking people. In this town, you either work in the mines or leave for a bush camp, seldom home to see family or friends. Everyone wants a new life, an opportunity. Karelia may just be the dream they need, but for me it's becoming a nightmare.

At the back of the room is a familiar face: Fredi Virtanen. What is he doing here? He's shown no interest in Karelia, and I've even heard him discuss the follies of it with my father. Has he changed his mind? I leave the hall and Korhonen's resounding voice, hopeful he can deliver on the promises he's giving these hopeless people, and me, this desperate woman.

Chapter Thirty-Four

February 1933

The streets are dark, but lights shine from the windows along Eva Street. The house I'm looking for tonight is near the top of the hill, and by the time I reach it I'm winded, but the porch light is on to welcome guests and I'm relieved. Cars are parked along the street, and Korhonen's is in the newly shovelled driveway. I pause at the top of the steps and knock, inhaling slowly to calm my nerves. I've been to several meetings already, but it still makes me nervous to speak to strangers about Karelia. Asking for donations is just as bad when I can see they have so little to spare.

There are loud voices within, so I knock loudly. Korhonen will be upset because I'm late, but there is nothing to be done about it. Millie and I had to prepare for Mrs. Wright's luncheon tomorrow before we left for the evening.

A woman with her hair tied back opens the door and motions for me to enter. She barely says a word, but nods at me in welcome. She's older than me but not by much. This must be the wife, Anu.

Behind her, people are making small talk in the cramped living room. Korhonen's voice booms over the others. He's not yet into his familiar lecture. I sigh with relief.

These meetings are getting tiresome, but Korhonen expects me to attend unless they interfere with my work at Dr. Wright's house. Most take place in individual homes with a few families squeezed into a small living room. This time, three families sit in the living room: the homeowners, a husband and wife with three children; the husband's brother's family of four; and a husband and pregnant wife with a toddler. It's an average-sized house on Eva Street, a few streets over from my boarding house, with a living area, small kitchen, and two bedrooms. The furnishings are sparse but clean, with rag rugs neatly laid out on the light plank floors. A beautiful *raanu* hangs on the wall above the low sofa. I wonder if the wife, Anu, wove the wall hanging herself or if she brought it with her from Finland.

Korhonen launches into his usual speech, and I get restless, probably because I've heard it so many times. He may not convince everyone to go, but he's remarkable at opening their wallets for donations. I must admit, he is captivating to listen to, and even though he's said the same thing to different audiences, he never looks bored. His enthusiasm could be called infectious.

Anu quietly rises from her chair near the kitchen, securing her child on her hip. The child is fussing. Anu whispers into the girl's ear, brushing away strands of white blond hair from her eyes, and rubbing her back as she slips away from the meeting and into the kitchen.

Korhonen lights a cigarette. I glance at the men. Most are leaning toward him, and their eyes are intense, captivated by his descriptions of this new society and the passion with which he describes the comradeship and opportunities awaiting them there. He doesn't mention what Jussi wrote about to me: the rough conditions, the rations, the disease, the long hours, the arrests, the disappearances. Everything is described in a positive light, as an opportunity, a promise of a better life. Only one guest is leaning back, his arms crossed, looking unimpressed. He asks about the rumours, and Korhonen smiles, shaking his head. He glances at me and gives me a quick nod. I know what he wants, and I'll try my best.

I excuse myself as I squeeze past a man and make my way to the kitchen. Like a good host, Anu's preparing refreshments.

"Can I help you with the coffee?" I ask. The kitchen is tight, with only room for the two of us to manoeuvre.

Anu shakes her head but doesn't smile or change her expression. I'm not sure she needs, or even wants, my help, but Korhonen made it clear I needed to focus on persuading the women of the house. He would take care of the men. I don't know whose role is harder.

Anu fills the kettle and places it on the stove. She uncovers a freshly baked pulla from beneath a tea towel and places it on the butcher board to cut into slices for the guests. The scent of cardamom reminds me of home. "Is there anything I can do?"

"Cups and saucers there," she says, nodding toward a shelf, but never taking her eyes off her task.

"Have you been thinking of moving to Karelia for a long time?" I reach for the cups, careful not to drop anything. The child stares at me with wide eyes and clings to her mother as she works.

"My husband thinks it's a good idea," Anu says in Finnish.

"And you? Do you want to move?" Anu doesn't look much older than I am but already has a husband and a child.

"He lost his job. He's had no work for many months. I go where he goes."

"And your children? They're excited about the possibility of moving?" I smile at the little girl, but she just blinks and turns away.

Anu's eyes well with tears, but she quickly looks away and arranges home-baked cookies on a chipped plate. "My children have friends now. They are happy here, and they like school. Only the little one was born here." Anu glances at her daughter. "She's a Canadian girl," she says with pride.

"I'm sure they'll find new friends in Karelia. There are many excellent teachers in the communities. They can even study in Finnish. I know it's scary to move, but you left Finland for Canada, and it turned out well for you, didn't it? Imagine a place where everyone speaks Finnish and is working toward a common goal." I feel like a fraud, telling this woman about a Karelia I've never seen. A Karelia that's swallowed up my fiancé. A place I now fear. A place I am desperate to go to, but not for the reasons Korhonen extols.

Anu wipes a few tears from her face. "If my husband wants to move, we move. I'll be fine. The children will be fine." She says this as if to convince herself.

I feel sorry now for Anu and don't want to persuade her to do something she clearly doesn't want to do. She'll do her duty: follow her husband. I admire her courage and her loyalty, but part of me wants to tell her to trust her instincts. But the reality is not so simple.

Anu and I work in silence, arranging the few offerings she has on a tray and pouring the coffee. She fills a small bowl with cubes of sugar. I imagine it is a luxury she can barely afford, but she won't allow the others to see how difficult times have become. I know many proud Finns who will give what little they have to others.

"Will you go there?" Anu asks, pausing over the kettle. "To Karelia?"

No one has ever asked me, although I've visited many homes and had many private conversations with the women. Occasionally, someone asks if Korhonen and I are a couple, although neither of us wears a ring.

"Yes. My man is there waiting for me. I will go to him as soon as I can, and we'll be married." The cup I hold trembles in my hand and clinks against the saucer as I place it down.

"Don't worry. He'll wait for you. You seem like a nice girl." Anu gives me a shy smile, picks up her tray with one hand, her daughter still propped in her other arm, and turns toward the sitting room. She pauses. "But you be careful. With him," she says in a low voice as she nods toward Korhonen.

Anu enters the room. Korhonen's voice booms. "Coffee time. Kiitos." Thank you.

"Ole hyvä." You're welcome, she replies. She keeps her eyes averted from Korhonen and the guests. What does she know about Korhonen? I offer the plate with slices of pulla around the room.

We drink our coffee and nibble on the coffee bread, chatting with each other about various topics now, as though we weren't strangers an hour ago. I am weary of the small talk, of answering the same questions. I don't care for the attention, although Korhonen seems to thrive on it.

The night wears on, and the room feels stuffy. I long to go outside into the chilly night air and clear my head. When the last cup of coffee is drunk and Korhonen's last words have fallen, I help Anu collect the dishes while her daughter sleeps curled up in her father's arms.

"What did you mean about Korhonen?" I whisper to Anu in the kitchen. The rattling of china cups in the sink covers my voice.

Anu just shakes her head. "He wants people's money. Nothing else. He doesn't care about the people he sends there or what happens to them." A scowl crosses her face.

"Do you know him, Anu?" I'm confused about her relationship to him. "How do you know this?"

Anu glances behind her, and I follow her gaze. The others can't hear our conversation. "Women talk. I know families who have gone to Karelia and others that plan to go. Korhonen tells them the cost. They sell everything. They get ready to go. Suddenly, the price goes up, and they must pay Korhonen. No choice." Anu shakes her head with a look of disgust. "He makes money. Dirty business. I suspect the police are involved. But people who want to go to Karelia need him." Anu shrugs. "You can't tell my husband anything. He thinks Korhonen is wonderful."

I believe Anu is right, but I don't admit that I share her suspicions. Korhonen might sound like he believes in the socialist ideals of Karelia, but he's only in it for himself. Once, I overheard him talking to a colleague who travelled by train from Toronto, presumably to check on Korhonen's progress. "I'd never go to that hellhole," Korhonen said. "Those poor suckers will work themselves to death before any good can come of it. I wouldn't trust a Russki even if you paid me. And they do!" He and his friend laughed and clinked their glasses. They change the subject to numbers and recruits. The other man cautioned Korhonen not to let anyone at headquarters get wind of his views. They were serious socialists and wouldn't put up with him.

After the meeting, Korhonen and I pause outside the house and breathe in the cold air. He lights a cigarette and takes a deep inhale. "Matti, I know we've discussed it, but I really need to get there soon. I still haven't heard from Jussi."

"Hold your horses, little girl," Korhonen says, taking a long drag of his cigarette and watching the smoke drift into the still night. "I've got my feelers out, and they're asking questions about your boyfriend. Your paperwork is ready to go, and your fees are almost paid. What are you worried about? Karelia ain't going nowhere."

"Karelia isn't going away, but I'm worried about Jussi. You read his last letter. Things aren't right. How do people just disappear? How can officials just arrest foreigners for no reason? Where are they sent? Jail? A gulag?"

Korhonen sighs and offers me a cigarette. "To tell you the truth, Hanna, I don't know what the hell is going on over there. There were a few good years, but now? If you want my advice, I'd stay the hell away from that place."

I take the cigarette, and he lights it for me. My fingers tremble as I bring it to my lips and inhale. Nothing he says reassures me, and my darkest nightmares seem more possible now. Despite Korhonen's warning, perhaps because of it, I'm more determined than ever.

Chapter Thirty-Five

February 1933

I want nothing more than to stay away from the Wrights' house, away from the doctor and his wife, but I don't know what else to do. The familiar walk from the boarding house to my workplace seems more daunting today, as though it is sapping all my energy. I trudge up the long hill parallel to the creek, under the railroad bridge and its trusses, and past the rows of houses on Beatty, winded by the time I arrive on the corner of Elm Street. A few blocks from the house, nausea rises from my belly. A sudden surge to my throat and I vomit in a snowbank, momentarily feeling tremendous relief, although I am crouched over on the street.

From my pocket, I pull out a handkerchief on which I've carefully embroidered the initials J.K. and wipe the remains from my lips and chin. The handkerchief, one Jussi gave me on our first date, needs washing, so I fold it carefully and place it in my pocket where it will remain until I can soak it. I can add it to the laundry, so long as Millie doesn't notice its distinctive lettering.

I stand and look up and down the street, conscious of how I must appear. Two women are walking my way, chatting in Italian. One of them is pushing a pram. When they see me, they pick up their pace and avert their eyes. The woman with the baby glances back at me, but her expression is judgemental. She thinks I'm a vagrant or a drunk. I try to smile at her, to show her I'm as respectable as she is, but she turns away and resumes her discussion with her friend.

I approach the house, looming large and unwelcoming. Every day is a challenge to enter the place I once coveted, but I am thankful the doctor has not tried to lay hands on me again. He's likely moved on to some other victim. Millie says he has a new mistress—one of Mrs. Wright's socialite friends—who keeps him busy on the side. It's good news for me, at least for now.

The path to the side door needs shoveling, and I trudge through in my heavy boots. By the time I enter the house, I'm feeling faint. Millie looks flushed from kneading bread dough in the hot kitchen.

"Lordy, where have you been, girl? Late again, eh?" She shakes her head and tut-tuts while I remove my outerwear.

I don't respond. It's none of her business. Instead, I take my apron from behind the door and tie it over my simple work dress. Dishes need to be done, and a stack of laundry is waiting for my attention. Sharp smells from the kitchen summon the nausea.

"You're looking a wee bit pale. If you're sick, you'd best stay away from me with those germs. I don't have any time for getting a cough, nor the flu, these days."

She'd like me to ask her why she doesn't have time, but I ignore her as I pour the steaming water from the stovetop into the sink. The scent of the soap, so different from the homemade lye soap we use at home, mingles with the odours wafting from the dirty dishes. My stomach churns.

"I don't mind telling you, an illness would just knock me out right now. I'm so tired. Didn't get any sleep." Millie chuckles to herself and shakes her head. "That man of mine sure does like his late nights, if you know what I mean."

Millie has told me about the new young man, George something-or-other. He's a miner who recently went back to work. It seems like all the eligible young men either work deep underground in the near dark, slaving away for the precious nickel that keeps this town running, or hope to get a job there. I don't envy them, though. So many others have lost their jobs. I see them lined up waiting for a chance at a few hours' work. Every one of them looks desperate, and tired, and hungry. I imagine the families they have at home, hoping their men will get a good day's labour, or more.

Millie keeps chattering away, although it's unclear whether she's addressing me or just filling the space. At least she seems to be in a good mood today. I soak each pot and scrub until my knuckles turn red, trying to avoid the smells, and thinking instead about what to do about my problem.

"He's going to get me a gift." Millie thwaps the dough on the table and kneads again. "I don't know what it is, but I think it's a you-know-what for my wee finger." She raises her flour-covered ring finger in case I didn't catch her meaning.

I feel my ring against my skin, hanging alongside my family charm on the gold chain around my neck. "You're going to marry him? You barely know him." For the first time, I'm hit with a pang of jealousy. Her man is here, in town, and I'm separated from mine by a vast ocean.

"Don't be so surprised. I mightn't be a looker like you, but I have my own attractive qualities. I catch the eye of many boys. I have my pick, really." She tosses her head and gives me a wink. "Before you came along, even Dr. Wright couldn't get enough of me. But that's all done now. I got my George. He mayn't have much money, but we'll get along just swell."

Another wave of nausea wracks my insides. I rush to a bucket in the corner and toss the mop aside and empty what little remains in my stomach. It takes a moment to stand straight again, wipe my face, and catch my breath. I pause in case another wave assaults me. When my body settles, I slump on the floor and lean my head against the wall. The cool surface feels good against my skin. When I finally turn, Millie looks at me with a knowing smile.

"You don't have no flu," she says. "You have a secret."

"I don't have a secret," I say. "I'm just under the weather. It must be something I ate."

Millie shakes her head. "You've got a wee one in your belly. I can't see no bump yet, but I know morning sickness when I see it. That's why you're so pale." Millie folds her arms across her chest, flour floating from her fingers to the floor. She has a mischievous look. "Who's the father, then? Is it that man who came here the other week? The one you sent away?"

Millie must have seen Matti Korhonen. I'd told him to go away; angry he should invade my workplace. He wanted me to meet him after I finished work, he'd said. I'd agreed, but I couldn't have him in the house, not with Millie's prying eyes. She knows nothing about Jussi or my plans to go to Karelia in search of him.

I pick myself up from the floor, hoping Millie will let it go. "It was nobody, Millie. Just a family friend." Is Millie right? Is this why I've been feeling unwell?

"He's quite a looker, but a bit on the old side. Must be a Finlander like you. Barely moved a muscle in his face when he was talking to you in your foreign tongue—sounded like gibberish. He was pretty interested in you."

I move back to finish the dishes. Although I rarely cry, and never in public, I can feel hot tears streaming down my face. I must stop; my shoulders shake uncontrollably as I grip the sides of the sink with my raw, red fingers. What if Millie is right and I'm pregnant?

"Come on, then. No need for tears." Millie's voice is gentler than I've ever heard it. "You can tell Millie. You're not the first girl to get herself into trouble. Not the last either, I venture. There are ways to deal with it, you know. I can help."

Why is Millie taking such an interest in me?

"I haven't gotten myself in trouble," I say, my tears bursting forth again. "This is not my fault." What would Jussi say if he were here? Would he leave me now that I am pregnant with someone else's child? Would he accept it as his own?

"Do you have a man, then?" Millie pulls up a chair and tells me to sit. "Is he gonna marry you? It's the gentlemanly thing to do."

"He's not here. It's not his," I say. I'm reluctant to tell Millie about Jussi in Karelia. The less she knows about my life, the better. I don't trust her, despite her kindness today.

"Not your man's baby? Then whose baby is it?" Millie paces the floor, bringing a hand to her chin like a detective in a movie trying to solve the mystery.

I don't answer, just stare at my hands in my lap, thinking about what to do. Should I confide in her? I can't tell Essi. And I certainly can't tell my mother. I'm too ashamed. But Millie might have some advice. She knows the kind of people who know about these things.

"Wait a minute. You said this wasn't your fault." Millie stops, then swivels, and points her finger at me. "Well, don't that beat all. It's his. You're having the doctor's baby." She claps her hands with delight, as if guessing the answer might award her a prize. She can't understand how painful the idea of carrying Dr. Wright's baby is, how I wish to scream, or run away, or hurt myself. "I've hit the nail, haven't I? I can tell by the look on your face."

She knows. I am carrying Dr. Wright's child, and I don't know what to do about it. I've never felt so alone in my entire life, not even after Martta's death or my mother's decline. If only I could tell Essi, but how to explain the secrets I've been keeping from her for months, and now this.

"Well, well, well. Perfect little Hanna is with child by her own employer. You should have known to use something to stop it from happening. But I guess you're just a child yourself. Too inexperienced." Millie's tone smacks of her usual sense of superiority.

I don't disagree with her. I've heard of ways to stop a pregnancy, but I've never imagined I'd need them. There certainly was no discussion about how to prevent a baby. I'd only wanted to scream, or fight, or run away.

"There's only one thing to be done," Millie says. "If you want it, keep it. I dare say the doctor will give you some money to go away and keep the whole thing quiet. If you don't want it, even better. Dr. Wright has contacts who can take care of things for you. He'll pay, I know he will. And then you'll make sure he pays you to keep quiet."

I stare at Millie. Is she telling me Dr. Wright will pay me to get rid of this child? What kind of man is he? I'm horrified.

"Don't look like that, Hanna. It might be illegal, but women get abortions all the time. You need to know the right people. It can be done quietly. No one even needs to know you were pregnant." Millie looks positively enthusiastic about the prospect of my going under the knife.

"I don't know, Millie. I don't think I could go through with it." I touch my belly with one hand. With the other hand, I clutch the ring hanging around my neck.

"Don't be foolish, girl. This might be your windfall. Men like him will pay for their sins. Who knows how many little offspring are out in the world or whose lives have ended abruptly? I thank the good Lord he never made me pregnant, but I took care of those things for the both of us. Now that I think about it, I should have let it happen. I might be better off." Millie stares into midair. I wonder if she's dreaming of what could have been. I wish we could change places because this certainly doesn't feel like a windfall to me. She shakes it off. "Nah. I wouldn't want to deal with Glenda. She's a nightmare."

"I'm not telling anyone about this. You must promise to keep it a secret." Millie's such a blabbermouth, I don't know if I can trust her to keep this to herself. "I need this job, at least for now."

Millie's pacing with her hands behind her back, as if she's making important battle decisions. "You'll have to decide and then tell him. Demand it of him. He may seem like he's a know-it-all, but he's just a man with base desires and a fear of strong women. Especially his wife. And his mistress. If they get one whiff of this, there will be hell to pay. You understand what I'm saying?"

I nod and sit straighter. Millie's right. Dr. Wright needs to deal with this situation. He forced me, and if I must, I will tell Glenda Wright everything. I'm feeling buoyed by Millie's confident tone and the indignation I feel about what happened to me. Someone will pay.

"You let me think on this a bit more," Millie says. "Get to work. Those dishes ain't gonna clean themselves."

Millie turns back to her dough, whistling a cheerful tune. I feel anything but lighthearted. Should I keep this baby? How will I tell Jussi? Doubts cloud my mind, and my thoughts are as muddy as the dishwater.

Chapter Thirty-Six
February 1933

Millie leads the way from Dr. Wright's house through back-alley roads and narrow paths between the houses. I can barely pick my way along the uneven ground in the dim light. Here and there, a few house lights turn on in the early evening dusk, and the full moon is slowly rising, gleaming through the trees. Darkness is a small blessing. It's unlikely anyone will recognize or even notice us as we trace our way. Even so, I glance down the alleyways and the rows of houses, but I see no one and only hear the chirps of birds who flutter from nearby branches, berating our approach.

I trudge behind Millie's footprints, lost in a neighbourhood I thought I knew so well. No number and no street sign to speak of. Millie knows the way. She has led others here. "I don't know about this, Millie. We should go back."

"You're lucky he'll see you," Millie says. "He's a very busy man, and he does this as a favour to Dr. Wright. He doesn't take just anyone."

I am strangely thankful to Millie. She arranged everything, even speaking to Dr. Wright and insisting he pay while I stood in the background, avoiding eye contact and wishing the floor would swallow me up. We approach a house with an unassuming door facing a back alley.

She knocks twice, then lets herself in. I expect someone will greet us, a nurse or an assistant, but no one is in the dim, dank room. I want to flee, but Millie gives me a sympathetic smile and tells me to sit on one of the two chairs. It doesn't look like a proper doctor's office, but like someone's old garage tidied up to look like a waiting room.

"I'll see if he's ready for you," she says, knocking on the door. Footsteps approach, coming down a set of stairs. "Don't worry. Dr. Young is the best and very discreet."

I sit on my shaking hands, wondering what I'm doing here, and with Millie, of all people. Ever since she found out I am with child, she's gone from enemy to friend. Well, almost. Even though I'm grateful for her interest in my situation, and even for her advice, I can't help but wonder what's in it for her. Why does she want to help me?

My heart rate increases, and I tremble. "I can't do this."

"Don't be ridiculous. What do you plan to do? Have your employer's baby? Lose your job? Raise it on your own? No one will ever marry a single young woman who has spoiled her reputation and has a kid. Screw your head on straight." Millie scowls and leaves me to reflect on her words of wisdom. She's not wrong. It doesn't make it any easier. I wish Essi were here. She thinks I'm working tonight and am staying overnight. I didn't lie about the second part. Mille suggested my staying overnight while I recover.

The wait seems interminable. Wallpapered walls are peeling, and the large stain on the ceiling suggests water damage. A layer of dust covers the only table in the room. Someone used their finger to write *help* in the dust. Is it meant to be funny? It gives me chills. The small waiting room has no windows, but it's just as well. I have no desire to see outside and even less desire for anyone to see me here.

I guess I'm supposed to feel special or thankful Dr. Young will see me, but I feel nothing like that at all. Just helpless. And scared. How many other women were here? I'm afraid in so many ways. I'm giving up a baby, one I didn't know I might want. I'm trusting my body to a stranger and a procedure that could kill me. I'm listening to a woman who, only days earlier, cared nothing for me, and who is now trying to help for no reason. No one knows where I am. Not Essi, and not my parents. What would happen if I simply vanished? And I haven't had the courage to write to Jussi, the one person whose opinion on the matter is most important.

But I'm young. I have the rest of my life to have babies. Why would I want to carry the child of the man who violated me? Will I even be able to love it? What if I become like my mother, so distant she's almost not a mother at all? Could Jussi accept this child? Or will he reject me? Letting go of this baby would be like starting fresh. No one needs to know. My head aches with the swirling thoughts.

"Hanna?" Millie motions toward the door.

Behind her, the doctor looms in the hallway, a mask covering his face. Dr. Young nods toward me. "Get her ready," he says to Millie, and retreats into the shadows.

"You're sure he's done this before, Millie?" I whisper as she helps me remove my coat and hangs it on a hook.

"Of course, honey. There's nothing to worry about. The doctor has performed this procedure many times. He's trusted by Dr. Wright, you know. They're friends."

My mind whizzes. "You mean Dr. Wright has sent other girls here?"

"Of course. Sometimes they're his patients, and they want his help. He doesn't do it himself, you know, but he'll arrange it for his special patients. I help him out from time to time. We can't have him bringing girls here himself, after all." Millie laughs as though it is the most ridiculous thing she's ever heard.

"But other girls? Servants? Like me?" I'm panicking now.

"You mean girls who got themselves into trouble?"

"Girls he's violated ... girls he's raped." I gasp to say the word. It's the first time I've admitted what happened out loud.

Millie gives me a stern look. "Now, Hanna. You've got this all wrong. You've been flirting with Dr. Wright for months. I've seen it with my own eyes. Why, I was even jealous you caught his attention, I'll admit it. Don't worry. Most girls are attracted to handsome doctors with money and power. Dr. Wright and you— well, it was bound to happen."

I'm sitting on the edge of the bare table, my feet dangling. "That's not what happened. He cornered me. He forced me. I didn't want it to happen, but I couldn't get away. He ... he was too strong. I said no over and over—"

Millie laughs again. "That's what all the good girls say when they get knocked up. Blame it on the man as if you didn't want it. Take off your clothes and put this gown on. I'll talk to the doctor."

I look at the gurney with its cold stirrups and the tray of surgical devices and hyperventilate. I can't be here any longer. My mother lost a baby and never really recovered. And then she lost Martta, and it affected all of us. How can I give up this child?

I tiptoe to the door and open it quietly, peering out to see Millie and the doctor down the hall, deep in conversation. I grab my coat and purse from the hook.

"You know, it's the second one this year, and it's only February, Millie," the doctor says. "I don't approve of this. I'm not comfortable taking care of Wright's problems."

"She's a good girl," Millie says. "She's got a fiancé and plans to marry. You know how it is, Doctor. She's not like the other ones I bring you. They're professionals, in their own way. Getting knocked up is a risk of their job. Besides, Dr. Wright is compensating you. He wants it kept quiet."

I glimpse them in the dim hallway. Millie looks coy, and the doctor concerned. "I wouldn't do this if—"

"There's no need to explain," Millie says. "Everyone is having a tough time of it these days. Your wife is sick. You need extra cash. I'm not judging you. Think of it like you're providing a service for these girls. And this one, Hanna, is as innocent as a budding flower."

The doctor pulls down his medical mask. He's so young, barely old enough to be a doctor. Millie hands him a wad of cash. He counts out some bills and gives them to Millie. "Thank you, Doctor. It's a pleasure doing business with you," she says, folding the bills and putting them in her purse.

So that's why Millie is here. She's on the take. Dr. Wright, Dr. Young, and Millie have an arrangement, and they all benefit. They're playing with girls' lives, and I'll be damned if I'll have anything to do with it. I couldn't live with myself knowing how my mother would do anything to have her children back. I just hope Jussi will understand. Before they can notice me, I slip out of the building, leaving them to wonder where I've gone.

From the alleyway, I steal past houses on a well-worn path, bringing me to a street I recognize. I look left and right but see no cars or pedestrians. The moon is high and lights my path home. I take deep breaths, trying to calm myself and rethink my situation. Essi will know what to do. But how can I tell her? In a few more months, I won't be able to cover up my secrets.

I don't know if I've made the right decision, but it is a decision, at last, and my body feels more relaxed than it has in days. If only Jussi were here, I'd tell him everything. He would understand. I would make him. I must find the courage to write to him.

Chapter Thirty-Seven

March 1933

"Hanna! Letter for you." Rouva Ruusa's voice calls me from downstairs, and my heart leaps. I ask her every day if there's been mail, and she just shakes her head.

Essi looks surprised. "Who is it from?" She smooths the handmade quilt on her bed and plumps her pillow.

I shrug, trying to hide my excitement. "Probably a letter from cousin Aili in Finland. I wrote to her a few weeks ago, asking about her parents." I throw my quilt over the bed, not worrying about how it looks. "Do you want some coffee while I'm downstairs? I can bring you some porridge."

Essi shakes her head. "No, thanks. I'm off to work. I promised Mrs. Johnson I'd see the children off to school this morning. Her husband has a doctor's appointment, and she's worried about it. He's been unwell for quite some time now." Essi touches my arm as she passes by. "See you tonight?"

"See you then," I reply. I hurry down the stairs, holding the bannister with one hand.

Yvonne pauses on the landing to let me pass. She is carrying a basket of laundry, and I get a strong whiff of lavender soap. "Where's the fire?"

"Sorry, I can't talk now," I say. I hear her footsteps resume, heavy under the weight of the basket.

Rouva Ruusa is in the kitchen, tugging at the corner of a wayward linen tablecloth. Without turning around, she pulls a letter from her pocket and holds it out to me. "You've been waiting for this?" She smiles as I nod and grab it from her outstretched hand. "Looks like it's from your friend overseas."

I hold my breath, hoping against hope it's from Jussi. It's been many weeks since I heard from him last, but it feels like years, and I fear I'll never hear from him again. There, scrawled across the envelope, is Jussi's unmistakable script, his slanting letters and curving numbers. I let out a cry, and Rouva Ruusa turns with wide-eyed curiosity. I'm like a schoolgirl, clutching the letter to my chest and willing my tears to stay behind my eyes.

"Must be good news," Rouva Ruusa says.

"I hope so, but just the fact that it's arrived is good news to me." It's an understatement. I'm so ecstatic I can barely breathe. I turn from the too-hot kitchen, down the hall past the parlour, and up the creaky stairs. By the time I return, Essi has left for the day. I'm relieved she's gone; it gives me a chance to savour the letter without prying eyes.

I sit on the edge of my bed as the light streams in through the curtains and plays on the floorboards, afraid to open it. Before, I would have eagerly ripped open the thin paper and devoured his words, reading and rereading every word, analyzing every sentence for signs of his love for me. Before everything changed. Before I was carrying a baby.

A light knock on the half-open door startles me.

"I heard a noise. Everything okay?" Yvonne peers in. "Anything I can do?"

"Oh, Yvonne. You startled me. Everything's fine. Thank you, though." I attempt a smile. Yvonne shrugs and withdraws, closing the door gently behind her.

I take a deep breath and let it out slowly, staring out the window across the yard to the street. In the distance, the train rumbles on the tracks where it will pass by Nolin Creek. The world continues, even as I sit on my bed, worried about opening a letter I've desired for so long.

I slip a fingernail under a slight edge and cut open the envelope. To my relief, it is recent.

Dearest darling Hanna,

I miss you every day and can't wait another heartbeat until you are with me. These are confusing times, but I have faith life here will be everything that was promised to us. I can't write much now, but know I am safe. I don't want you to worry about me. Everything will turn out for the best. Will write more soon.

All my love,
Jussi

I turn the letter over, looking for more, and even check the envelope, but it is empty. Why is his letter so short? There are no details about what is happening in Karelia, about where he is and what he's doing. It's so unlike him. Why does he say these are confusing times? Has he changed his mind about Karelia? Why can't he write more?

Jussi's alive. He misses me. Loves me. Wants me to join him. The rumours about people being arrested or disappearing in Karelia have been enough to haunt my dreams and shatter any hope of Jussi thriving in a faraway land, but this letter proves he is alive.

I read and reread the letter, putting his words to memory, exhausted by my shifting emotions. From the table, I take up my pen and a fresh piece of paper, eager to write to him in return, but worried about how much I should reveal and what should remain a secret, at least for now. I read the letter a third time, contemplating every sentence, every word. I begin my letter, crumple it, and throw it away.

We will be a family. I'm certain he'll accept this baby. I touch the tightness of my belly. Jussi will understand it is right to raise the child as his own. I start my letter again, this time pouring out all the details about Dr. Wright and the baby. I tell him about working for Korhonen and the money I'm setting aside. I don't trust Korhonen, but it's the only way. I must join him soon. It is here in black and white, everything I've yearned to tell him. For a few moments, I stare out the window.

I fold the letter and put it in an envelope addressed to my love, place it in a wooden box under the bed with his stack of letters, and push it to the back where it will go unseen. I will need to send it, but not yet. I want to tell him I am coming to him soon.

First, I need to confront Dr. Wright. He may have agreed to the procedure, even covering the expenses, but now he needs to help me financially with this baby. I'm willing to keep our secret, provided he gives me enough funds to cover my journey across the ocean. Then, I need to find Korhonen. I want to be on the next ship. My heart is lighter, if only because I have a plan. I'll go to Karelia on my own terms to start a new life with Jussi.

Chapter Thirty-Eight

April 1933

Dr. Wright's office door looks imposing at the end of the hall. Heart racing, I approach, listening for some sound within. It is the scariest thing I've ever done, apart from my clandestine trip with Millie to Dr. Young's back-alley office. There are no other choices for me.

With a deep inhale, I knock on the door and stand back, holding my ground, but it's not Dr. Wright who opens it. Instead, Glenda Wright appears. "Hanna? What do you want?" Mrs. Wright purses her lips, and she stares at me with those small, but intense, hawk-like eyes, ready to swoop down on some unsuspecting prey. Millie once said Mrs. Wright avoided her husband's office, keeping mainly at the other end of the house. In fact, we rarely even see her in the kitchen except to give a few orders or arrange a menu with Millie for a party.

"Good morning, ma'am. I'm here to see if Dr. Wright has any paperwork for me to do today." I'm not a good liar, but this one is close to the truth. She knows I pick up extra work for him a few times a week.

"Dr. Wright no longer requires your services. A girl in your condition has no business working in a reputable doctor's office. And not in our house either, for that matter. Gather your things. You are no longer under our employment." Mrs. Wright's tone is always unfriendly, but this time she's incensed.

I'm so startled I can't move. The only people who know about my condition are Dr. Wright, Millie, and Dr. Young. As far as I know, none of them would have told Mrs. Wright.

Nausea fills me. "I understand, Mrs. Wright. I'll gather my things, but I just want a few minutes with Dr. Wright and then I'll be on my way," I say.

Mrs. Wright crosses her arms, her round figure filling the door frame. "You have nothing to say to my husband or to me. Clear out right away and never show your gold-digging face here again." I try to steady myself with a hand on the wall as I turn to leave, not knowing what else to do. She grabs my arm. "You would do well to stay away from reputable folks. And you'd be wise to keep your trap shut about this baby. If I hear you've been telling tales, I promise I'll shut your mouth myself." Glenda Wright is positively seething as she snarls at me. The pressure of her knotted fingers against my skin makes me gasp in pain.

I pull my arm away and take several steps back. Mrs. Wright always disliked me, but I didn't think she'd threaten my life. "I did nothing wrong. It was your husband who did this to me."

"Go on now. You're not wanted." Mrs. Wright waves her hand at me and then slams the door shut. I'm stunned.

What do I do now? When I turn around, Dr. Wright is striding down the hall toward me.

"Hanna? What's the matter?" As he gets closer, he slows down and approaches me cautiously, like I'm some wild animal about to bolt. His voice is quiet, which is more than I can say about his wife. "Millie tells me you didn't go through with it." He pauses, waiting for a response.

"I couldn't do it. I just couldn't." Tears well in my eyes. I cover my face with my hands and feel the torrent release into my fingers.

Dr. Wright reaches out a hand but withdraws quickly. He must see the panic on my face, the way I recoil from him. This man is my attacker, and the very idea of his touch repulses me. If I didn't know better, I'd think his face expressed remorse.

"Your wife fired me, and now I have nowhere to go. I'm going to have a baby. Your baby. How am I going to take care of it?" I blurt out the words. "And you ... you're to blame for everything. She accuses me, but I did nothing wrong. You did this. But I'm paying the price!" I'm so angry, I want my words to cut into him like barbs, expose his guilt.

"Quiet down," he says. "Let's be clear. I don't know for certain that it is my baby. I don't like this situation any more than you do. If you'd just taken care of it like we planned, it would all be over, and no one would be the wiser. Millie was right. You're a naïve girl." He grabs my arm and drags me down the hallway to the top of the stairs. I can only assume he doesn't want Glenda Wright to hear or see us together. "Listen, I've already provided more for you to deal with your little problem and extra for your inconvenience. What more do you expect of me?"

His grip on my arm tightens, and he backs me up to the edge of the top stair. I look down at the steep and narrow staircase, the one only the servants use, afraid one false move and I'll plummet to the bottom. My heart is beating faster now, and I reach for the bannister, trying to grip on to something..

"This is what's going to happen, you understand. You're going to work for a few more weeks, enough time to sort yourself out, find a new job, move, whatever you want to do. And then you'll go. Forever."

"But Mrs. Wright said—"

"I'll handle her. Do your job and stay out of her way. She can start looking for your replacement. She won't like it, but she'll see my reasoning. It's the best I can do."

I nod, still trembling.

The doctor leans toward me, his nostrils flaring. "I assure you. I am no monster. I'll supply some monetary support and you will leave my employment, but once you are gone, I don't want to see you again. Do what you want. Have it. Get rid of it. I don't care; just leave me out of it. You'll speak to no one about what happened. You got it?" The friendly version of Dr. Wright has transformed, like Dr. Jekyll and Mr. Hyde, into the version that terrifies me. The one who doesn't care whether I live or die.

I agree, tears soaking my face. I'm shaking as badly as the night he assaulted me. I want to be strong and stand up to him, show him I'm not afraid, but I'm like a frightened child worried for her life.

"Do you understand? You'll disappear ... or else." He shakes me as if to make his point more real, but there is no need. I believe him. In this moment, I know he will hurt me, or worse, if I don't do what he says.

"I understand. Please, please. Let me go. I won't tell a soul. I promise." I hope this man has an ounce of humanity left, and that he will release me without harm. He could push me down the stairs or strangle me with his large hands. I am no match for his physical strength. In this very moment, I know that if I don't do what he says, he will kill me.

Dr. Wright nuzzles his face against my cheek and neck. I'm frozen in place. His breath is heavy, and his words are slow. "It's such a pity, Hanna. I liked you. We could have had a long and wonderful relationship. But you're just like the others, a little whore who deserves what she gets," he whispers in my ear. My arm throbs where he has me in a vice grip. His other hand steals up from my waist and across my breast until it reaches my neck. His fingers enclose my throat, and I gasp.

With no warning, he releases me. "Get out of here," he says.

I rush down the stairs, my legs quivering so much I might collapse. When I reach the kitchen, Millie is nowhere to be seen. I grab my coat and boots and run out of the house and down the street until I can't breathe another breath. I don't look back at the old house I once thought of as splendid and stately. Soon, I'll turn my back on this house forever.

I take the long way home, letting my tears dry and summoning my resolve. My mind races. I have enough time to convince Korhonen to get me on the next ship to Karelia. I dream of being with Jussi in a new world where we can be a family. I cling to the hope that it's only a matter of a few weeks and everything will be resolved for the best.

Chapter Thirty-Nine
April 1933

The dinner party has gone later than expected, and the guests are milling in the foyer chatting with Dr. and Mrs. Wright. When the last guests finally leave and the door closes behind them, Millie rolls her eyes, and I sigh with relief. With everything that has happened, I avoid Mrs. Wright and the doctor. Even as I served the guests tonight, I could feel her eyes boring holes in my uniform.

My body aches, my back is sore, and my feet feel swollen in my tight shoes. The apron feels like it will strangle me, but I get straight to clearing dishes.

"Don't dilly-dally," Millie says, although I am working as hard as she is. I ignore her as I struggle to the kitchen with my heavy tray. She'll have someone new to boss soon.

The dishwater is prepared, and Millie hums as she washes. I dry, changing the soaked tea towels several times, and put away the dishes and cutlery.

"You seem happy tonight," I venture.

"I just might be," she says. "I guess I can tell you, since you know something about it. Dr. Wright has invited me for a little drink this evening."

I flinch at the mention of his name. I place the last set of plates in the cupboard and throw the dish towel into the laundry basket. "I thought you had a new man, someone who wants to marry you."

"Pshaw," she says, waving her hand in dismissal. "He's a poor boy. I'll see what the good ol' doctor can offer me first. That boy will wait for me, I'm sure. And he'll be right happy I have some jewels or cash if I decide to marry him. Don't you worry, Hanna. Millie always has a plan." She points to her temple and smiles.

"Oh, Millie, please reconsider."

"Don't be ridiculous. I told you he'd give you up and come back to me. You were just a flash in the pan."

"Listen, you can do what you want, but I think you should be careful. He's not who you think he is. He may seem charming, but he's ... dangerous." I'm compelled to tell her, even if we aren't friends.

Millie shrugs and takes off her apron, hanging it on a hook behind the pantry door. "I'm sure I already know everything about him—and you." She straightens her skirt and calms her stray hairs. In the window's reflection, she pinches her cheeks, letting the colour rise to the surface, and smooths a red lipstick over her lips. "How do I look?" she asks.

"You really shouldn't, Millie." I glance behind, but no one else is in the kitchen. "He can be violent. Trust me, Millie. Don't take any chances."

"I don't know what you mean. He may like it a little rough, but he's not violent."

I want to stop her, but I think she knows exactly what she's getting herself into. Despite their mutual desires, I fear for her. Dr. Wright is not a good man. He treats women like us as his property to be toyed with and discarded.

I gather my boots and coat and take one last look around the room. Once I leave this house, I will never return. As agreed, I will not contact Dr. or Mrs. Wright again, and that's fine with me. I've already taken the envelope of cash he gave me and stored it under my bed with Jussi's letters. I'm filled with relief. I can't help but feel a little sadness for the next girl who will take my place. As for Millie, she knows what she's doing, and if she wants to play with fire, she can get herself singed.

I leave the same way I came on my first day, through the servants' entrance. It's a cold, dark night, and I shiver after the warmth of the kitchen. My lungs fill with air as I take a deep breath. Above, the azure sky is dotted with bright stars and a full moon, but clouds are quickly approaching. Smoke from nearby chimneys travels straight up to meet the Milky Way. Somewhere, Jussi is looking up at these same stars, thinking about me and waiting for me to join him. And now I can. I know deep in my heart he'll accept this little one I'm carrying, and we'll raise this child together.

I take one last long look at the Wrights' house. Tonight, I will tell Essi everything: Jussi, Karelia, Dr. Wright, the baby. There's no reason to delay. She'll be upset with me, even angry, but I know my sister. She's always been my biggest supporter, my best friend, and she deserves to know the truth. Leaving her behind will be the hardest thing I'll ever do, but she'll understand I need to go to Jussi, to Karelia, for my baby. She'll help me tell our parents. I turn away from the house, a lightness in my steps I haven't felt in a long time.

Snow falls, landing on my eyelashes and lips. I stick my tongue out to catch a flake, like I did as a child. Tonight marks a fresh start for me: leaving behind my old life and embarking on a new adventure.

At the end of the lane, a figure looms in the shadows. I hesitate. I should go the other way, take the long way home, but the man steps into the light and raises his arm in greeting. I recognize his form and wave back. What is Fredi doing here at this time of night? If he's been waiting for me to finish work, he must have been here for ages.

"Hanna," he says, striding toward me. "I was hoping to meet up with you."

"Fredi? Is Essi with you?" I'm surprised to see him, but at least it's a friendly face, someone who has known me for a long time. Knows I'm a good person and doesn't treat me like a common tramp.

He shakes his head. "I was down at a pub on Station Street and thought you'd like someone to walk you home." He looks up at the sky. "Storm's coming."

"Where's your truck?" I ask, glancing at the spot where he sometimes parks.

"Left it downtown. Had a few too many drinks. I need to clear my head before I drive home." Fredi weaves a little as he walks, but he's not staggering.

"Very sensible of you. If you drive the way you're walking, you'll end up in the ditch." I'd been looking forward to being by myself, clearing my head, and enjoying my newfound feelings of freedom, but I can hardly reject him, especially if he's been waiting for me, even if it is a little irritating. "I welcome the company."

We make our way down Elm Street, turning left on Beatty. For several blocks we walk in silence, our feet crunching in the snow. Clouds obscure the previously clear, starry night, and the snow thickens. Fat flakes swirl around us.

"You didn't have to come all this way to walk me home." Truthfully, I'd prefer to walk alone, but I don't tell him my feelings.

Fredi clears his throat. "I had another reason. I needed to see you."

"Oh? Is something wrong?"

"There are rumours. About you. I wanted to talk to you first."

From here, I can just make out the train tracks above the creek. The snow is driving harder now. I adjust my collar to keep the flakes from hitting my neck like tiny little knives and lower my head as we continue our trek downhill.

"I don't know what you mean. What rumours?" I try to read his face, but his hat is pulled down low, and I can't see his eyes.

"You've been keeping secrets," he says. I hear the caution in his voice, and the concern. "I know about him. You can't deny it."

I don't reply. What does Fredi know?

"Hanna, I want to warn you. He doesn't want what's best for you. He doesn't care about you the way I do."

"What do you mean?" Dr. Wright only wants what's best for himself, and I know I mean nothing to him. I've been given money and told to go away. And that's what I'm doing. But how could Fredi know about this?

Fredi stumbles, and I reach out to steady him. "I care about what happens to you," he says. "I've always cared."

I'm annoyed now. "I don't know what you know or how you know it, but what's done is done, and I'm going to move on with my life."

"Don't you understand? He's putting you in danger." The anger is rising in his voice.

"No, I've made my decision. I've left my situation, and he's paid handsomely for what he did to me."

"What did he do to you?" Fredi turns to face me and grips my arm. He looks confused. "What happened? No more secrets."

I'm flustered. Fredi's grip is powerful, but I pull away. At the bottom of the hill, we cross the street toward the creek and onwards to the tracks. "I've taken the money he offered, and I'll go to Karelia. It's the only way to keep us safe." My voice quivers, saying the words aloud.

"Liar. You are such a lying bitch." He grabs me with both hands, holding me in place by my shoulders. I've never seen such rage on his face. "Tell me what's really going on."

My heart is beating faster now. Why is he so angry?

"Please. Let me go," I say. "I'll tell you everything, I promise." My voice pleads, but his grip tightens.

"You were going to leave. Go to him. Go to Karelia. You're making a big mistake. As soon as I saw you with Korhonen, I knew you were keeping secrets from all of us."

What does he know about Jussi and me? "I want to be with Jussi. He loves me." I try to squirm away from him.

"*He* loves you? I've loved you since ... forever. We're meant to be together."

"Please, Fredi ... let go."

Fredi's grip tightens as I try to pull away from his grasp. We struggle, and I cry out for help. "No, Fredi. You're my friend. Why are you doing this? Let's talk about it." I beg, but he is unmoved. "Please don't hurt me. Don't hurt my baby." I wrap my free arm around my middle.

My voice pierces the night air, and for a moment Fredi looks startled. "Your baby? Whose baby? Kallio's?"

"No, it's not his. I was ... It's Dr. Wright's. He forced me." Will Fredi let me go now? If I tell him the truth, will he listen?

Fredi's grip loosens. This is my chance. I yank away from his grasp and run. The fast-falling snow blinds me, and I can barely see where I'm going. My foot slips and I fall down the embankment toward the creek. On my hands and knees, I pray the ice will hold my body weight. If I can get across, I'll run up the other side toward the boarding house.

Fredi grabs my legs and tugs me through the snow. I grip the ground and kick my feet, but he is bigger than I am. Stronger. More forceful.

Flashbacks of the night in Dr. Wright's office flood me with fear and a sudden, fierce energy. I twist out of his grip and lunge forward. The ice cracks under me.

Everything is in slow motion. Muffled sounds and blurry vision. Frigid water engulfs my body. I fight to break free, but a weight forces me down. Cold water. Arms flail. Feet kick. The weight releases, and I gasp for air but am shoved down again.

This time, I'm crushed into the bottom of the creek, the water enveloping me. It is cold, so very cold. I gasp. The water fills me with such a shock, but my mind knows what my body resists. Lungs will fill with water. Pounding heart will slow. Blood in veins will turn to ice. In seconds or minutes, I will cease to be. But I fight. I fight until I can't fight any longer.

PART 3: ESSI

Chapter Forty
May 1933

The night drags on in the cold jail cell. I must have fallen asleep, because I jolt awake from a disturbing dream of water, of snow, of drowning, of ice. Of Martta. Of Hanna.

"Have you slept?" I ask Rouva Ruusa in a whisper, rising from the cold floor and wrapping my sweater around me.

"I'm watching over my girls," Rouva Ruusa replies. "The wolves are on the other side. I don't want any of those men getting the wrong idea about their role in this business." Rouva Ruusa looks haggard. Her lines on her face seem deeper, and the circles under her eyes have darkened. With little makeup, she seems older than usual, although her actual age is still a mystery to me.

"Any news? Are they going to let us go?" I ask.

"Not yet, but I have friends in high places. The girls. I worry about them," Rouva Ruusa says. "This must be very scary. Some of them will move on to other work now, if they can find it. Not necessarily a bad thing, but they make a decent living and have some control over their lives here. Some of these girls don't have anyone looking out for them."

We sit in silence for a few minutes. A set of boots strides down the hall toward our cell. The clink of jangling keys gets louder. At the sound, all the girls come alive and wait with bated breath. Yvonne stretches and rubs her eyes. Her wide-eyed bewilderment returns as she realizes where she is.

The door swings open. Robert Cane's familiar face appears, but he isn't smiling, and my stomach knots. "Esteri Kivi?" he says, glancing down at a clipboard.

I stand up from the bench, straighten my dress, and push the stray hair behind my ear. "Here," I say. I look at Robert Cane with inquiring eyes. Does he pretend not to know me?

"Come with me," he says. I glance at Rouva Ruusa, and she gives me a solemn nod.

This more official version has replaced Cane's usual friendly demeanour. More like the man I first met on the day he came to the boarding house with O'Rourke, the day he told me my sister was gone. I've trusted him and believed he wanted to help me. Have I been wrong?

The door clangs behind me, and Cane locks it again. I follow him down the hall to a familiar office. It was here I told him about the death threat, about my suspicions surrounding my sister's murderer. By the time we enter the cramped office, I'm angry. Cane motions for me to sit and closes the door behind him.

"What's happening?" I ask. "What's the meaning of this?" I'm not yelling, but I want to. "You know I don't do the work they're accusing me of."

"You mean you're not a prostitute?" Cane asks, raising his eyebrows. Sits down on the edge of the desk, close to my chair.

"I live at the boarding house, but it doesn't mean I'm one of Rouva Ruusa's girls. I work in the kitchen and laundry. The rent is cheap. It's the best Hanna and I could get. And besides, who are you to say those girls are doing anything wrong? They're making a living." I know I am blustering, but I can't seem to help myself. All the frustrations I have bottled up are pouring out and directed at Robert Cane. I want him to know better. Do better.

Robert Cane softens. Then he chuckles. His posture relaxes, and he looks genuinely concerned. I search his face for answers.

Cane smiles. "Essi, I know your story. Don't you think I've found out about you?"

"You've been investigating *me*?" I'm shocked.

He shakes his head. "I haven't been investigating you. I've been trying to find out about your sister. Inevitably, I'm learning more about you. It's part of the job, Esteri Kivi. I think you were right about your death threat. It was probably someone who knew both of you. Someone who worried you were getting too close."

Relief washes over me. I want Robert Cane to be a good person. Someone I can admire. Someone I trust. He is a good man. A kind man. It means I can still have hope for the right outcome: the discovery of my sister's murderer. And then, I hope, justice for both of us and closure for our family.

"What's going to happen? Am I being charged?" I sit back in the hard chair and cross my arms.

Cane shakes his head. "No, I pulled some strings. You're being released. I know enough about you and your past to verify your employment. Besides, Madame Rose has already denied your involvement. She said you live there as a boarder, and you are strictly working as a domestic and nothing more. She's been very compliant in our questioning."

"I appreciate that," I say, warming to him. He really seems to care about what happens to me. "What about Rouva Ruusa and the girls?"

"There will be charges. Her business is illegal, as you know. One girl is underage." Cane's voice is serious. "Could be the end of her establishment."

"Yvonne? She has a family to take care of. She needs the income. What will she do now?" I'm thinking aloud but can't help but worry about her and the others.

Cane nods. "Everyone's just trying to survive, but not everyone is doing so legally. There are still laws in this country. You know it's my job, right?" His look softens, and he touches my shoulder.

My mind is racing. "Those girls don't have many opportunities. You don't know what it's like out there. It's hard enough to find a good job, let alone a good employer who treats you well. Just look at my sister. Her boss was a philanderer. Millie says he had affairs with other employees. And the girl who worked there before Hanna just disappeared. What happened to her?"

Cane reaches for his notebook and pencil and starts writing. "Dr. Wright? What else did you find out?"

I can barely think straight. "You'll want to talk to their servant Millie and to the Wrights, of course. Millie's been there for years and knows all about Dr. Wright and his affairs."

"You'd better be careful, Essi." I detect concern for me in his eyes. "Dr. Wright is a highly respected doctor, and some people will be very upset if you slander him."

"But if he's done something wrong, something illegal even, shouldn't he pay the price? You say Rouva Ruusa's activities are illegal and you're going after her."

"I'm not going after her personally. The police department is, and I'm just doing my job. Madame Rose runs a bawdy house and serves bootlegged liquor. She's facing fines, maybe jail time. The mayor wants the city cleaned up."

"What about the girls?" I sigh with frustration.

"That's different. Prostitution isn't illegal, but we may charge them with being found in a bawdy house."

I raise an eyebrow. It's all so confusing. "So, you're saying you'll charge Rouva Ruusa with criminal activity while someone like Dr. Wright, whose reputation is more important than his actual behaviour, will be ignored? What if he's responsible for my sister's death?" I want Cane to see what I see, a pattern of interconnected links leading to the guilt of one man: Hanna's employer. He's the last man to have seen her on the night of her death. It's all falling into place for me now.

"You may be on to something. I'll look into it, I promise. Listen, Essi. I know you don't work for Madame Rose, but I recommend you find another place to live. Anyway, they'll shut her down. I don't know if I'll be able to help if you're arrested with these women again."

"Why weren't the men arrested? Rouva Ruusa's house wouldn't exist if those men didn't spend their money there. Why aren't there consequences for them?"

Cane's face reddens. "Madame Rose earns money from illegal activities, and it's our job to follow through."

"But those men choose to pay. They are participants in these illegal activities. Why should she be punished if the men aren't?" *Nothing makes sense to me. How can there be justice when people are treated so differently?*

"I get it. It's not fair. A lot of high-profile men could be implicated here." Cane massages his forehead. "I shouldn't be telling you any of this."

"So, the mayor doesn't want his cronies involved? He wants to protect them from any stain their associations might bring them. That's rich." I scoff. "You know that's ridiculous, right?"

Cane shrugs. "I have a job to do. I don't get any say in how these things play out. The best I can do right now is free you."

"Is it, though? The best you can do?" I stand and glare at him, trying to bore my eyes into his.

He shifts uncomfortably but then reaches for my hand. "Essi, I want to help you. I really do, but it's no good if you're locked up in here. You won't get any closer to solving your sister's murder if you're in the clink."

I don't pull away, just let him hold my hands in his. "Do you believe Hanna was murdered?"

"I don't know. But between you and me, I'm compelled by everything you've told me about her, about your sister Martta, about Hanna's situation. Time will tell, but I trust your gut on this one, and the death threat against you is compelling. Something's rotten in the city of Sudbury."

I am so relieved that I embrace him. "I'm sorry. You don't know how important it is to me to have someone believe me."

Cane returns my hug and holds me a little longer than I expect. I feel safe here in his arms, but pull away. Our relationship is professional after all. "So why haven't you talked to O'Rourke about it?" Cane's not getting off this easy. If he's going to get this thing solved, we need to move forward, and now.

"The first time I approached him, he accused me of ... being sweet on you ... and suggested I stay away from the whole thing. Since then, I've been tied up in other investigations."

I soften a little. He likes me. Do I like him? Even if I did, there's no time for romance now.

Cane's smile suggests my embrace wasn't completely unwanted. "I want to help you."

"I know you do." And I mean it. I trust this man, who has done more for me than anyone else and goes against his orders.

"But first, we need to get you out of here." Cane stands up to retrieve an official document and slides it across the desk, releasing me from police custody. I sign it. "You're free as a bird, Miss Kivi."

He passes over the few personal items they took when we arrived. The small envelope reminds me that Hanna's belongings are missing. I look inside to find my bracelet with Martta's button. "Did you ever find out if Hanna had a necklace on the night she ... I mean, did the coroner have it?"

Cane shakes his head. "I asked the coroner after we spoke about it, and he checked his file. There was no necklace on her when she arrived. She may not have worn it that night, or it was, as you suspected, lost in the creek."

I'm saddened by the news. If it had come off, it would have been swept away by the strong spring current.

"I guess it's lost forever," I say as I put my bracelet back on my wrist. "Thanks for trying." I attempt a smile, but the bad news is worse than the glimmer of hope I'd felt earlier. My friends are still in jail, and I'm running out of leads. I turn to the door and open it to the long corridor.

"Will you at least tell me what you know about Matti Korhonen? All I know is my sister was involved with him somehow. It must be a lead."

A scuffle in the hall makes us both turn to look. Two police officers have a man in handcuffs, and he's not happy about it. The man scowls as he passes us, but I recognize his face. It's Pekka Peltonen, and judging by the fumes he leaves behind, he's drunk.

"Essi Kivi? Is that you?" Pekka slurs as he says my name. "You gotta help me out, Essi. She don't want me no more. It's not my fault." I can make out only some of what Pekka says. Most of it is ranting or babbling. He looks utterly distraught. It looks like he's slept in his wrinkled clothes, and his hair is standing on end. I don't think he's had a bath in quite some time.

The officers don't slow down, but Pekka tries to look behind him as they drag him down the long corridor. "Essi! I didn't do it. I didn't hurt her." He struggles against the handcuffs, and I notice the blood on his knuckles.

I'm stunned. Nothing he said makes any sense. "What's happening? Where did they find him?" I know Pekka's history of drinking problems and involvement with the police, but is it possible he murdered my sister? Where has he been all this time?

Cane doesn't look surprised to see Peltonen. "We got the call that he was in an altercation at an establishment on Borgia Street. According to the bar owner, the other guy's face is mashed like a potato, and is in the hospital. It looks like Peltonen will need to dry out before we can interview him."

"He's not here because of Hanna?"

"No, it has nothing to do with your sister's case, but I'll get the investigator to look into your claims. Are you okay?"

I gaze down the now empty corridor, wondering where I've gone wrong. I don't know who to believe anymore. I believe and suspect everyone I've spoken to about Hanna's death. How am I supposed to sort out the truth from the lies?

Robert Cane sticks his hands in his pockets and leans against the wall. "There's one thing I've learned. The person you presume to be guilty is often not the guilty party. Everyone has secrets. Uncover the evidence, and it'll lead to the truth. I'll see what I can find out. For now, he'll have to sleep it off."

I thank Cane and exit the building onto Elm Street. It's a proper spring day, and the bright sun shines warmly on my face. I take a few deep breaths and try to calm my racing thoughts.

Chapter Forty-One
May 1933

Fredi's truck is parked across the street, his window down. He waves and I jog over. I couldn't think of who to call, and there was no way I could contact my parents in Wanup. What would I tell them?

"Need a lift, jailbird?" he asks, but he doesn't crack a smile.

"I appreciate you picking me up. There's no one at the boarding house, and I don't feel like being by myself." As I make my way to the other side of the truck, I realize I have no one here—except Fredi. Cane assured me they'll release Rouva Ruusa and the girls soon, but I'm not holding my breath. These days, I'm learning to expect the unexpected.

As usual, the passenger door sticks, and I roll my eyes at Fredi. He reaches across and gives it a good whack.

"You really ought to fix your door," I say, as I wiggle into the seat, moving aside his old work gloves and his metal lunch box.

"Yeah, yeah," he says and grins. We both know there's no cash for repairs.

"I could have just walked home." I feel guilty relying on Fredi again.

"I don't understand," he says, his brows furrowed. "Why were you in jail?"

He turns the ignition, and it stalls. He tries again, and the truck sputters. A third time, and the truck roars into action. Fredi lets the engine idle, looking at me for an answer.

"I got caught up in a police raid. Apparently, the city is trying to shut down the illegal bootleggers and fine the prostitutes. Obviously, Rouva Ruusa's place is a prime target. But don't worry—no charges." I don't want to alarm Fredi. He's already made it clear how he feels about Rouva Ruusa's establishment.

"Listen to you, talking about being in jail like it's no big deal. No good could come from you living there," Fredi says. "I've always said you should move away from that evil woman and her associates."

"Rouva Ruusa? Evil?" I look at Fredi, bewildered by his attitude to these women who are my friends. "They're trying to make a living. It's difficult, you know, being a woman with no prospects and no family to support you."

Fredi grips the steering wheel. "They should shut her down, and those girls should be sent to prison until they're reformed. Your Rouva Ruusa should never be let out again." Fredi's tone startles me. He's crosser than I've ever seen him, even angrier than the time Walter Beverly called him a dirty Finlander. They fought in the schoolyard until the teacher broke them up. Walter was left with a bloody nose, and Fredi's eye was black and blue for days.

"Be reasonable, Fredi. These women are like family to me. Ever since Hanna ... they've taken care of me. I can't thank Rouva Ruusa enough for her friendship. She's like a second mother." Like a first mother.

"A mother?" Fredi sounds irate. "If Hanna hadn't lived in that den of illicit activities, she'd still be alive today." He turns from Elm Street toward the Donovan, taking the corner more sharply than usual.

I'm stunned. "Are you suggesting they had something to do with her death?"

"I'm saying Hanna was not the person she was before you moved into the boarding house." Fredi's eyes are squinting hard against the bright light. His foot is heavy on the accelerator as we travel down the hill.

I reach over and touch his arm, clad in an old wool plaid shirt. "Slow down. Take it easy."

Fredi does not ease up. I feel every bump and rut on the road. It feels as if we are flying.

"Don't you know, Essi? Can't you even see what happened to your own sister? She gets involved with a socialist who drags her all over the countryside to do his dirty work for him. She's planning to leave the country for some man no one knows anything about. And then, and then ..."

I grip the door with one hand and the dashboard with the other, trying to keep myself from sliding across the bench as we take a curve. A large pothole throws me toward the ceiling.

"Slow down, Fredi. Let's stop and talk about it." I try to keep a calm voice, but fear has entered every limb. He's out of control, and I don't know how to stop him.

Halfway down the hill, with the creek on the right and tracks in the distance, the honking of an oncoming truck assaults my senses. If Fredi doesn't get back in his lane, we will collide.

"Fredi!" I scream and reach for the wheel, but he smacks my hand away.

As he swerves to the right to avoid the truck, he hits another pothole and loses control. The truck slams into an old birch tree. Branches snap. Pain shoots up from my wrist where I've gripped the dashboard. I feel a warm ooze along my forehead and touch the spot. It is throbbing, and my forehead is bleeding. Strands of my hair are stuck in the cracked glass, the cracks spreading like a spiderweb across the windshield. I don't remember hitting it. Had I blacked out?

Fredi is leaning against the steering wheel. "Fredi, wake up! Wake up!" I jostle him.

He blinks a few times. "What happened? Where are we?"

"We had an accident. You lost control, and we hit the tree." Fredi groans and closes his eyes.

I fish around in the glove compartment for something to dab the blood. An old handkerchief, a little greasy on one corner, will do. I pull it out. Something catches my eye. A gold chain. I glance at Fredi. He groans and raises a hand to his forehead, but his eyes are still closed. Why is there a necklace in the glove compartment? When I try to remove it, I feel it snag on something. My stomach knots. I move some articles around until I free the necklace. Hanging from it are a rose gold ring and a pendant. I've never seen the ring, but the charm is unmistakable. It belongs to my sister. It belongs to Hanna.

A vision of Hanna and Fredi, of all the times he looked at her with love in his eyes when she was kind, embarrassment when she reprimanded him, frustration when she ignored him. All this time, since we were kids, Fredi has been in love with my sister. How did I not see it?

As I cradle the necklace in my hand, my heart beats faster, and I glance toward Fredi, trying to decide what to do. I have an urgent need to run, but I'm frozen in my seat. He opens his eyes, looks at my startled expression and then at the necklace held in my palm, and his eyes widen. He stretches across the seat to grab it from my hand.

In a second, I close my fist around it and reach for the door. The broken handle does its usual trick and refuses to open. I jostle it as Fredi lunges for me. I shove him away and scramble to dislodge the door, falling in a heap on the ground with my legs kicking at the truck and Fredi.

"It's not what you think, Essi!" Fredi stumbles out of the truck. "Essi!"

I scramble off the wet ground and sprint away. Fredi is yelling and running after me. He's a big man with long legs, but he's not fast. I cross the field toward the river, clutching the necklace in my hand. I don't turn around. I want to put as much distance between us as I can.

Above are the iron girders of the bridge. Below is the creek. The water is moving rapidly, high for this time of year. I shudder at moving toward it, but I don't know where else to go.

"Please, Essi, stop! I can explain everything," Fredi yells. He's catching up to me. I can hear his laboured breathing behind me, his heavy footsteps struggling in the soft, wet earth.

As I get closer to the creek's edge, I make a quick decision. I swivel to my left, aiming toward the tracks in the distance. If I can make it across, someone will help me. I catch my foot on a tree root and hurtle to the ground, landing on my shoulder. My injured wrist takes much of the weight. I cry out in pain. Still, I clutch Hanna's necklace in my palm, my knuckles raw from the impact.

It takes only this one stumble for Fredi to catch up with me. "You're the one who sent me the death threat."

"I just wanted to scare you. Stop you. I wasn't going to hurt you," he says, getting closer.

"You killed my sister. You killed Hanna!" He's so close now; I fear he will grab me at any moment. I get up and face him, walking backwards. "Why, Fredi? Why did you do it?"

"You don't understand." His eyes are wild with fear. "It was an accident."

"She drowned in the creek. It was no accident." I keep my eyes on Fredi, watching for any sudden moves.

"I didn't mean to hurt her, Essi. I was just so angry. I could have helped her, but she didn't want me." Fredi is crying now, but he's coming toward me.

My heart is pounding against my chest, my wrist is swelling, and I think I've dislocated my shoulder, but I hold the necklace like my life depends on it. I try to make sense of Fredi's words.

"What did she need help with? Why were you so angry?" The water roars against the rocks. We're getting close to the edge of the creek.

"I was the one who loved her. I was the one she should have married. I was the one who should give her a baby." Fredi's tears are streaming now. His eyes look maniacal.

I'm shocked. "A baby? Hanna was pregnant?"

"If she hadn't been living at the boarding house, she would have been a good Christian girl. You let the devil get to her!"

"Who was the devil? Was it Peltonen? Did he hurt her?" I'm edging away from him, but I want answers. "Or Korhonen? Is he the one? Did he make her pregnant?"

Fredi lunges at me. "The doctor knows what he did. I'll kill him, too."

My foot slips down the embankment, and pain reverberates through one side of my body. The bridge is just ahead. I can make it. I scramble up, digging my fingers into the ground.

Fredi grabs my ankle and pulls. We both tumble toward the creek. We come to a crashing halt, partially submerged. I scramble to my feet, frozen and shaking.

Fredi's hands are on me. I twist and turn, trying to get away from his grip. Was it like this for Hanna in those last moments? "You're hurting me!" I scream into Fredi's face. He looks startled and releases me for a second, long enough for my foot to deliver a blow to his thigh. He stumbles and trips, falling backward into the creek.

I'm about to run when I realize he's not moving. I crawl toward him through the shallow water, pain in my shoulders and wrists, and my hands raw from the creek bottom. Blood oozes from his head where he's struck a rock. The water edges around the contours of his body.

"Fredi?" He doesn't respond. I kneel beside him, feeling the sharp rocks on my knees, the water soaking my clothes and skin. I jostle him, but his body remains still.

My body shakes, and I am disoriented. Above us, the steel girders loom. In the distance, a train whistle blows. A murder of crows settles into a nearby tree, cawing at me. Or him. But I can't move.

Tears stream down my face, merging with the water of the creek. "Why, Fredi? Why did you do it?" My words are a mix of cries and whispers and pleading, but he will never respond. I will never know the answer. I pound on his body, allowing the anger within to release on this man I thought I knew. Reliving the intense grief of my sisters' deaths. He has always been part of our family story, but I never imagined it would come to this.

Finally, my tears spent, I crawl up the bank and lie on the side of the creek, my feet still submerged, staring at my old friend, and weeping for them all.

I don't know how long I am there, keeping vigil over his body. Perhaps hours. Or minutes. I am surrounded by people. Robert Cane wraps a blanket around my shoulders and holds me close to his chest, saying something I can't comprehend. Others are removing Fredi's body from the water on a stretcher, covered in a white sheet.

"He's dead," I say. I feel nothing now. "Fredi is dead …"

"Yes," Robert Cane replies. "Let's get you taken care of, Essi Kivi." Cane guides me from the water's edge. The pain in my shoulder and wrist returns, and I wince as we pick our way up the knoll.

Chapter Forty-Two
May 1933

Days pass and I slowly emerge from under the sheets, feeling the emptiness of the room more acutely than ever. The tears I've been holding back flow now, unbidden, and I let them. Yvonne brings trays to my door and removes the empty ones as my appetite makes a slow return.

The house is quiet now. Many girls have packed up and moved away, to where I cannot say. Only a few remain.

I make my bed for the first time in days and sit on Hanna's, hugging her pillow to my chest. My head and my body ache, but it's nothing like the grief overwhelming me now. With precision, I fold her clothes and her quilt, placing them in a large box, along with her few personal items. Under the bed, a pair of her Mary Janes looks like they are waiting to be stepped into. I reach into the far recesses of the dark and dusty space until I touch a familiar wooden box. Our father made them when we were children, and over the years, they have always housed our treasures. I knew better than to open hers without permission. Now, I sit cross-legged on the floor, wiping the dust off the lid with my sleeve, and hesitate.

"May I, Hanna?" I say into the room, but the answer is only a squawk from a crow landing on the windowsill. It cocks its head as if curious about the contents, too.

The lid opens to reveal an envelope filled with money and a stack of letters bound with twine. They are from Jussi Kallio in Karelia. I lean against my bed and read each letter from the first to the last, imagining the person who wrote them and how my sister must have felt about receiving them. In the box, I find an open envelope addressed to him in my sister's handwriting, a letter left unsent and dated shortly before her death. It reveals everything. When I am done, I weep again for the life she lost, her unborn child, and the life she wanted to create. Any secrets she has kept from me are no longer secrets, and I know she planned on telling me everything. If only she'd had the chance.

I pull myself from the hard floor and open the window, letting the warm air filter in, feeling the sun on my face. The crow eyes me and shifts from claw to claw, then swoops to a nearby branch.

I read and reread the letters. I am angry with Jussi Kallio. If he hadn't left, she wouldn't have been in this situation. I am angry with Hanna for not telling me about him and what was really happening at her workplace. I am angry with myself for not listening to her, for not knowing something far worse was going on than I imagined.

I find a leaf of paper and Hanna's pen and stare into the distance through the window of our shared room, the room I am leaving behind with all of its memories, both good and bad. What I know for sure is that Hanna loved Jussi Kallio and wanted to build her life with him. And she deserved to have that kind of love in her life. He must hear from me what happened, as painful as it is to write.

Dear Mr. Kallio,

I have no words to express my deep regret in writing to you. My name is Esteri Kivi, and I am Hanna's sister. There is no easy way to communicate what happened except to say my sister is dead. I know this will come as a shock to you, and I should have told you sooner, but I didn't know about your relationship with my sister. Forgive me, but I read your letters to her and saw how committed you were to one another. The circumstances of her death were suspicious, and it took time before we found the murderer. It was our childhood neighbour and friend, Fredi Virtanen. We believe he acted out of jealousy. You see, he loved my sister, too. I will share with you all the details, but for now I want you to know what happened from me, her sister, who loved her with all my heart. I hope someday we may meet.

My sincerest and deepest sympathy,
Essi Kivi

I've told Jussi what he needed to know, but I can't bring myself to share everything in this letter. Instead, I will take my time to write her story, every detail, and send it to him. Perhaps someday we will meet. Until then, I'll leave him to his grief.

A knock at my bedroom door startles me, but it's only Yvonne peeking her head in. "Officer Cane is waiting for you outside. He's looking very handsome," she says, giving me a wink.

"I'll be right down," I say. I unclasp the necklace and take the rose gold ring off the chain. I wrap it in one of Hanna's handkerchiefs and tuck it into the envelope with the letter to Jussi Kallio. For a moment, I trace the lines of the Hannunvaakuna charm and attach it to my bracelet. It feels good to have something of hers close to me. I tuck the letter into my pocket. I'll post it from the Wanup Post Office on the way to my parents' house.

Hanna's box is full of her personal items, but I remove the stack of letters and leave them on the table beside her bed. They belong to Jussi Kallio. For now, I will be their caretaker. The rest—things I know my mother will treasure—will go home, to the farm, to our parents.

Chapter Forty-Three

May 1933

Everything at home appears the same on the surface. Daisies nod their sweet little heads, and bright buttercups dot the yard. I long to cross the field and escape into the woods in search of lady's slippers or trilliums, but today is not the day for idle wandering.

Robert Cane turns off the engine and turns to me, but I sit with my hands crossed on my lap, studying this familiar landscape like I've never seen it. Everything is different now. He pulls the keys from the ignition and moves to open his door, drawing me back into the moment.

"Hold on." I touch his arm. "I need to do this alone. Will you wait for me?"

"As long as it takes," he says, giving me a warm smile. "I'll take a walk."

I nod, and he exits the car, coming around to the passenger side to open my door. I take a deep breath and step out, taking the hand he offers. I trod up the stairs to the front door of the farmhouse.

Should I knock? I hesitate. Robert strolls down the driveway toward the main road, his hands clasped behind him. It's strange to see him here in this familiar place, but somehow, he fits right in, like he's always been part of this landscape. He leans down to pat one of the barn cats, who seems quite happy with the attention.

Another deep breath. There's no reason to delay. I must go inside.

"Essi?" Father's voice calls, and I squint against the bright sun as his figure approaches from the field. "What's wrong?" he says.

I run down the steps and into his arms; the tears streaming down my face, soaking the front of his overalls as he holds me like he did when I was a little girl.

"Oh, Essi, let it out," he murmurs into my hair. "Hush now, it will be okay." His Finnish sounds like a song to my ears, a song I've heard all my life. It comforts me now. The tears keep coming, and I try to blurt out why I'm here, but my voice sounds like great gulps between my sobs. When my tears finally slow and my breath returns to a regular rhythm, my body relaxes, but I stay cuddled in his arms for a moment longer.

"I'm sorry, Isä," I say, pulling myself away from his arms and wiping the tears from my face. "I came as soon as I could."

He raises his eyebrows and wrinkles cross his forehead, but he puts an arm around my shoulder and directs us toward the house. "You have news?"

I nod and wrap my arm around him, leaning my head against his shoulder. "I should have told you right away, but ..."

"It's okay, Essi. Wait until we are inside. Your mother will want to hear this."

He opens the door at the top of the porch, and I step over the threshold I've passed over so many times, dropping my shoes at the front entrance and making my way to the kitchen table. The afternoon sun is streaming in, flooding the space with light.

My mother appears from the kitchen, her hair neatly pinned back and her clothes tidy, looking better than last time. She nods a greeting, but her eyes widen as she studies my face. My eyes are swollen from my endless crying. All the tears I could barely shed when Hanna died flow freely now.

Her brows crease, and she frowns. "Coffee?" she asks.

I nod, knowing the moment requires it. When she returns, we sit around the table, taking sips, leaving the fresh bread and jam untouched.

Father puts his cup down and clears his throat. "Essi has news for us, Ida. About Hanna."

Mother's eyes meet mine, and Father reaches for her hand. She nods. I can begin.

I tell them about Hanna and Jussi. About Fredi. I spare them from hearing about Dr. Wright and their unborn grandchild. It's a story I will need to tell them someday, but I can't bear to trouble them more than I already do. It comes out as one long story, with no pauses, afraid I'll break down and not be able to start again. When I tell them about Fredi, Father expresses anger and shock, but also sadness that the young Fredi we knew as an awkward child and troubled boy could commit such an atrocious crime against someone he claimed to love.

When I am done, I pause and search their faces. For several moments, they are silent, her hand still gripping his.

My mother sits still and straight, her eyes on me. "Thank you," she says in Finnish. "This news brings me great comfort, like cold water for a weary soul. Your sister would be very proud of you. We are very proud of you. There is some justice for your sister, and for that I am grateful, but also saddened that Fredi's parents will know the grief of losing a child—the grief I've lived with for so many years."

I'm overcome with emotion and relief and love for this strong and broken woman who has lost so much in her life. I reach over and put my arms around her neck, allowing the tears to flow again. She touches my head and smooths my hair, a gesture I remember from childhood. "You're a good girl. You've done a good thing."

As Mother and I hold each other, I glance at Father. He wipes the tears from his eyes and looks as proud as I've ever seen him. We once were five, and now we are three. But we are together, and although I can never undo the past, I finally feel like I am forgiven. Hanna is not here, but I feel her presence. I hope she is with Martta, looking down on us. We're doing the best we can. Without them.

Chapter Forty-Four
June 1933

"I don't know how I'll move on without her," I say, searching Robert Cane's face. "But I know Hanna would want me to."

"More coffee?" The waitress asks, holding a steaming pot in one hand, with the other hand on her hip. I nod and hold out my white cup and saucer, breathing in the scent and watching it pour into my empty cup. These seemingly everyday moments are, at least for the time being, so extraordinarily fulfilling. One minute we're ignoring everything that gives us pleasure, taking for granted our simple lives, and the next we're wishing we could savour every moment, never knowing when the last moment will be.

"What about you, honey?" The waitress turns to Robert. He smiles and nods as he holds his cup to her.

We watch her amble off to the next table. Robert takes a bite of his half-eaten lemon meringue pie, his appreciation for the flavour written on his face.

"I just didn't see it coming," I say. "Fredi was there for me when they found Hanna in Nolin Creek. We've been friends since we were little." I shake my head, still trying to grapple with the events of the last few months.

"You know, people are more likely to be murdered by a family member or an acquaintance than a stranger," Robert says, fiddling with his napkin.

"But you can't tell me I wasn't off track when I was looking into Dr. Wright," I say. "He was no stranger to my sister."

Robert finishes the last morsel of his lemon meringue pie and takes a sip of his refreshed coffee. "We're investigating Wright and Young. I have a feeling we'll find more evidence to link them to some unforeseen deaths in the community." He pauses. "Of course, I can't talk about it."

"I understand," I say. Robert wants to confide, but he's still a police officer with protocols. He's already told me more than he should have. "I can't believe Hanna never told me she was pregnant."

"And the coroner did not uncover that fact either. Of course, she wasn't very far along." Robert looks embarrassed. "He's a good man, but he made a mistake. He focused on the drowning and missed Hanna's pregnancy."

I nod and stare into my cup. A few bubbles float around the edge. If my mother were here, she'd tell me they meant something, but I can't fathom what they have to say to me now. "I guess I was on the wrong path with Pekka Peltonen, too. The fact his wife disappeared made me think he was someone who could murder a woman."

"Pekka's wife lives in Timmins with her new man, and Pekka was there trying to win her back the night of your sister's murder. It turns out Pekka's story about Hanna wanting his help was true, but he claims she only asked him to scare her employer, not harm him." Robert takes another sip of coffee and looks out of the window at the bustling sidewalk. I follow his gaze, wondering where everyone is going.

"And all this time I thought the death threat was from Korhonen, but it was Fredi all along, trying to throw me off track."

"Korhonen has been lining his own pockets, preying on people's dreams for a better life. We've been investigating him for some time. I shouldn't tell you this, but it seems O'Rourke was on the take, too. He had some arrangement with Korhonen, so when O'Rourke was supposedly investigating the claims, he was really just covering up. It won't go well for him,

I'm afraid. I think your questions brought more scrutiny on Korhonen, and that turned up information about O'Rourke. But the people he's swindled are speaking up. We'll soon have enough evidence to charge him."

"You enjoy this, don't you?" I say, smiling at the handsome police officer.

"Seeking justice? You bet I do. It seems you have quite a knack for it yourself."

"I don't know ... it seems I've been going around and around in circles, seeing some things and not others. I still can't believe that Hanna was engaged, planning to leave Canada, and I didn't know any of it."

"Sometimes these things get complicated. Jussi was a socialist, and from what I gather, your father would not have taken too kindly to his politics. Sometimes one little lie just leads to another. She probably didn't want to disappoint you. Or your parents."

I scrunch my nose to stem the tears from welling. "She could never disappoint me. I would have helped her." But maybe that's what I need to believe about myself. Hanna tried to talk to me. She wanted to leave her job at Dr. Wright's, but I pushed her to stay. I said she was being selfish, looking for more. I didn't listen. Oh, how I regret that.

"Have you broken the news to Jussi Kallio?"

"I've written a letter. I don't want to be the person who shatters his dreams, but there it is. Hanna would have wanted me to tell him." I pause and look outside at pedestrians trying to dodge the gathering puddles. "I'll meet this mystery man someday. If he were worth travelling across the world to be with, I'm sure he's someone I'd like to know." The idea of meeting Jussi Kallio makes me smile. Somehow, he is one of the last connections I have to my sister. And he would have been my brother-in-law.

"I never thanked you, you know," I say.

"For what?"

"Rouva Ruusa said you never left my side at the hospital. A few times I woke up in the dim room and I could see you slumped in the chair, and it made me feel safe. Why did you stay?"

"I don't know what I would have done if something had happened to you ..." Robert's voice cracks with emotion.

I'm about to ask him how he would end the sentence when the waitress passes by with the coffee pot and the moment is gone.

"What's next for you, Esteri Kivi?"

I shrug. "I'm not sure. I'm wanting to write about my sister's life, and everything that happened to her, but I need a job. The local newspaper is looking for a reporter, so I'll apply. I'm interested in what's happening in the city, maybe uncover what's really going on, you know."

"And leave the police work to others this time?" Robert laughs. "But seriously, you'd make a fine reporter. You have a keen eye for detail."

"And Yvonne helped me find a room to rent on Borgia Street. It's not much, but then, I don't need much. But first, I'm going home for a while to be with my parents. I'm all they have now."

Robert reaches across the table and takes my hands in his. "Don't be gone too long, you hear, or I'll have to come to Wanup and get you." He leans over the table and kisses my fingertips.

I shiver. My heart fills with love for this man. "I'll be back before you know it. And I would love for you to come down and meet the old folks. If you want to."

Robert beams. "Yes, indeed. I want to very much."

I reach up to trace the lines on his face, searching his eyes. In them, I see my future. Someone who will be my rock, my supporter. From my bracelet, Martta's button dangles against

Hanna's charm. Whatever the future holds for me, I will always have them near me, and with Robert at my side, I can face anything.

Epilogue

Restlessness has kept me swirling like snowflakes in a gust of wind. I'm drawn toward the earth when I yearn to float up and far away. I see it all from here, wherever here is, in the air, the ether, the place between known and unknown. There is no time. No place. No past. No present. No future.

There is only I am and all I have known and everyone I have loved reflected against one another. Like a kaleidoscope, I see all the moments at once, a symmetrical pattern of multitudinous lights and spectacular colours, moments and feelings and people and places revealed and shifting into new patterns and dazzling new arrays.

Four figures stand at the edge of a creek. An older woman clutches a photograph of a family with three daughters. It's bent and faded with time, and quivers so slightly as to be almost imperceptible. The woman's eyes are closed, and she is praying so quietly her voice disappears in the air. But I hear every word.

The older man plants his feet on the soil, his back stooped. He fixes his eyes on the water as it flows gently away.

A couple stand close together. He wraps an arm around her waist, and she leans her head on his shoulder. He watches over her with love and tenderness, and she feels safe. The young woman fusses with the flowers in her hand, arranging and rearranging them until they are perfect. She inhales their scent, looks up at the sky. She reaches to touch her bracelet, revealing a charm and a bright blue button. May they bring her comfort and good fortune. She knows what I know.

My body is buried beneath the soil in the wooden box constructed by my father's own hands, and marked by a simple white cross, but my soul has been here. Waiting for this moment.

Another figure arrives, a young man with sad eyes. He nods at the others and shakes the older man's hand. My love. I surround him and feel his soul reach out to mine. Not yet, I whisper.

No judgement remains within me about what I have done or left undone, what others have inflicted on me or neglected to do, what was said or left unsaid. There is only this spectacular display of a life, an energy that can't die. There is no space for the petty concerns of the living. I observe them with patience, knowing their grief may overwhelm them now, but will dissolve one day into the vastness of love.

The energy I am lingers, one last time, with the ones I've loved most dearly. I can hear the steady progress of the new grass as it pushes its way through the soil, the music of the light as it filters through the pale leaves, the whisper of the breeze as it brushes the cross marking my body's place of rest. I hear the crow caw at me, dropping toward the water, and swooping away. I will follow soon.

I feel their presence even more than I see them: my father, Edvard; my mother, Ida; my sister, Esteri; her young man, Robert; and my love, Jussi. There is great sadness in them, and I want to tell them there is no reason for these emotions. In Ida, there remains a struggle she will never part with for her remaining days. Edvard's grief is buried so deep it may someday drown him from the inside. In Robert, a desire for justice and a fiercely protective love. In Jussi, a bright flame and a deep loss. He will find his way in this world, and I will guide him. And in Essi, a strength, a resolve, a sense of peace. I know her sisu will serve her well.

I yearn to be free and move beyond this plane of existence. I feel the energy of all the others gone before me and within this energy a spirit my soul recognizes as part of me. Every particle of my being is drawn to this spirit, my child, and is filled with complete joy.

Before I release myself from this earthly captivity, I surround my sister and fill her with my energy, my essence. Her spirit responds. She smiles and releases the flowers into the flowing river, watching them float downstream. She knows I am here. I am not gone, only transformed. And it's because of her. Because of Essi.

Acknowledgements

Writing fictional characters in historical times requires a great deal of research, but it was made all the easier by the thorough work of researchers writing about Sudbury, Finnish immigrants, and Karelian Fever. I was inspired to write about Finnish domestic workers and prostitutes after reading Varpu Lindström's *Defiant Sisters: A Social History of Finnish Immigrant Women in Canada 1890-1930*. Samira Saramo's *Building That Bright Future: Soviet Karelia in the Life Writing of Finnish North Americans*, and Alexey Golubev and Irina Takala's *The Search for a Socialist El Dorado: Finnish Immigration to Soviet Karelia from the United States and Canada in the 1930s* were instrumental in my understanding of the draw of Soviet Karelia to Finnish Canadians, and the devastating consequences for some involved. *Sudbury: Rail Town to Regional Capital*, edited by C.M. Wallace and Ashley Thomson, is an invaluable source for Sudbury history, as is Oiva W. Saarinen's *Between a Rock and a Hard Place: A Historical Geography of the Finns in the Sudbury Area*. Any errors or inaccuracies, intentional or otherwise, are solely mine.

Thank you to those who read versions of this novel and provided valuable feedback at various stages of the process, including editors Kim Reynolds and Ellie Barton, beta readers Nancy Daoust, Emily De Angelis, Kelly Rodriguez, and Christina Wells, and proofreaders Michael Jensen and Megan Jensen. To Marion Agnew, Eleanor Albanese, Emily De Angelis, Kim Fahner, Susan Scott, and Caroline Topperman, much gratitude for your kind words. I am so grateful to the individuals who read advanced review copies, including Debora Clark, Jeany Dohm, Laurie Elmquist, Holly Gutwillinger, Melanie Marttila, Brenda Niskala, and Kristiina Skogberg. Your thoughtful comments and feedback helped to shape this story. And to my launch team, Emily Andrews, Vera Constantineau, Emily De Angelis, Greg Gralien, Holly Gutwillinger, Kim Reynolds, and Shanon Stewart, big hugs for your help launching this book into the world.

Continued gratitude to the Ontario Arts Council for supporting my work, and this novel in particular, with a Literary Creation Project grant. And thank you to the Canada Council for the Arts and The Writers' Union of Canada for supporting my launch through the National Public Reading Program.

I am forever grateful to my circle of support. Thank you to my writing group, Holly, Emily, Greg, Shannon, and Lindsay for bringing joy and laughter to the work. Thank you to my current and former book coaching clients, and the members of the Women Writing Circle, who continue to support each other by showing up to write and inspire me with their incredible stories.

Love and thanks to Francine, Tom, Carita, Judith, Kristin, Hideki, Megan, Russell, and Jeanna and my lovely nieces and nephews. Most of all, love and gratitude to my mom, Anja, my husband, Michael, and my children, Mia and Kieran.

I dedicate this novel to my brother, John, an adventurous and fearless soul who continues to inspire me to take risks and dream big. You are missed.